# The Baggage Handler
By Colin Browne

West St. Floyd Books
London | Johannesburg

ISBN: 978-0-9572039-0-7

Published by
West St. Floyd Books
4C Garfield Road,
Twickenham, TW1 3JS
United Kingdom
publisher@weststfloyd.com
www.weststfloyd.com

First Edition

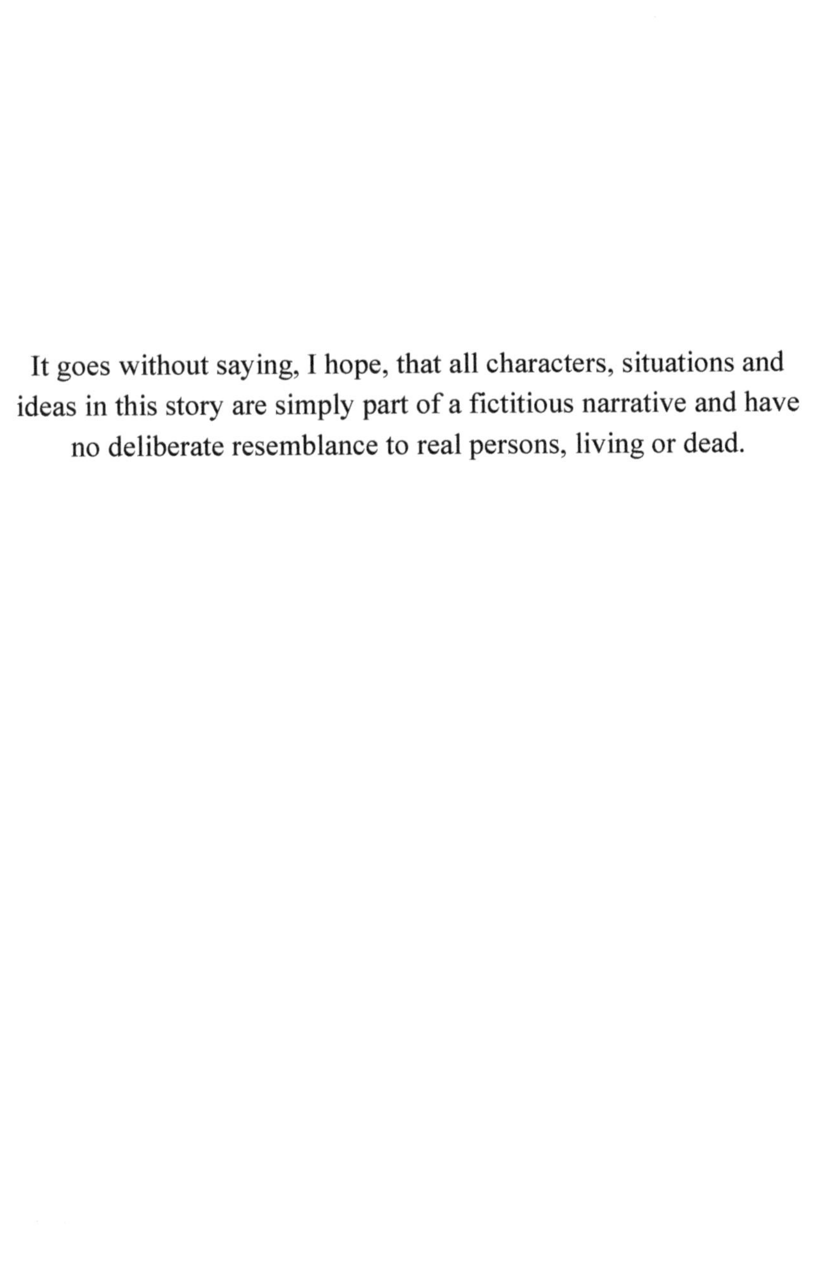

It goes without saying, I hope, that all characters, situations and ideas in this story are simply part of a fictitious narrative and have no deliberate resemblance to real persons, living or dead.

To my muse who for now shall remain unnamed.
She knows who she is.

## Chapter One

Martin White looked at his watch. All around the floor of the open-plan office, people gathered in groups, then split into others, mingling through the murmur of after-work plans that had thankfully long since stopped involving him.

It was after five which meant he was heading into his favourite time of the day when he would have the place almost to himself and get the best of his work done. In the longest part of a London summer when daylight beats the night by two-to-one, Martin thought of the extra hours of sunlight like plundered loot from a captured galleon.

All he asked for was solitude.

He rarely got it.

That evening was to be no exception.

As he began tearing open the envelopes he'd gathered around town that morning, his radar picked up the almost-silent fidgeting just beyond the walls of his burnt-orange cubicle. He glanced up to see who it was this time.

"Is this a bad time?" said Penny, a writer for one of the magazines on the other side of the editorial floor where they both spent too much of their lives.

Martin smirked. Like his convenience ever really mattered to anyone. He sighed out loud, realising as he heard himself how frustrated he sounded, and instantly regretting it because he had a soft spot for Penny, and because she was clearly in distress.

"I have a few minutes. Shall we go and make some tea?" he said.

She nodded, with a sad smile.

"Come on then," he said, leaping to his feet with feigned enthusiasm. He led her across the hallway from the editorial office to a break room, which looked precisely as it would had IKEA designed it as a showpiece. Red and white plastic chairs and chromed metal tables made it functional but uninviting, which was probably the intention.

Martin clicked the kettle on and pulled two mugs down from the cupboard.

He turned to Penny, who stood awkwardly and far too close. "Have a seat," he said, joining her at the closest table. "Now what's on your mind?"

"Oh it's really embarrassing," she said.

He smiled gently and sat back.

"I think my boyfriend's cheated on me. In fact, I know he has."

"Oh dear."

"It's just shit."

"That it is."

"So I think I have to leave him."

"I'm sorry Pen."

"But I've gone and got a tattoo of his name in the small of my back. And his name's Jerome. Where the hell am I going to find another Jerome? My only choice is to stay with him really."

"Oh. Wow, that's um ... sort of a committed step, isn't it?"

"Well you said getting someone's name tattooed on your body was the greatest act of love of all."

Martin's eyebrows nearly flew off the top of his head. "No, I'm certain that I said it was the greatest *leap of faith.* But I certainly didn't suggest you should do it."

"Oh."

"What's the point here though, Pen?"

"Oh it's just embarrassing."

"Don't tell me if you don't want to."

"I ... well, if you were to shag a girl with someone else's name tattooed above her ass, would that put you off? You know, I mean if it was doggy so you could read it."

As often as Martin was relied upon for a listening ear, peoples' capacity to stun him never seemed to diminish. "I honestly don't know how to answer that."

"I mean since I got the tattoo on your advice ..."

*"I didn't tell you to get a tattoo, Penny,"* Martin interrupted.

"Well, what would you do?"

"I can't answer that. I've only got a tiny portion of the story here. All that matters is what *you* want to do."

"Oh. Well, I think I'm going to forgive him. It's cheaper than having it removed, and anyway it's really lovely. Do you want to see it?"

"No."

She showed him anyway. Apparently Gerome was spelled with a G.

Martin shrugged it off. "Look Pen, my advice is the same as always: stop listening to all the other voices and just do whatever makes you happiest. As long as you're being honest, you're probably right."

"Do you think I'm being an idiot?"

"For what? For forgiving him?"

"Yeah. I mean it's shit, isn't it?"

"Yeah, but that doesn't mean there's only one rule here. Your militant friends will tell you to kick him out, and I'd guess you're already hearing some of that. But they're not inside your head or your heart, so what the hell can they really know? There isn't only one rule here."

She grinned. "Yeah? Oh thank God. That's what I needed to hear. You really are good with baggage, you know?"

"That's what they tell me," Martin said.

"Yeah. You're so figured out. I wish I was. Thank you, Martin," she said, kissing him on the cheek and dashing out of the break room just as the kettle clicked.

Martin laughed quietly to himself. *If only you knew,* he thought.

He sat for a moment watching the steam rise from the kettle and then decided to abandon the idea of tea and head back to his desk. As he stepped into the hallway however, he knew without question that the rancid smell now permeating the air would somehow require his involvement.

It was bad. Asian food perhaps. *Stale* Asian food. And way too much cologne. His instincts were well-enough honed for him to know it could only be Rich. He braced himself as he stepped towards his cubicle but even so, he wasn't close to being prepared for the extent of the damage.

Rich was sitting in Martin's spare chair; a complete shambles. Normally very dapper, now he was crumpled and wilted with days-old stubble as if he'd spent a week in a grimy drunk tank or the boot of an abductor's car. The lace of one shoe was undone and there was a splat of something white on the other. He smelt terrible.

"What the hell happened to you?" Martin blurted out, aiming for casual but missing by a mile.

"Tokyo," said Rich.

"You mean the city?"

Rich yawned and made as if to stretch, but apparently decided that he couldn't be bothered. His arms simply flopped to his sides. "None of the good bits. I never even got out of the airport."

"*Tokyo* airport? *In Japan?*"

"Yeah, for fuck's sake."

Martin shook his head slowly. "Well, do you want tea?"

Rich nodded. "I'd kill my mother for a cup of tea right now."

"Right." He pointed a firm finger at Rich. "Don't go anywhere."

Rich brought one hand up to his temple and gave what looked like a painful squeeze. "Wasn't planning to," he said.

Martin took his time making it, deliberating all through the process whether he should just make a run for it. Whatever Rich wanted, it looked like more than he wanted to have to handle. Loyalty, and the fact that he hated going home without his MacBook were the most convincing arguments however. He returned with two steaming mugs to find Rich rubbing away vigorously at a stubborn crease in his lapel with a wet finger.

Martin gave him the once over again. "I wouldn't bother with that to be honest," he said.

Rich looked up with eyes that hadn't had enough sleep for a good long while. He sighed.

Martin nodded, coaxing him to begin. "Tell me what happened. You look like crap."

Rich managed a smile, though weary and humourless. "No bloody wonder. It's twelve hours to Narita airport. Sixteen-and-a-quarter back via Moscow and I was on the ground for twenty-two and a half. That makes fifty hours since I last had any real sleep or a shower or a decent meal. This has been the most wretched experience I've ever had," he said.

He ran a finger between his collar and his neck. Impressively, he was still wearing his tie, though the neck of his collar was stained with sweat. He picked up his tea and attempted to sip it, recoiling at the heat and putting it down heavily, splashing a little over the rim onto Martin's desk.

"You actually followed her all the way to Japan?"

"I mean, you said go and have a Hollywood moment, so I did."

"I said go and speak to her at the airport. Tell her how you feel. I didn't say get on the bloody plane, Rich. Did you travel *with* her?"

"No. To be honest, the only way I could think of to get hold of her once I got to the airport was to buy a ticket and find her in the departures area. I thought an economy class ticket would be an easy investment, especially since I didn't plan to actually use the fucker. But I couldn't find her so as I ran out of time, my only remaining option was to board. I mean, if it'd worked out, she'd have told every single one of her friends."

"But ...?" Martin dragged the word out expectantly.

"But it turned out my ticket was at the back of the plane between two irritating little Chinese fuckers while she was somewhere up in business class or better. A nightmare. I asked one of the crew to send a message to her that I was on board and wanted to have a word, but they couldn't have been less interested. Spontaneity isn't a very Japanese thing, you know? All they cared about was getting 300 tubs of crab and noodles out of the oven. I upended mine all over me, by the way. That's that bit there." He pointed to a stain on his jacket below the bottom button, and on the front of his trousers.

He reached out to test the temperature of the mug again. Still too hot.

He finally decided to loosen his top button and pull his tie down slightly.

"So you didn't see her?"

"No, I did. When dinner was over, I went up to the galley and asked again, and at first I had the sinking feeling I was on the wrong plane because they couldn't find her on the passenger list. Finally, I'm guessing one of them opened their eyes because suddenly it was all *aaaah, Miko Mikada, business class*," Rich waved his hands in the air to mimic them. "So off one of them went while I suddenly had heart palpitations at the realisation of what I was doing."

"And she was ... what? *Happy* to see you?"

Rich shook his head, slowly. "You know what it reminded me of? When I was about ten, my friend Harry had this massive dog that used to just sit around, silently watching with these dead, rheumy yellow eyes like it was some sort of land shark. It used to absolutely scare the living crap out of me. When Miko came through the curtain, she looked just like I imagine I did whenever I saw that dog. And that was just to start. She asked what I was doing there and I said, *I've come to get you*. Oh, for fuck's sake, I told her I loved her."

Rich buried his face in his hands, then rubbed his tired eyes violently.

Martin's eyebrows broke ranks with his resolve not to judge. *"You love her?"*

"I don't know," said Rich, slumping even further into his chair. "But it seemed like the right thing to say. But let me tell you, she made it absolutely plain she didn't share the emotion."

"What did she say?"

"She has a fiancé. She was going back to him and really looking forward to it."

"Oh shit. How did that manage to never come up?"

"I don't really know. I thought about that a bit on the plane and I suppose our conversations were always about me, not her. She was here to learn about western business and it could have been that I was just a living case study for her. I really don't know."

Martin looked Rich up and down for the hundredth time. "Wow. So you obviously haven't been home; are you just in from the airport now?"

"Yeah. I needed to talk to you."

"Well is there any chance you can be friends? Do you even want that?"

"Nope. That's off the cards. I ended by telling her she was a cock tease and she slapped me. There was a real to-do about that. They ordered me to sit down and stay in my seat until the plane landed while she stormed off to her seat. And then when we landed, I was met by the Japanese airport police who wanted to have a little word. They didn't much like the fact that my return ticket was for the next day and that I didn't have any luggage. They apparently thought I was a drug mule or something."

"Oh don't tell me ..."

"Yep."

"Noooooo ..."

"Oh yeah." Rich leaned in. "They cavity searched me Martin."

"Oh my God." Martin put his hands to his head. "Oh God."

"Latex gloves on, snap, snap and next thing I know I have some bloke's fingers up my ass."

"Jesus ..."

"It's not entirely bad to be honest."

"Oh no, for fuck's sake Rich ..."

"Anyway, I remained a guest of the police for nearly 24 hours and then I was put back onto a plane and now here I am, looking and smelling like this. Not quite the intended result. I think this suit needs to be burnt. I know my underpants do."

"I don't know what to say. Did you at least get frequent flyer miles?"

"I don't know. It was Japan Airlines. I don't have a card for that one. I'll have to look it up and see if I can redeem them. Right now, I need a shower and some sleep."

"Yeah. You really do."

"Thank you for that. You're a good bloke Martin. I needed to tell you this. Thanks for listening as always."

He grabbed his lower back and groaned slightly as he stood up, and then he was gone without another word.

Martin stood to watch him as he shuffled slowly, painfully, disgustingly away, with a broken heart and a ruined suit. He hated that his overwhelming thought was a slight pang of jealousy.

## Chapter Two

It was getting on for seven by the time he was able to focus again, but he'd lost all of his momentum. He rolled his head back and stared at the ceiling for a moment then leaned forward and smacked his MacBook shut.

He meerkatted briefly over his cubicle wall to see if Drake the Robot was still in his glass office, though he already knew he would be. He packed his things away and then stood, hoping to get away with a single wave good night before he headed out but Drake the Robot beckoned him over instead.

So much for that plan.

Martin muttered under his breath, but half smiled in mock-acquiescence as he crossed the floor and opened the door.

Drake the Robot flapped his hands around. "I have to show you something bloody brilliant," he said. "Put your ass down."

Martin sat in one of the chairs in front of the desk as Drake the Robot disappeared behind it, rummaging through a bag. Finally, visibly delighted, he pulled out a cowboy boot, setting it down carefully on the desk.

"What do you think?" he asked.

Martin gestured to pick it up and Drake the Robot nodded enthusiastically, so Martin examined it. "What are they made of?"

*"They?"*

"What is this? Lizard?"

"It's a monitor. I killed it."

"Oh."

"Not on purpose. It was an accident. I ran over it. But I saw the skin and thought, bloody hell, that's bloody brilliant. So I scooped it up, had it skinned and made a boot out of it."

"*A* boot?"

"Yeah, there wasn't enough undamaged skin for two."

"Oh. If you'll forgive me, what's the point then?"

"Glad you asked. Let's have it back," said Drake the Robot, reaching out and tugging it from Martin's hands. "It is a sign of my appreciation of aesthetic and of my tenacity Martin. I'll have to go back to Australia one day and find another monitor and kill it to get the second boot. But it'll be worth it. I mean just look at it."

Martin obliged. The last thing he felt like was a conversation with Drake the Robot and he had a strong sense of where it was heading. "Well it's great Drake, just great. Congrats."

Drake the Robot beamed at him and placed the boot back in the middle of his desk for them both to admire as he settled deep into his chair for what Martin recognized as the beginning of a pep talk.

"So how's it going Martin?" he asked.

"Everything is just great Drake. Couldn't be better."

"You're still the resident agony aunt I see."

"*They* come to *me* Drake."

"And I'm not trying to tell you what to do Martin. Just to help, you know? But you know what I'm going to say, don't you?"

"Yes, you're going to say that every meaningful human connection I make carries a risk that I'll lose myself and that the board requires me to take a monastic vow of shallowness in order to feel safe about their investment. And I'm going to tell you once again that I invented the Shallow Review of Books and I know what it needs. These things are not related."

Drake the Robot chuckled, but there was no real warmth in it. "Martin, nobody wants you to be a monk. But your social detachment is precisely what makes the Shallow Review the roaring success it is. I just don't understand why you care about other people's problems anyway."

Martin cringed. Drake the Robot always shortened the name and it didn't benefit the product one little bit. A bit like shortening Buckingham Palace to Buck House or The Rolling Stones to The Stones; how hard is it to just say the whole thing?

"Drake, if anything, all the crap people invite into their lives only strengthens my determination to avoid it. You can probably take comfort in that."

Drake the Robot beamed at him once again as if it was a new thing of his. "Take it from me Martin, when we acquired the Shallow Review, you and your attitude and your reputation were an important part of the package. It's all less interesting to us without that, you understand?"

Martin nodded. He'd heard all this before, countless times though every time Drake the Robot rolled it out, he apparently thought it was fresh. He wanted to go home and he especially didn't want to have this conversation. Just agreeing was usually the quickest way to get Drake the Robot to shut up.

He was ignoring Martin however and leaned forward to run his knuckles gently down the boot, getting obvious pleasure from the act. "Look Martin, I'm not saying don't live a normal life. Just live a normal life for *you*. Your life is perfect for your work. The one always affects the other. Just exercise caution when people are trying to suck you into their problems, that's all."

"*I'm not getting sucked in Drake*. That would be counter to everything I stand for. My entire life is about avoiding that. I don't know how I could possibly be less involved without becoming a hermit. And don't think I haven't considered that."

He had too. The only thing that really switched him off about being a hermit is that it is actually *more* work, not less. You have to cut your own hair for instance and cook everything yourself. Grow everything you cook for that matter. Being a hermit may seem like a simpler life, but investigation doesn't bear that out.

"Just remember our mutual goals Martin, that's all I ask," said Drake the Robot.

"Right. And now I'm out of here. So should you be."

"We'll see."

"Don't you ever go home Drake?"

“Have a good evening Martin.”

Martin paused. But he didn’t push it. He’d invented Rules of Shallowness to keep his life simple and to keep the Shallow Review of Books pure. Pressing Drake the Robot for details of what looked suspiciously like baggage was a far cry from simply handling what was dropped off uninvited outside his cubicle.

Martin’s flat was on the second floor of an apartment building in Highgate where he actively ignored his neighbours.

Sneaking past Rupert’s place so he wouldn’t hear him if he was in, Martin got to his front door, put the key in the lock and quietly opened up, shutting it gently behind him.

He flicked the light on and went to the window to pull the curtains. Across the road, Polly was home and on this warm summer’s night, she was wearing only shorts and a little top as she bounced away to the music on her iPod. Over the year since she moved in, taking the second floor flat directly opposite him, she and he had developed a sort of friendship, waving hello and good night and on one evening when the X-Factor was on, running to the window after every act with a thumbs up or down for each in a joke that ran longer than it was actually funny.

Polly was the name he had given her; actually he had no idea what her real name was. He thought that it would be a terrible tragedy to find out it was something less pretty.

As she danced, she threw her head back and suddenly caught sight of him watching her. She laughed, a little embarrassed, but not enough to do anything about it. He laughed back and pretended to dance to the music he couldn’t hear. She gave him a thumbs down and they both laughed again. When Martin waved Polly good night before he pulled the curtains, all he knew was that it made him happy she was there to wave back.

## Chapter Three

His hand smashed his bedside table and knocked over the remains of a glass of water as he lashed out at his BlackBerry alarm just before seven. Pain flashed across his knuckles and he shouted out in anger while the opening bars of *Eye of the Tiger*, a ringtone he'd vowed repeatedly he would change, continued to taunt him.

Realising that rage could be useful, he threw his duvet aside and rolled onto the floor to get straight into his early morning push ups. A chart at eye level, next to the bedside table, told him how many he had to do today, day 63 of his routine.

*One. Two. Three. Four. Five.* No problem so far. *Six. Seven. Eight. Nine. Ten.* Getting harder, but okay. *Eleeeeeven. Tweeeeeelve. Thirteeeeeen.* Ugh. Forget it. Try crunches instead. He rolled onto his back and began to psyche himself up. Then he threw in the towel. Not his morning. That would make 19 days he had missed out of the 63. Not good, but Martin knew that without a more serious goal, he was unlikely to improve on that.

He shuffled into the kitchen, still not fully awake, and threw random frozen fruit pieces into a blender, yawning as he held the lid down while it roared into life.

He showered and dressed and pulled his door gently closed as he left his flat so that he didn't alert any of the neighbours.

The lift was already carrying the Spanish woman who lived in the flat directly above him. She was forty-odd, he guessed but dressed like she was permanently on the prowl. He supposed she was what was meant by the term *cougar*, and he had even, charitably, assumed her to be a call girl for a while; not judging, but occasionally wondering whether he should enquire about her services.

That myth had been put to bed when he'd passed her on the phone in the car park one morning, talking business. She either owned or ran or maybe just thought she ran, a marketing consultancy.

He'd been a little disappointed at the discovery.

She always wore sunglasses so he'd never seen her eyes, but he thought if they were even half as spectacular as her suntanned legs and perfect calves, they'd be remarkable.

On one occasion many months before, she'd smiled at him as he got into the lift, though he still had no idea why. This time around, like normal, she nodded a silent good morning as he entered and then ignored him entirely. He returned the favour.

It was a perfect early-morning walk to the Archway tube station and would have been just five stops down to Goodge Street if he was heading straight into the office. Mornings for Martin however were crucial times to check in with the Peepers. Down to Leicester Square, he walked around the corner to Hair by Margot, where Red Stella waited for him outside.

"You all right?" she asked in London vernacular, hiding not a shred of her Russian accent.

"Hello Stella. You got the goods?"

"Summer in this city, we always got the goods," she said, slipping her hand into the pocket of her little black shorts for the sealed white envelope.

"Who we dealing with?" he asked.

"Kate Winslett. And that girl from that show. The other girl told me who she is. And also the blonde singer. The Australian one."

"Kylie?"

"Could be. Perhaps. I didn't know her."

Martin flicked his eyebrows in appreciation. It was a good haul. "That sounds great. I can't wait to see who else. You're right, you have to love summer," he said.

Red Stella nodded, but as usual she was all business. Let him make small talk; she just wanted her money. Martin pulled out another envelope containing five twenties and handed it to her.

She smiled, rare for her. “Thank you. Today I think will also be good. Janet is coming to the shop to work which means she has a big client.”

“That’s the stuff Stella. Keep those eyes peeled, and thank you for the risks you’re taking,” he said, and then he left her. They’d done this dance for too long to bother with small talk.

Back on the tube, this time he popped out of the ground at Bond Street and made his way into Mayfair. Shannon the Bombshell was also waiting for him, smoking a cigarette and looking like a seduction in a little red flowery summer dress. She had no bag and apparently no pockets and Martin wondered briefly where she got the cigarette from, and where the lighter went to.

She played it cool as was her style, and let him come down the road to meet her where she leaned.

“Marty,” she said in a false New York accent.

“Shannon,” he said, taking her lead.

“I’ve got some real goods today,” she said, handing him another white envelope.

“Do I want to know right now?” he asked.

“That depends. Are you the sort of boy who likes knowing your Christmas presents in advance?”

He handed her an identical envelope to that he had given Red Stella. “In that case I’ll wait,” he said.

“When are you going to ask me out?”

Shannon the Bombshell had often hinted she was ready to party if Martin was, though he had absolutely no idea whatsoever what that meant. Was it sex? Was it dinner and dancing? Was it paintballing? While he was safely away from her he often thought of how sensational she would be in bed. Under her direct gaze however, he simply didn’t have the courage to find out.

“When they build a restaurant good enough for you,” he said. The sort of stupid line that made him cringe as soon as it left his lips.

“I could name a few.”

"Yeah, but who's the man here, you know what I mean?"

He actually said *who's the man. Smooth like someone who never wants to get laid, ever. Idiot.*

Shannon the Bombshell smirked at him, took a last long drag from her cigarette and then flicked it far away to her right where it hit a man making his way down the pavement, squarely on the chest. He gave his suit a brush as he frowned at her and Shannon the Bombshell, with characteristic attitude, maintained eye contact with him all the way past. The advantage of the intimidatingly pretty girl.

"On that note, I'm off," said Martin.

"See you next week lover," said Shannon the Bombshell, producing a little stick of lip balm from out of nowhere, and applying it to her sensational lips.

Too much. And trouble with a capital everything, he thought. A pity.

He got back on the tube for his final stop of the morning to find Nelsinho the Grave Digger whose principal interests were Brazilian rock band Sepultura and girls with tattoos. It was a pretty serious violation of Rule #1 of Shallowness: *Never, ever, get involved with anyone beyond the superficial,* that Martin even knew that, but Nelsinho the Grave Digger wasn't one to keep his thoughts and opinions to himself. "As long as you don't talk about this thing of ours," Martin had said to him once.

"I give you my word. It's stronger than hate," he had replied.

"Huh?" Martin had really only grunted.

"From *Beneath The Remains*," Nelsinho the Grave Digger had said. "It's a total classic. I'll make you a flash drive."

"No. Don't make me a flash drive. Don't share music with me and don't tell me about your business. Shallowness pays our bills, right?" Martin had said.

That was six months ago however and Nelsinho the Grave Digger had turned out to be completely reliable, producing the goods often. The coffee shop where he worked and above which he lived, was frequented by BBC types and it often made his lists brilliant.

"I'm especially excited about yours today Nelsinho. Is summer working its magic here too?"

Nelsinho the Grave digger looked at the sky. "Is that what you call this?"

"Fuck off, it's a beautiful day," Martin said.

"Yeah, for London. But anyway, yeah, I have a good list this week. Maybe the best. You paying extra?"

Martin snorted, and snatched the envelope, exchanging it with the payoff.

Back on the tube, his collecting done for the day, he thought of Shannon the Bombshell as he did every time he saw her. She was the only one of the Peepers he really wondered about. A ragtag assembly of predominantly Europeans, they were selected as much for their places of employment: a top five restaurant, an in-the-loop hairdresser, a sublimely located coffee shop as for their personalities. He had other Peepers on the Eurostar and on the airlines and in the summer he had them on Mykonos, Santorini and Majorca to Drake the Robot's initial alarm. He had them in Los Angeles and New York. He was the ultimate spy master.

But Shannon the Bombshell intrigued him not just because of her long, smooth legs and her incredible breasts and the fact that she never failed to eye-fuck him when he approached her, but for the fact that she was the only English girl he had yet met who didn't declare herself too cool to load up her eyeballs when faced with a celebrity.

Nothing about her was normal and as Martin told himself every time he thought about her, nothing about her was for him. Rule #2 of Shallowness was *never like anyone as much as they like you.*

## Chapter Four

When Martin walked through the front door of the unkempt tower which housed among other things, his fourth floor cubicle, Jane the receptionist was close to panic. "Quick, quick, quick," she said to him, leaping up from behind her desk and practically shoving him into the glass door that stood between reception and the inner sanctum as she swiped her security card to release the latch. "You've got a member of your hate club here."

"Where?" Martin looked around the empty reception area as the doorway leading to the men's room flew open.

Jane's face told him unambiguously to get the hell out of there and he slipped around the corner out of sight, choosing the stairs over the lifts which were in full view of reception beyond the glass doors. Doors which it turned out were secure enough to stop unwanted visitors, but powerless to prevent their bouts of rage from reaching his ears.

By the time he got to his desk, the phone was already ringing. He picked it up.

"So that was pleasant," said Jane.

"Jane, I'm so sorry."

"Jesus, Martin."

"Who was that anyway?"

"What, you don't even know the bloke? How is it possible you can piss someone off that badly when you don't even know them?"

"A talent, I guess."

"His name's John Stevens and he's an author of a book you basically told people not to bother buying last week apparently. He says the publishers won't deal with you so he has to come and do it himself and he says he'll be back here every day until you explain, and I quote here ... hold on, let me find it, because I wrote it down ... oh here it is ... *back every day until you explain why you're such a cock-banging, ball-sucking, bag of anti-intellectual shit*. I had him spell *cock-banging* for me to make sure it was hyphenated. So anyway, that's nice, isn't it?"

"He said that?"

"They *all* say that."

"That's a bit rude, isn't it?"

"You think?"

"Look, I'm sorry you had to go through that. Can security just take care of it next time?"

"It isn't in my job description you know, fending off the lunatic fringe of your hate club."

"Oh come on, it's not like it happens often."

"Martin, I promise you, you owe me for this. I promise you. He was shouting like a mad man. You can bloody well buy me a drink, this time."

"He doesn't know what I look like does he?"

"And that's the question you come back with? You're unbelievable. You really are a cock-swallower or whatever it was he said."

"That's nice," he said, but the phone had already gone dead.

He sat down heavily. *Not again.*

By its very nature, the Shallow Review of Books got Martin into regular trouble. He hadn't told anyone not to buy the John Stevens book. All he did was report that both Emma Watson and Rhys Ifans had been spotted putting it down and making another purchase instead. It baffled even him that such an inane observation could have a real impact on the following week's book sales, but there was empirical evidence that it did.

It was three years since Martin dreamed up the Shallow Review of Books and a year since it was bought by a big media house which had the ability to drive a significant increase in readership.

But he still struggled to lose the mindset he had when he founded it as an ironic blog and twitter feed. It was supposed to be a statement *against* shallowness; a veiled lashing-out at the people who believe that superficiality and substance are the same things. He guessed those people didn't care about reading good books anything like as much as they did about being seen reading the hottest book of the moment. Cheryl Cole may carefully select her beach time read, but the masses of brain dead who wear Burberry knock-offs on government benefits, care only that it's the latest must-have accessory.

Martin had watched in muted astonishment as his twitter followers rose rapidly into the thousands and then the tens of thousands. He'd never anticipated a day when hundreds of thousands of people would read his blog every week, or that it would be tagged on more than a dozen news services. And yet there it was. And people like John Stevens could pay a heavy price for a single celebrity's fickleness.

In selling it, he'd become moderately financially independent, had kept basic control and received a fat cat salary with the added shelter of a five year contract. The only real concession was Drake the Robot who gave Martin plenty of rope, but wasn't afraid to give it a neck-breaking tug when he attempted to deviate from the established format.

That morning it wasn't a neck-breaking tug that pulled him from his thoughts about the monster he had created however, but the arrival of a man at his cubicle, asking to know who he was.

*Oh Jane, you total bitch, you let him in,* he thought. "Who're you looking for?"

"Bloke called Martin," said the man. He was a big one, overweight, but Martin could tell that enough of his weight came from muscle for him to be just the sort of rival he hated most: one that could beat the crap out of him.

"And why do you want him?" he asked.

"Bloody hell, you're a suspicious one, aren't you? You're him, aren't you?"

He was way too laid back to be the shouter from a few moments before, but Martin remained on edge.

The man stuck out his hand. "Gerome. You spoke to my girlfriend yesterday. Penny?"

*Oh shit,* Martin thought. *This is worse.*

"Well, I wanted to thank you," said Gerome.

"Ah," said Martin.

"Yeah, well, I've done something stupid. I know she told you. But your advice has made her decide to give it a go. I thought she'd leave me. I'm really grateful."

"Oh," said Martin.

Gerome looked suddenly embarrassed. "Right, well, I'll be off. Just dropped Penny off and thought I'd come and see if I can find you. So, thanks a lot and ... well, thanks," he said.

Martin nodded but only watched as he walked away. And then, quite out of character for him, perhaps because John Stevens was still on his mind, he suddenly felt bad about being so offhand. Without thinking, he took off out of his cubicle and out of the office area to catch Gerome before he got into the lift.

But it wasn't to be. Because before Martin could get to him, he was knocked solidly onto his ass in a collision with an unexpected Pole.

## Chapter Five

Martin had collided with a pole once before. At school, at the age of nine, running while simultaneously reading the first page of a book he had just borrowed from the micro-library, he failed to notice the steel pole which held up one end of the volleyball net. The collision caused him to chip a tooth and require three stitches in the centre of his forehead to seal a cut which still carried a scar to that day.

This time around however, it was different. As Poles go, this was a much softer one. A nice looking one too, even from the floor on which they had both ended up sprawled.

"So sorry," she said in a heavy accent.

"My mistake."

"No, I don't look where I am going. My blame."

She began to gather the envelopes she had been carrying before she hit the floor and Martin scrambled to help, forgetting the reason he was in the hallway in the first place.

"No, really, I was running. I don't usually do that. I really do apologise," he said, blathering out of embarrassment.

They got to their feet together and he handed her the envelopes, trying to think what more he could say. But he couldn't say anything. And he couldn't think at all. She locked her eyes on his just for a second, but it was enough to arrest all of his thoughts.

They were an intense, hot copper colour, but they were neither particularly warm nor enthusiastic. They had a brilliant sparkle of crystal brightness, but it was clear they were unimpressed. Probably with him, for knocking her on her backside.

But they were magnificent. A flush of warmth washed over him as the hairs on the back of his neck and on his arms tugged at the air around him as if they were trying to work themselves loose. He held his gaze too long though it was just a second, and she looked away with what could have been embarrassment, could have been irritation. It didn't matter to Martin. She was a brief flash of bright sunshine through a break in the clouds on an otherwise gloomy day. Only it was as if he'd never seen the sun before; had never realised anything so splendid could exist.

And that wasn't all. She smelled like some of the happiest moments from his childhood. He'd long ago forgotten the violet-flavoured sweets he'd been so obsessed with as a boy, and hadn't seen them on sale for more years than he could remember. He hadn't seen them, hadn't tasted them, hadn't thought about them. But the memory was as vivid as if it was yesterday when he realised her very subtle violet scent; a scent of absurdly simple pure joy.

She turned to leave and he moved just a half-inch into her path. "Are you new here?"

She nodded. "Yes. I am working here, only yesterday and today."

From beneath the rising pedestal on which he had reflexively placed her, he tried to find his wits. “Oh right. Welcome. Where are you from?”

“Warsaw. I must go. Thank you.” She pulled the files closer to her chest, withdrawing, and Martin realized he was still staring, a little intimidating perhaps.

“So do you work here?”

“Yes. I tell you that. And now I must go.”

“What’s your name?”

“Kasia”

She didn’t ask for his.

Looking back, that was the moment Martin decided to give it all up, though he wouldn’t really pinpoint that until later. Back at his desk, he flipped open his MacBook and as he waited for it to boot up, he replayed the moment when her eyes met his. He couldn’t mentally conjure up the colour. It was impossible for him to get a handle on because they didn’t fit into any generic eye colour category he could think of. There were flecks of green there. There was what was almost orange. Who has orange eyes? The creature at the end of *Rosemary’s Baby* probably would have had orange eyes if you’d been permitted to see them. How beautiful would it have been after all, if you took that into consideration?

Her name was Kasia. Like strawberries in French. No, that’s fraises. Similar vowel structure, more or less. She reminded him of strawberries. Not for any obvious reason but that they were fresh. *Fresh* strawberries were anyway. And sort of exotic. He’d often wondered how nature, which created the Brussels sprout could also create strawberries. How, for that matter, it could create kittens as well as crocodiles. Kasia was more of a kitten. She was definitely a strawberry. But what colour were those eyes exactly? And what did they see? And what did they think of him? God, she probably thought he was a complete idiot. What did he say? Did he say anything stupid? He stared at his screen for a moment and then decided he needed tea instead.

As usual, the boys were in the break room, boisterous in one of their many debates.

Searching for quiet in his head to try to assess his new discovery, Martin considered for a moment just turning back, but Dave the Legend, editor of Sportfolio spotted him. "Martin, let's have your opinion on this," he called out.

Martin nodded with mock good will and went to join them, thinking momentarily of what Kasia would think of the gathering.

"Most annoying song ever recorded. We've got a list. We've got ... er ... *Blah Blah Blah* by Kesha, *Wannabe* by The Spice Girls and *Who let the dogs out* by the Baha Men. Um ... oh, here's a good one: *Lonely* by Akon with that squeaking wombat or whatever it was ..."

"Chipmunk," said Torpedo Steve, editor of the political satire magazine Railroaded.

"Whatever," said Dave the Legend. "*Achy Breaky Heart, Mmm Bop, YMCA* ... any of these making you want to kill yourself yet?"

Martin didn't want to think about it. "I don't know."

"Come on, get off the fence," said Dave the Legend.

"I don't know. *Love Story* by Taylor Swift."

"Really?"

"You don't agree?"

"How does that go then?" said Torpedo Steve.

"Don't act like it isn't on your iPod," said Dave the Legend.

"It *isn't*," Torpedo Steve came back, too vigorously, too affronted, confirming in the process that it probably was.

Dave the Legend rolled his eyes. "Anyway, why?"

"Because it's reckless," said Martin. "Romeo and Juliet get permission to get married and live happily ever after at the end of the song which is an outrageous corruption of one of the greatest works in the English Canon. It's also inaccurate in its reference to Nathaniel Hawthorne's *Scarlet Letter* and on the subject of Elizabethan-era wedding clothing."

Dave the Legend and Torpedo Steve exchanged a mocking glance. "You're crap at this game. You think too much. Why do you always do that?"

Martin ignored the comment and headed for the door. Then he

changed his mind. "You want to know something interesting?"

He had their attention.

"I'd bet you a month's salary you could be convinced to like any of the songs on your list by a girl."

"Oh, I think I might draw the line at *Blah Blah Blah*," said Torpedo Steve.

"*Any* of those songs," said Martin, pointing towards the list. "Or at least you'd let her play them and keep your opinions on the matter to yourself."

"Well maybe *you* would," said Dave the Legend.

"No. *You would*. I think we can agree I'm probably the only one here who would not," said Martin.

"Bollocks. The girl will come along who'll change you, mate," said Dave the Legend.

Martin smiled. *Maybe*, he thought. *If she does, I hope she has eyes like those.*

He ambled back to his desk, trying to find a reference for that colour, lost in thought so deeply that he nearly tripped over the red plastic cooler box that stood in the middle of his cubicle.

Frustration. He hated surprises. He threw up his hands, though nobody was watching. And then he opened it to take a look inside.

"What is that?" Dave the Legend asked, stopping as he passed by on his way to his desk.

Martin turned his head towards him as he lifted the lid to reveal the contents. "It's full of fresh fish. On ice," he said.

"Who's sent you fish?"

Martin handed Dave the Legend the invitation that came with it. It was effusively over-written the way the author who penned it tended to treat all prose, including that in his many successful novels. He wanted Martin to go deep sea fishing with him and his friends, off Dubai, all expenses paid, as thanks for the great mentions in the Shallow Review of Books.

Dave the Legend gave a slow, long whistle of appreciation. "Cool. I read his last couple of books. He's brilliant," he said.

"Yeah," said Martin.

"What? Don't you think so?"
"Doesn't matter what I think."
"Is this one of your rules then?"
"It's number three actually. *Never look at what's behind a name.* You're usually disappointed when you do, I find. Celebrity is usually unearned. It's the reason I refuse to handle the books."
"Have you ever read any of his books?"
"That's not what the Shallow Review of Books is about."
"Have you ever read anything that goes into it at all?"
"That's not what the Shallow Review of Books is about, Dave."
"Fucking weird man," said Dave the Legend, shaking his head.
Martin shrugged. "It's a formula that works. Anyway, do you want some fish?"

Because Martin focused best when the office was silent, he rarely got very much done during the day. Time at his desk was more of an obligation stipulated by his employment contract, but even so he'd usually get a little work done while he waited for everyone else to leave.

That day however, between aborted attempts at writing, fact-checking with his Peepers and a review with Drake the Robot, he found himself researching the origins of the name Kasia, reading the Wikipedia entry on Poland and following countless links to other information, and though he knew it was a step over an imaginary line, looking his latest fascination up personally on the company intranet. Only occasionally did he allow the mocking voice in his head to point out that he was a creepy crawling stalker.

When the day began to unwind, he was a little embarrassed to discover he'd violated every sacred Rule of Shallowness there was.

Normally he was politely patient when Dave the Legend came about asking if he would, this time, just for once, join them at the pub, but when his face appeared over the cubicle wall that evening, Martin was genuinely grateful to be pulled back into reality.

"Pint?"

Martin smiled. "What am I going to say?"

"It's England away, mate. This is the decider. Come and watch."

"Can't do it Dave. I'm sorry. I might catch some of it at home later but I'll be working through it."

"Worth a try anyway. You work too hard."

"I know."

"No, really."

"No, I know."

"Oh well. Have a good evening. We'll be at The Dog and Duck later if you're interested."

"Thanks Dave."

Martin meant it. He appreciated the gesture because he knew it always came from a good place and a lesser man than Dave the Legend would have stopped extending the invitation a long time ago.

He gave Martin his characteristic two finger-pistol, shoot-from-the-hip move and Martin more or less did the same in return, though with none of the John Wayne that Dave the Legend seemed able to channel.

He walked on and then clicked his fingers as if remembering something important. "By the way, you should put your head up more often. If you did, you'd have noticed you got a smile from that new Polish girl today," he said.

The way Dave the Legend recoiled in fright as Martin launched from his chair, he obviously hadn't thought that information more than an aside.

*"When?"* said Martin.

"You were on the phone to some bloke with your head in your barrel of fish there and she came past. Put some mail down for you I think," he said.

Martin looked at his desk. On the left hand side, just inside his cubicle, were two envelopes. They had been put there by her black finger nail polished hands, he thought, realizing suddenly that he had noticed those too. And her chestnut hair. And her ridiculously kissable lips. And then to his horror, he remembered her smile could have had an alternate meaning.

"Oh crap. Did she see my screen? What was I looking at?" he asked, out loud, but aimed into thin air.

"Er ... Why? What *were* you looking at?"

"Nothing. Just wondering," Martin said. "What did she do?"

"She smiled mate. I didn't think about it much beyond that."

"But like, a *friendly* smile?"

Dave the Legend let out a belt of laughter. "Martin, only you could think there is any other kind," he said.

## Chapter Six

He tried not to roll his eyes when he stepped out of the lift that evening to see Rupert unlocking the front door to his flat, but he wasn't sure he achieved it.

He didn't think his across-the-hall neighbour had noticed.

Rupert was bafflingly skinny for a man who appeared to be in perfectly good health and Martin dreaded that he would have the reason for it foisted upon him one day, leaving him with the options of getting somehow involved or looking like a jerk.

Rupert's face lit up when he saw him. "Hey Martin, how you doing?"

"Good, good, thanks. Just busy, busy, busy."

"Are you in this evening?"

"Um, yeah. Yeah."

"Well are you watching the match?"

"No mate. Wish I was. Got work to do." Years of lying to avoid commitments had made him an expert and he knew he'd got away with that.

"Okay, well if you decide to put it on, I'll be watching it. Company would be cool. You'll have to bring your own beer though because I don't drink any," Rupert said.

*No, you don't,* Martin thought. *You certainly don't drink beer.*

Martin put his TV on and clicked it to mute. There was no way he was going to miss that evening's Euro qualifier, which held the added excitement of being a grudge match against Germany, but he didn't want Rupert to know. He didn't seriously expect Rupert to come knocking, but if the TV was on mute, there was no risk of his secret being exposed.

He grabbed a Carlsberg from the fridge and then thought better of it. No sit ups this morning meant no beer this evening. That was another rule, albeit an unnumbered one.

Sinking back into his couch, his MacBook on his lap, he considered ordering a pizza. No sit ups meant no beer, but it didn't have to mean no pizza, did it? Beer was useless calories, but a vegetarian pizza offered plenty of goodness to go with the bad.

He allowed a brief, lopsided internal dialogue and then picked up the phone, dialled the number and ordered a Meat Feast Supreme. Then he put the idea out of his mind.

The thought of working bored him, the silent match hadn't yet begun and with the prospect of a thirty minute wait for the guy from Bella Napoli he put his head back and stared at the ceiling. Dave the Legend was both right and wrong. Martin didn't work too hard. In truth, he really didn't work at all in comparison to some of his colleagues. But he didn't do anything else either.

His general preference for being alone meant he was practiced at spotting and avoiding emotional social potholes. Ironically, that was the biggest reason he had any social connections at all: the basis for most of his relationships was his ability to see simple solutions to the common problems of his co-workers. But the more he learned of the daily dramas in the lives of the people around him, the more his initial distaste for relationships had swelled into a paralysing fear of any that were other than *shallow*.

He closed his eyes and exhaled deeply, a technique for clearing his head he had learned from a university lecturer a few years back. And suddenly, there was Kasia, smiling at him as he rummaged through his ice box of fish. There she was turning her eyes away from him as he stared like a half-wit. Those eyes that were so astonishing, so utterly beautiful. He replayed the moment again and again, like a loop. What was it about her? She was a pretty girl, but there were lots of those. In London, there were a million of them. There were offers on the table too, from Shannon the Bombshell and Jane the receptionist, both of whom were pretty overt. And there had always been women. That couldn't be it.

He tried to imagine what it would be like to be with her. Would she like him? Could he be enough for her? He leapt to his feet, vaguely aware out of the corner of his eye that John Terry was in trouble with the referee and realising that the match was now in its twenty-sixth minute. In his head he practiced a conversation with her, imagining how it would go and realising that he was struggling even in his head, to look her in the eyes. What if she laughed at him? What if he bored her?

And then there was a knock on the door and he froze. What the hell was this now?

"Pizza," came a voice, muffled by the door.

Martin felt his whole body release, aware only after the fact of how tense he had become.

He opened the door. "Hi. Thanks. How much is it?"

Fourteen Pounds later, he sat back down heavily, switched off mute and raised the volume just slightly, listening to the commentary as a lacklustre nil-nil first half drew to a close.

As he ate his pizza, he made up his mind that whatever Kasia was, she wasn't his. Shouldn't be his. Shouldn't be anything he should even want. What did those eyes say? What did they warn of? That afternoon she had been strawberries. Now she seemed more like a stick of dynamite.

*She'll embarrass you mate*, he thought. *You'll embarrass yourself. You'll make yourself look like a fool even trying it on with someone like her. And anyway, a girl is the last thing you need.*

Suddenly full of anxious energy, he flipped the TV back to mute, grabbed his iPod and looked for something loud. The Pretty Reckless. Female singer. No matter. He clicked play, leapt onto the couch, the table and across the floor, air miking Taylor Momsen, air guitaring and drumming along with the band, wondering whether his rock moves would have enough awesome to wow a girl like Kasia but realising with frustration that if that was her thing, he had nothing to offer.

As the match re-started and he grabbed absently at another slice of pizza, the only thing he could think was: please like me, like I like you. Just a little bit.

She stayed on his mind that evening and it took him a long time to fall asleep. He knew he was in trouble when she was the first thing on his mind when he woke up. Or the second anyway after the stuck record of *I have to change that bloody ring tone*. He lay in bed for a moment, staring at the ceiling, feeling worse for thinking about her first thing because he knew there was no way she was doing the same thing. Or if she was, it was only because she was looking at her bruises in the mirror and wondering about the lunatic that threw himself into her path the day before. He laughed a little at that thought, lifting his mood enough to roll onto the floor and take a look at where he was supposed to be on Day 64.

50 push ups was going to be a stretch since he hadn't yet managed them on any day even though it was supposed to be something he had built up to. He got through them in several sets, the largest consisting of 12, the smallest being seven, his arms quivering like jelly and scarcely having the strength to lift themselves, much less his entire torso.

He had the goal he had been lacking however. Today, he might see Kasia and since he had managed ultimately to finish that entire giant circular heap of cheese and meat last night, this morning he was going to work some of it off.

Crunches came next; never his favourite. The goal was 100; he managed 70, and the last ten were a joke. It didn't matter. Mentally he was fully switched on and the pain in his abdomen reminded him that this morning he had actually taken some of his life into his hands.

He tried not to think of her through his long shower, feeling that they weren't there yet and she deserved better, that to think of her while he was naked would somehow be disrespectful.

He'd noticed with idle interest over the years that when it came to washing his body in the shower he never seemed to get below his knees, leaving his lower legs and feet to take care of themselves. He'd noticed this, but until that morning, he'd never bothered to do anything about it.

And then, his shower done, a towel around his waist hiding his nakedness, he let her open her eyes inside his head once again so he could see them. And he decided to do something he usually tried to resist doing on a Friday. He shaved. Normally that was a thing for a Monday and perhaps a Saturday if he planned to go anywhere. One Wednesday per month when he had to report, with Drake the Robot, to the overlords upstairs.

As he got dressed, he played through the conversation he would have with her that day and it partly excited him, partly made him feel a little like vomiting for the sheer terror of it.

In the kitchen, he opened the fridge and absently pulled things out, playing through the possibility that if she found him amusing the day before, perhaps she would welcome the chance to speak to him.

All he would have to do is put himself in the same space as her and let her take the lead. Less risk there. She'd smile as she walked past and he'd stop and she'd say, *hello, I don't know if you remember me* and he'd say *sure I do* and they'd talk and arrange to go out or something. God, even he knew *that* was pathetic.

He put everything back in the fridge and grabbed a banana, his keys and his computer.

On the way out, he looked in the mirror, an act as alien to him as surfing a tube. There he was. Martin White, man of rules, commander of a life he had carefully crafted.

What the hell was he thinking of?

## Chapter Seven

When Martin was a child, he believed photographs could see him. As an adult, though he knew that was nonsense, he still felt an eerie discomfort whenever he was placed before a straight-on shot of someone he admired, especially female. On the platform at Archway that day, it was Olga Kurylenko, staring straight at him from a shampoo billboard. He wasn't sure what she was communicating ... was that smile taunting him and mocking him and tacitly explaining in immense detail how ludicrous his thoughts were ... or was it encouraging, willing him on, offering moral support? He couldn't tell. But just before the train obscured the poster as it raced into the station, he would swear that Olga winked.

His pre-office run around town that morning included Nick the Greek, Style Council Marco and Marina Triple Platinum, twenty; twenty-one at a maximum, and as commanding as a bad hangover, with long lashes that framed the greyest eyes he had ever seen on a human being. As grey as the North Sea in a winter storm, but as crystal clear as Vodka. She always played the game as if they were spies for real, writing only in Russian and forcing Martin to recruit Dimitri from TechToyland to translate for him. More than once he'd had to verify with her what he got back from Dimitri who insisted that Marina Triple Platinum spoke *some form of Lithuanian Russian or something, but certainly not the real deal*. Rule #1 precluded Martin from asking her about it and he didn't really care enough anyway. Like all of his

Peepers, Marina Triple Platinum always had the goods, and that was good enough for him.

Jane ignored him as he walked through the front doors, so he thought he better try to smooth things out. As he stopped in front of her she grabbed a phone and put it to her ear, looking down and saying nothing. He waited. She continued to ignore him, but after a minute she shot a glance at him. "How long are you going to stand there?"

"Morning. Just until you're off the phone," said Martin.

"Martin, I'm not on the bloody phone," she said, dropping the receiver back onto its cradle. "That was a signal to you to go away and leave me alone."

"Look Jane, I'm sorry about yesterday. That guy was an idiot. He shouldn't have put you through that."

"*You* put me through it Martin, not *him*. And you're going to have to think of a way to get me to forgive you."

*Oh shit.*

Martin had an unacknowledged red-blooded attraction to Jane, much he imagined like many other men in the building. She was hot. A real eight. A natural eight, unenhanced and effortless. Jane was definitely a potential ten, but she didn't acknowledge the importance of the final twenty percent. Martin was certain there were no natural tens, just enhanced eights. A strategic tattoo perhaps; obsessively-loved hair; the confidence to know your legs are amazing enough to go on display ... a ten was just an eight with an after-dark attitude.

Jane was an eight with an attitude of sweetness, which meant she'd be hard to be shallow with, appalling to hurt and therefore against his rules, making the next four seconds excruciating.

Their relief was immense when a UPS man arrived with a box, apologising as he bumped Martin's arm.

"I'm sorry," Martin said, pathetic and totally insufficient. He backed away as the UPS man looked from him to her and back, gingerly aware he had unwittingly thrust himself into the middle of something deep.

Martin felt dreadful when he got upstairs, late as usual for the regular

Friday Idea Workshop which was already underway in the fourth floor meeting room.

It was a meeting he hated and he took extra time to make himself tea before he walked into the room, miming an insincere apology as he did so.

The only parts of the Idea Workshop Martin liked were the ones in which he was doing the talking; for the rest of the hour it was to him a constant dirge of *cross-pollination* and *deadline progress reporting* that he knew hardly applied to his digital rag of nearly-unsubstantiated gossip. As usual, once he'd elaborated on his methods for recruiting Peepers for one of the new editors, he stopped listening and began to idly doodle on his notepad.

It came to him with some alarm that he had been writing the name Kasia in capital letters in the page margin and he worked quickly to disguise it, joining the letters together into an improvised image of a space ship, complete with flame-spewing rocket boosters and an alien with long antennae in the cockpit. He glanced to his left to see if Paper-thin Allan had seen anything, and was relieved that his attention was focused squarely on Drake the Robot as he held forth. To his right however, he wasn't as lucky. Dave the Legend grinned at his space ship with amusement and gave him a smirk that either said *great work*, thickly buttered with ridicule, or to Martin's intense discomfort, perhaps *I saw what you did just there*.

Martin pretended not to care, and even sat back a little with calculated indifference when over his shoulder, a new pad of paper was placed by a hand with sparkling black nail polish, attached to a thin arm in a pale yellow cardigan. The subtle scent of violets decorated the air. His throat suddenly closed up and his heart stepped up thirty beats as he felt his face begin to burn.

He heard Dave the Legend say thank you and watched as Kasia slowly came into view around the table, moving silently as she topped everyone up with new notepads.

She was masterfully unobtrusive, and she avoided eye contact, only responding to the occasional word of thanks with a very slight, but completely heartbreaking smile.

Her dress rustled slightly as she moved, and Martin wondered if anyone else could hear it besides him. He tried not to look directly at her, faking a stretch so he had a reason to raise his head and steal a glance but feeling a little silly as he did it.

She didn't look his way, but kept moving, slowly.

Her chestnut hair had a hint of red in it as she passed directly under the fluorescent ceiling lights and Martin realised that it was hands-down his favourite hair colour in the world. With those eyes and that hair, where had this girl come from?

He fidgeted slightly, hoping to get her attention without drawing that fact to anyone else. She smiled a little at the new editor in acknowledgement of his thanks, and Martin winced at the growing hollowness inside him as she did so. He adopted a pose, but quickly realised it was stupid, so he sat back with his hands behind his head as if he was too cool to take that dull old meeting seriously.

And then all at once he realised that she was moving slowly because she was listening to the conversation. Suddenly Martin could see a golden opportunity was slipping away, to get her attention by saying something clever.

"Good idea. I concur," he said out loud, too loud, too desperately, dealing as he did so, a self-inflicted near-fatal blow to his own ego. Oh Jesus. *Really though? Concur?*

Drake the Robot stopped what he was saying and blasted Martin with a piercing belt of irritation. "With what do you concur, Martin?"

All eyes were on him, including Kasia's which darted from him, to Drake the Robot and back to him. She had picked up the obvious sea change in the conversation.

Martin scrambled. "What you were saying. With what you were saying. It's great. Sorry, just thinking out loud."

"Okay. So Martin concurs that the publishing world is in a state of chaos and thinks that's a great idea," said Drake the Robot. "Fantastic. Thanks for the input. Now perhaps if you could put the lady down for a moment ... my apologies to you, Kasia is it?" he glanced up at her.

She nodded.

"Well, perhaps you could then pay some attention over here, Martin."

There was a little embarrassed laughter, but it was uncomfortable. Martin's face began to burn for the second time in two minutes as he tried to fake incomprehension for Kasia's benefit.

She met his eyes head on but her face registered nothing whatsoever. What is it about some people that you can't tell whether they're interested in a good or bad way? What could be withering disdain could just as easily be delight.

She left the room without acknowledgement as Martin shrank back into his seat, feeling more than a little battered. Across the table, Torpedo Steve gave him a supportive, sympathetic wink.

The rest of the meeting was a black hole he was relieved to be able to climb out of. Drake the Robot could be a real asshole but his behaviour had been unusually brutal even for him.

Martin went to his desk and sat down heavily, falling forward to rest his head on his bag.

*No, this wouldn't do.*

He couldn't leave things as they were. He knew that if he didn't act on it there and then, he may never have the nerve again.

He rehearsed a new scene in his head where he found her alone and said *Wow, that was amusing, but also completely misunderstood. You realise that, right?* and she would instantly see he wasn't the idiot he must have appeared.

He needed to clear the air or he would die for sure. Maybe even just seeing her would be enough. Just taking a look at her, being near to her, getting another smell of her perfume. And just to be cool and casual. And just because he wanted one of those stunning faint smiles to be aimed at him.

He scoured his floor and the one below, and then, through the doorway of the specialised publishing department, there she was.

A smoother guy would have just walked right up to her and said, *may I just apologise for that, I was just distracted because you look really nice today and frankly in that boring meeting I was delighted that someone could bring some sunshine into the room.* Martin almost had himself worked up into enough of a frenzy to do that too, but then Kasia smiled sweetly as she handed files to someone he couldn't see inside a cubicle with whom she exchanged some words and even laughed a little, and his confidence completely collapsed.

What if she didn't remember him? How stupid would he look if he dealt her a smooth line and she said, *sorry, who are you?*

His plan gave way to panic and as she turned towards the doorway, he jumped out of sight to the left.

Dilemma.

If she was coming, he would look like a outright weirdo for skulking out of sight. He could pretend he was tying his shoe lace or something. Could he get away with that? What if she saw him?

*Oh for God's sake ...*

Grabbing the moment impulsively, he launched into action, stepped boldly into the doorway, and dealt her a full-force body blow, sending her to the floor once again.

"Oh *shit, shit, shit*, I'm so sorry. Are you all right?" he said.

She sat up, stared up at him, and it didn't take a relationship specialist to know that she wasn't feeling the love. "Yes, I am fine. You again? Why?"

"Oh, no, it wasn't on purpose. I was just coming here to do something and ... and it is all a bit of a shock."

He extended his hand. She ignored it and got up on her own.

"I saw you looking at me. Before you attack me."

"No, I didn't attack you. No, no, no. It was a mistake. I just had to tie my shoelace and so I did that and, and, well actually, I didn't see you there. So you saw me did you? That's interesting."

It wasn't enough to say she ignored the comment. She wasn't even listening. "I must go."

Martin's mouth began to fly ahead of his brain as it so often did when he was out of his depth. "May I walk you to where you're going?"

Kasia heard that, and she looked properly spooked. "I go to the file room. Why do you want to walk with me?"

"Oh, just to chat actually. I ought to go to the file room anyway and see if there is anything there for me. Save you the trouble of having to bring it up."

"It's my job."

"Yes. Yes it is, isn't it? I see. All right. Well, in that case I better let you get on with it. It was nice to see you again Kasia."

Her eyes seemed a little less beautiful as they flicked an irritated parting glance.

That Friday didn't get a lot better. He struggled in completing that week's Shallow Review of Books. Though there was lots of great content and Drake the Robot even made it out of his glass shrine to pay him a visit in his cubicle and congratulate him, Martin put it together without joy.

He was just spinning his mental cogs when Youla from accounts knocked on his cubicle wall with a distraction which for the first time practically ever, he welcomed.

"You got a minute?" she said.

"I've got lots of minutes. All I have is lots and lots of slowly dragging minutes, torturing me one by one, like an army of biting ants."

"Oh. Perhaps I should come back."

"And leave the ants to bite me? What are you, a sadist?"

He could see she didn't have a clue how to react, so he squeezed out a smile.

"Youla, it's fine. I have a minute. Take a seat."

"Oh, all right. Because I can come back."

He waved to the seat. "Please."

"I think this might turn out to be a bit daft actually, considering."

"Considering what?"

"Well, you're obviously having a harder time about something than I am."

"That depends on what you're strung out about."

She winced. "Cars."

"Cars?"

"I told you it was stupid."

"No, not necessarily. Though you're asking the wrong guy because I don't own one."

"No, well, I just need a guy's perspective. I'm going to buy one, and I just need to know what to buy."

"Wrong guy, Youla."

"No, hear me out. If you were a guy ..."

"I *am* a guy."

"Yeah, but okay then, speaking as a guy, would you be put off if I had a better car than you? I mean, if I was looking at buying a new one and I wanted to buy something flash, and you didn't make as much as I do?"

"There's a bloke, is there?"

"Yeah. And he can be a little sensitive."

"Well what do you care, aren't you just going to buy a red one anyway?"

"Don't be a wanker."

"I don't understand the point of the question. Really, I don't. Buy what you want to buy. But if your primary goal is to not upset him, I would say don't buy a car that's likely to be better than his because cars are things men use to impress women, but it rarely works the other way around."

"Isn't that sexist?"

"Yes."

"And you're okay with that?"

"It's genetics. What do you want me to do about it?"

"So I should buy a heap of shit so I don't offend him?"

"Do you want the truth or would you prefer me to give you a sugar-coated story?"

"The truth, of course."

"Buy a heap of shit. Buy thigh high boots. You'll save thousands of pounds and have a better chance of keeping him loyal."

"That's outrageous."

"I don't make the rules Youla, I just know what they are."

"You're just talking about sex."

"Well what are you talking about? Family holidays at Disney World?

Are you planning on buying an Audi TT so he'll start a vegetable patch with you?"

"God, men really are wankers."

"If you want a TT, buy one. But buy it for you."

"It's an Alfa Romeo Spider."

"Oh. Nice."

"Not anymore."

"Youla, it's the dance. Having a better car than him is like having a bigger cock than him, if you'll pardon the expression. We're challenged by that. That's all there is to it. Buy your TT if you want, but don't insist on driving him around all the time."

*"It's a Spider."*

"Your Spider then."

"You think this is a stupid conversation, don't you?"

"Not if I can help you keep Mr Right, I don't."

"I'm going to buy it anyway."

"Good for you."

"What's on *your* mind that's so troubling?"

"*On* my mind? Not much anymore because I think everything is tipping off it as it turns over and sinks once and for all."

"Wow. You *are* in a state."

He was too. And how stupid it all was. He found a sort of reassurance in something he had once offered a colleague in a similar situation: that in the mission of making an impact on Kasia, he was scoring all the way. He now had her attention. No doubt about that. Whether it was good or bad, at least he wasn't wallpaper.

He hoped she would stay away from him that afternoon but felt like he might die if she did so.

She did.

He didn't.

But he did something else totally out of character to end that thoroughly ridiculous day. At five o'clock, he went to the pub.

## Chapter Eight

The Dog and Duck in Soho isn't the biggest pub in the world. It probably isn't the smallest one either; nor even the smallest one in London with all its quirks and oddities. But the cosiness of the interior means that in good weather, the pavement outside isn't just for the smokers anymore and it was for that reason that his approach, virtually from the time he appeared out of Soho Square, was the worst kept secret in town that afternoon.

"Bloody hell, it's the Baggage Handler," shouted Michael Courtney Hole, the Sicilian-born editor of computer dweeb magazine Byte Me, nicknamed for The Godfather of his nationality and the Godmother of his musical preferences.

Dave the Legend put his head up and threw his arms wide in greeting, sloshing lager onto Torpedo Steve. Torpedo Steve didn't mind, so fascinated was he with Martin's appearance. Rich, who remained the only ad salesman in the company to manage a friendly relationship with the editorial crew, stepped out into the middle of the road and applauded him.

By the time Martin completed the 90 second approach, more than a few of the patrons were wondering who he was.

"Well bugger me senseless," said Michael Courtney Hole. He'd lived in London since he was eight, but still either retained or affected a slight Italian accent so that most such idiosyncratic English expressions sounded even more ridiculous. "What are you doing here this fine Friday? Don't tell me you've finally broken down."

"Leave him alone," said Dave the Legend. "Good to see you mate. I think this first one's on me."

Martin asked for a lager. Any would do. Dave the Legend went inside to get it while the others gathered around.

"Everything all right Martin?" Rich asked. He looked much better. If the first 72 hours of that week had been thoroughly wicked to Rich, the last 48 had apparently fully restored him.

"Yes, sure," Martin lied.

"I heard about Drake the Tosspot this morning. I reckon that was out of order," he said.

"It was complete bullshit," said Torpedo Steve. "He tried to make you look like a complete wanker, mate."

"He succeeded actually," said Martin. "Mind you, I sort of started it with that stupid comment, didn't I?"

Dave the Legend appeared with a tray of pints which he carefully balanced on the sandwich board. It was his speed at the bar that had earned him the nickname. He handed one to Martin.

"We talking about the meeting?" he asked.

"Yeah."

"You know, I'd have to say the most interesting thing about this morning was your behaviour Martin. Are you having a fling with that girl?"

Rich's ears visibly pricked. "Oh hold on a minute, you mean Drake the Robot was *right?"*

Already embarrassed, Martin tried to downplay it. "Oh, she's just ... no, anyway, we're not. At all."

Rich grinned at him. "You saucy little fucker. You've spotted something you like haven't you? Where does she work, I'll have to give her the once over for you. See if your eyes are working properly."

Dave the Legend glared at him with uncamouflaged outrage. "For Christ's sake Rich, I thought you lost the greatest love of your life, not 48 hours ago."

"Yeah, but she's gone isn't she? Time to pick myself up," said Rich.

"Unbelievable," said Dave the Legend.

Rich ignored him and returned his attention to Martin. "So who is she anyway?"

"She's ... I don't know really. The mail girl? Do we have one of those? She does admin stuff I guess."

"And is she fit?"

"Yeah. Well, yeah, I guess."

"You guess? Right, so she's a hound then, is she?"

"No, she's no hound," said Dave the Legend. "You fancy her then mate? Is that why you were doodling her name?"

*Oh shit*, thought Martin, *so you did see that.*

"You were doing what?" Rich laughed. "You *do* fancy her then?"

"I don't know. I like the look of her. I don't think she likes me," Martin said.

Rich snorted into his beer. "It's just hit me. You're here for girl advice. You realise that if you were anyone else, that would be like taking carrion to a pack of vultures and asking for advice on how to eat it? It isn't yours and it isn't safe," he said.

"Murder," said Torpedo Steve.

"What?" said Rich.

"It's a murder of vultures," said Torpedo Steve.

"No, it's a murder of crows," said Michael Courtney Hole. "Actually, it's a colony of vultures."

"Oh do me a favour," said Martin.

"Right, give him a break," said Dave the Legend. "So because you're Martin and we all rate you, you can more or less rest assured that if you've got a Kasia thing going on, you have dibs. But why is it that the Baggage Handler is here asking for girl advice? I thought you were the one to dish it out."

"*Oh wait, is it Kasia?* She's a bit of a belter actually. I've seen her too. I've had my eye on her a little bit actually mate. Are you actually giving her a go then?" said Rich.

Dave the Legend sputtered again in real outrage. "Jesus Rich, she only started working here when you were already on a plane to Japan. How the hell have you had the time to have your eye on her?"

"I don't believe in moping," said Rich.

"I don't know about any of this," said Martin, already regretting his decision to open up at all.

"All right, well, here's what I think: I think if there is a girl in our midst who can make the Baggage Handler come out of his shell, then she's all right with me," said Dave the Legend. He turned his attention to Rich with considerable aggression. "And I think the rest of us should stay the hell out of his way. Agreed?"

The others raised their glasses, but Martin could tell Rich was already elsewhere.

## Chapter Nine

He unlocked his flat door quietly, but to no good use. He yelped out loud when a light flicked on from deep within the darkness and shot a look of pure acid at the woman sitting in the chair next to the reading lamp.

She ignored it. "Oh don't be such a girl."

"You're sitting here in the dark. You don't think that's a little creepy?"

"I was thinking. If anything, you're the one inconveniencing me."

"It's *my* fucking flat."

"Nice language in front of your mother."

"When did you get here anyway?"

"This evening. A few hours ago I suppose. I was supposed to be at the Connaught, but they're doing road works or something just as ghastly outside and aside from the vulgarity of it all, the noise and the dust means there's no chance of any sleep there tonight."

Any old excuse, Martin thought. "I doubt if they do road works at night, Isabel," he said.

"Perhaps, but I have no intention of finding out. I've decided not to stay there. They loaned me their car and brought me here."

"So you're staying here then?"

"Yes Martin, I thought I'd stay with my son. Like mothers do all over the world. It isn't like you need the solitude to write your magnum opus, is it?"

"And there you go, straight into it."

"And so it will remain, Martin."

"Have you come here to fight, Isabel?"

"No. I've come here to take you to dinner. And you're late."

"Sorry about that. If you want someone to be on time, you ought to tell them what time to be there."

"I didn't know I was going to be in England today. I got the Eurostar four hours ago. Have you been drinking?"

"I had a couple of beers with some guys from work. Why?"

"Are you socialising now then?"

"I did today. Is that okay with the police?"

"Don't be so fucking belligerent, Martin. I just want to make sure you're going to be able to share a bottle of something. If you've had a couple of drinks, well done. I'm glad to hear you've found some friends. If you're stewed, less so."

"I'm fine for some wine mother."

"Good. Not every question is an interrogation you know."

"You should hear yourself. I feel like I'm an environmentalist trying to sue one of your fat cat clients."

She stood and walked over to him, embracing him tightly. "Oh dear. I think you're spending so much time with the down-and-dirty pop culture set you've decided to lead that you're beginning to grow an anti-establishment chip on your shoulder."

He hugged her back. "And I think you're still so pissed off that I'm not using my degree that you can't help sneering at everything I do."

"But darling, isn't sneering the way you make your living? You sneer at the people who write books and the people who read them alike."

"Where the hell are we eating?"

"Scotts."

"You're paying."

"Of course."

"And I'm having lobster."

"I'd expect no less."

Martin wasn't kidding about the lobster, but Isabel met the challenge and topped it by starting with Beluga caviar, the most expensive thing on the menu.

Dinner started as all social events did when his mother was present, with a low hubbub of drama. As a leading partner in a Parisian law firm, his mother lacked any semblance of a victim gene and related the day's events as a simple recap of facts that would have driven Martin to seek refuge under his desk. She had an army to take care of her petty inconveniences so she could don her steel breastplate and spend her time in combat and very little got into her way that she couldn't simply brush aside without ado.

Normal working people weren't among them. France Telecom drillers outside the Gare du Nord, a stewardess on the Eurostar and road workers in Mayfair had all crowded her calm that day, and where Martin would have walked on, relieved to leave them behind, Isabel had locked horns with the lot of them, one-by-wretched-one.

He let her talk while he quaffed Bollanger, amusing himself greatly at the thought of the word *quaff* and receiving scathing impatience in return as Isabel completed her summing up.

"Anyway. So how's your love life?" she asked.

"Same as it was last time we saw each other. One small difference I suppose. I have my eye on someone."

"What does that mean?"

"I mean I've met someone I like."

"What does *like* mean?"

"Christ, Isabel."

"Just answer the question. You have a teenage crush on her? You're sleeping with her? What?"

"You disapprove?"

"Of *what?* What does it all mean?"

"Oh forget it. She's just a girl."

"Martin for the love of God, I'm just asking. I haven't heard you speak about a girl with any interest since the Charlotte incident, so I'm trying to gauge what you're saying."

"I'm just saying there's a girl. At the office. Her name is Kasia and frankly I don't know what the hell she's done to me, but she's blowing my mind if you really want to know."

"Blowing your mind? That's very contemporary of you. What is Kasia? Where is that name from?"

"She's from Warsaw."

"Oh Christ. Not a gold digger from the East."

"No. Why would you immediately assume that? That's typical of you."

"All right, let's hear it. How far has it gone?"

"It hasn't gone anywhere. We've hardly spoken. I'm getting to it. But I don't think she deserves to be called a gold digger and I don't think she deserves your prejudice."

"Is she one?"

"No."

"And you know this, how?"

"I just know, all right? I can tell by her demeanour."

*"By her demeanour?* So in other words, you have no idea whatsoever whether she is or isn't a gold digger, but she has long legs and a pretty smile, is that right?"

"It's her eyes actually."

"Ah."

"But why do you have to go all the way to the most unpleasant conclusion anyway?"

"It may be stereotyping Martin and I'll admit that those can sometimes be incorrect. But generally they are not. I just live in hope that you'll take up with a nice English girl rather than leaving us all to integrate a foreigner into our lives."

"All your friends are French."

"That's different. The French know that the English are superior to them and they're appropriate about it. The Eastern Europeans on the other hand have no sense of place. All that communism has them thinking that everyone really is of the same class and we are absolutely not. But they don't know that."

"Oh my God. That's cynical even for you."

"All I'm saying is this: I have no problem at all with you screwing her. In fact, I would be delighted to know that my son is physically involved because I worry about you. Your challenge, and the thing you should have learned from Charlotte, is that a physical relationship doesn't have to be anything more than that. You don't have to become all doe-eyed just because you've been to bed with her. Take the lesson and leave the relationships on the side. She's Polish. They're just too complicated."

"Well maybe I'm ready for some complication."

"Oh God, you've slept with her already haven't you? And you can feel your little romantic heart beginning to puff out can't you?"

Martin leaned in abruptly. "You realise that no other mother in the entire world speaks about love to her children this way, don't you?"

"Just promise me you're using protection."

"Mother, I haven't even got past hello with her yet."

"Oh well then Martin, well done. That's the first bit of sense you've spoken this evening. Keep it that way. Just take my advice on this. I don't care how pretty her eyes are or how perky her little tits. You've never been committed enough to go after a girl of real quality, but that doesn't mean you have to bottom feed."

## Chapter Ten

Dinner ended badly and Martin and his mother didn't speak at all in the taxi home. She wished him goodnight when they got inside his flat and said she would be out before him in the morning for a Saturday client breakfast and was heading back to Paris straight after. He gave her a peck on the cheek, withholding affection like it really even mattered.

If the avoidance of situations that risked commitment was his first instinct, proving his mother wrong was his second. As unhealthy obsessions go, it was one that preoccupied his mind most actively whenever she was around because her rapid and unremitting condemnation of anything she didn't personally approve of, all too often ran to things that he did.

As he brushed his teeth, he wondered why her dismissal of Kasia had stung him so deeply. He wondered why it was that he was losing his head like this. He was embarrassed at the return of his sudden neediness. He'd been convinced that was all in the past.

He began thinking about some of the girls he might have let down along the way. Jane was the most recent example although if it carried any weight at all, it was way out of proportion. It was always hard when someone laid their cards down for someone who declined to pick them up. He suspected she'd get over it and in fact, she'd ultimately come out best in their little standoff.

Anyway, he wasn't that special; it was ridiculous to think she might require more than just that evening to pull herself together.

But that was ultimately his problem. He wasn't different enough to stand out to Kasia apart from his constant habit of physically assaulting her.

And yet he was well aware that despite his focused attempt to deflect any sort of relationship, or maybe because of it, there was something about him that girls seemed to like. Jane did. Shannon the Bombshell did too. Who else did?

*Sarah!*

Now there was a girl who threw herself full force up against his barricades and kept chiselling away long after she should have stopped. It was nearly two years since he'd last seen her and he still wasn't over the fact that he knew he'd embarrassed her terribly. And there were moments when he felt he should have just gone for it. At the very least it would have led to sex. But Sarah wasn't the sort of girl you got away with nailing quickly on a one-night-stand and he refused to let someone into his life who he would be answerable to and who had a hold on him in any way.

Refused.

That was a laugh.

Like he had a choice.

But he wasn't able to explain himself in a way that wasn't hurtful either so he continued to pretend nothing was happening until the awkwardness of the imbalance caused everything to collapse spectacularly one evening when she walked into the pub to discover she was the only one of those close to him who hadn't been invited to drinks to celebrate his birthday.

In his defence, drinks had been sprung on him too, and he would have far preferred to have avoided the whole charade.

But in getting wind that a now ex-colleague might be planning a surprise get-together for him, he had to admit he had been the one to say "just please don't invite Sarah."

Thereafter, days in the office were excruciating and he was on the brink of quitting when mercifully, she beat him to it.

As he climbed into bed, he wished he could call her and ask her what he had done to make her fall for him so heavily.

Most bad late night ideas reveal their folly in the cold light of day. As Martin watched the sun come up at the end of a sleepless night however, he had created a handful of flimsy rationalisations for making one particular lousy idea a reality.

The weekend was a waste. He didn't leave the flat on Saturday, eating toast for every meal, twice with cheese and Marmite and once with peanut butter, and drinking seven cups of tea.

That night, worn out, he slept better and when he woke after ten on Sunday he pulled himself together and went for a walk through Regent's Park, eating ice cream, enjoying the sun and trying to rally himself to face the fear he felt for the coming week.

He wondered what Kasia was doing.

He knew that if she knew half of what he was putting himself through over her she'd be seriously disturbed by it and that would be the end of it. With good reason, too. It wasn't normal and it sure as hell wasn't healthy. She'd be like Miko Mikada, walking into that galley and seeing Rich waiting for her.

Oh Christ, was he like Rich?

Martin had often been alarmed by his own darkness, by the fact that he could lock onto an idea and stalk it relentlessly. Was Kasia just one of those? He hoped not, but by the time Sunday was done, he couldn't answer that question with real certainty.

The only certainty he could come to was one that drained what little energy he had when he woke up on Monday morning: he was going to call Sarah.

*"Martin?"*

She picked up on the fourth ring, just before it would have gone to voice mail. She had input her number into his mobile phone one evening at the office in an overt and frankly very brave attempt to make her availability known. He had never deleted it, partly out of guilt, and partly out of the fear that if she ever called him, without her details in his phone book, he wouldn't know not to answer. He was surprised that she still had his, though she obviously was able to identify him from it.

"Hi Sarah," he said. "How have you been?"

"I'm fine. This is a surprise."

"Yeah, probably not a welcome one I imagine."

"What do you want?"

He hadn't paid enough attention to her two years back to recognise her voices, but it was obvious that though she wasn't brimming with affection, she didn't still wish him dead.

"Oh, I don't know. I probably shouldn't have called. I need some advice."

"*Advice?* On what?"

"Can we meet?"

"Are you *joking?*"

"No. Look Sarah, I know I'm the last person you would expect to hear from and probably would want to hear from. But there is something I need to ask you about. It's stupid, but it's practically killing me and I really could use your perspective. Especially in light of the way I know you probably feel about me."

"You don't know how I feel about you."

"Well I can guess. But anyway, that aside, can you meet me today?"

*"No. No chance."*

"Right. Right. Yeah. Okay. It was worth a shot."

"I can meet you later in the week if you want."

"No. Don't worry. I'm sorry I called. I shouldn't have bothered you."

"Maybe I can cancel my thing today."

"No, don't do that. Just forget it. Are you well otherwise?"

But neither of them had any conversation in them and the call didn't last.

Martin looked at himself in the mirror and considered not shaving at all. The way he was feeling, he was sure to nick himself somewhere, but he set about lathering up with a grim resignation, knowing that sometime within the day to come, her eyes would see him.

And then his BlackBerry buzzed, announcing the arrival of a text message.

*Cafe Rouge, Leicester Square, 12h30.*

Sarah would meet him after all. Perhaps, just perhaps, there was the chance of some mental relief. He typed an effusive thank you and then thought better of it, sending a simple acknowledgement instead. But his mood lifted from charcoal to sunshine yellow and he gave himself a grin in the mirror. *You fucking loser,* he thought, chuckling just a little.

## Chapter Eleven

The thought leapt about in his mind that he didn't have a logical reason to be relieved; that what advice Sarah had to offer was likely to be flavoured by outrage that he even had the audacity to consult her on the matter.

Nevertheless, Monday morning was his best since Kasia had walked onto centre stage and blinked into the spotlight and he didn't much care to think about what was to come.

However much better he felt, each of his collections that morning reaffirmed the toll the weekend had taken. "You got the flu or something Martin?" asked Jenny Lucie Manette, nicknamed for the main female character in Charles Dickens' *A Tale of Two Cities*. She was in uniform at St. Pancras, running a little late to board her Eurostar service, but took a few extra moments out of genuine concern.

He liked Jenny Lucie Manette. She was like butterscotch ice cream with her rich yellow hair and every time he saw her he wondered what her lip gloss would taste like.

"Tough weekend. I'm good though," he said, though he didn't think she believed him.

On the way out of the station, he grabbed some pain au chocolat from Le Pain Quotidien and scurried back to the office while it was still warm. Whatever Jane had intended for him that morning, she could only laugh in surprise when he handed them to her, asking her to share them with the other receptionist.

"I want to hate you, you know," she said.

"But it's chocolate," he winked, getting another chuckle from her.

"It's just about enough," she said.

So far, so good. He practically sprinted up the stairs, emerging onto the fourth floor a little out of breath, but feeling quite pleased with himself for making it all the way.

He looked around for Kasia with a faint feeling of anxious nausea, but mercifully she was nowhere to be seen. He realised he should have bought her a pain au chocolat too and hoped she wouldn't see Jane eating hers and ask where she got it.

That would be great. *"Martin bought it for me,"* would be certain to be misinterpreted. If someone said that to him, he'd certainly assume the unspoken part of that sentence to be *"and gave it to me in bed this morning."*

The obvious subtext being *"and that means he's off the market. So back off you Polish bitch."*

He knew it was stupid and he wanted to slap his own head to try to get some sense into it. But at the same time, he couldn't help thinking he was missing an opportunity. He seriously considered running out and getting her one so he could take it to her as a little surprise gift.

In fact, he was heading out the door to do so when Drake the Robot called him into his office to tell him once again that he'd loved last week's edition. And that he'd discovered a spelling error in it.

But calling Sarah and the pending, black comedic irony of their meeting, seeing the delightful Jenny Lucie Manette and pulling off the spontaneous coup of pleasing Jane had lifted that Monday considerably and even Drake the Robot couldn't scuttle his mood.

It seemed to perplex him. "I take it you had a good weekend then Martin?"

"Don't worry Drake, lunch promises the potential for a real buzz kill," said Martin.

He began to wonder if Kasia was even in that day when by mid-morning she hadn't turned up. Conflicted once again between the terrified flutter bug sensation of seeing her and the fear that she may come around looking stunning when he wasn't there, he kept his head down and his ears pricked while resisting the mounting urgency of a full bladder.

By twelve, he could resist no more. It being such a warm day, he wanted to walk down to Leicester Square anyway and the extreme physical discomfort of the past thirty minutes finally prompted him to his feet.

He decided to take the stairs down to the third floor to use the men's room since Kasia certainly wasn't on the fourth. She wasn't there either, so he tried the second, finally giving himself and his bladder a break when he got there.

Jane was on the phone as he passed her by, but she gave him a nod. Peace continued to reign.

The day had cooled somewhat and the sky threatened rain later, but the walk was pleasant. Sarah had had the foresight to book a table which happened by chance or by plan to be near the window. Martin sat down and ordered some water and waited.

She was late. He didn't blame her. He applauded her.

And then she arrived, making an entrance that he had to believe was anything other than chance.

His eyes weren't the only ones on her as she came through the door and he knew it wasn't entirely casual when she slowed her stride for a second to lift her scarlet mini dress just enough to adjust the top of her patterned black stocking.

She had lost some weight, her legs were nothing short of magnificent and her hair, much longer now than it had been, looked like strands of beautiful glossy silk.

He stood up, fully appreciating the show and she smiled with what appeared to be genuine pleasure.

"Hi," he said, leaning in to kiss her on the cheek in spite of his misgivings.

"Well hello stranger," she said, obligingly turning a cheek towards him for his lips to brush.

"What's new?" he said as they sat down. He poured her some water and topped his up.

"Oh, lots of things. It's been a while. What's new with you? You're looking tired."

"Yeah, a little. No big deal. Shall we order and get that out of the way and then we can chat?"

"Why not? Call it foreplay," she said.

"Huh?"

"Just an expression."

Martin put his menu down. "Oh shit, Sarah, I think there's been a misunderstanding. Oh God, I'm sorry."

Her smile dropped, not quite into a frown. "What are you talking about?"

"This just isn't what you think it is, I don't think."

That was incredulity on her face, no doubt about it. *"What do you think I think it is?"*

"Did you think I was asking you out? Because I wasn't. Oh God and now that sounds so unkind. That's not how I meant to put it."

Sarah was visibly stunned. "Oh ... My ... God. I don't actually know how you could be more insulting. Do you honestly think I'm that pathetic?"

"Oh. No. It's just that you seem really warm and ... well playful if I'm honest. Sorry, I've obviously got that wrong."

"Well maybe I'm just pleased to see you. Could that be a possibility in your mind? What the hell is the matter with you?"

"Oh God, I am so sorry. I'm just sort of all over the place at the moment Sarah, and you wouldn't believe the conclusions I'm drawing about the most random shit. I really do apologise. And to make matters worse, I've actually called you here to ask something totally stupid and arrogant, even I'm sort of shocked by my brashness."

"What?"

"What? It's a little ... oh to hell with it ... you used to have a bit of a thing for me. You know, in the past, and we've established that's over, so let's say no more of it. But you did. And I've been wondering lately, why that was."

"What do you mean?"

"I mean, I was wondering what it was I did that attracted a girl like you?"

Sarah sat back slowly, stunned again. "Did ... wait ... did you call me ... did you call me for girl advice?"

"Yeah."

She looked towards the window, shook her head and began to laugh. Not a great sign. Then her eyes were on him again with intensity.

"Do you like the way I look today, Martin?"

"Yeah, absolutely. You look fantastic."

"Fantastic is a lazy adjective. I know what I look like. I've looked in the mirror a dozen times today. Martin, I look sensational. This dress is sensational. I had my hair done, my nails done. My legs have never looked sexier. Jesus, I want to fuck myself, the way I look today. And you haven't even noticed."

"Sorry, I'm confused. Did you want me to notice?"

"Yes. You think I look like this every day? I don't. I did this for you. Because I'm feeling great lately and my life is going really well. My career is going great. And I'm seeing an amazing man off and on and at no point whatsoever am I sitting around waiting for you. So when you called this morning I thought I'd pull out all the stops to show you what you can't have any more." She began to laugh again, this time with merriment. "And you didn't even notice."

"Yes I did. But anyway, fill me in on why this is funny?"

"It *isn't* funny, Martin. It's tragic. That's how little charm you have. That's how self-obsessed and out of touch with anything that isn't inside your head. And that's your fundamental problem. You should at least have done me the courtesy of embarrassing yourself for me so I could have batted you down. Almost any other man would have done."

"Oh shit, really? But sorry, I'm not sure how that's helpful."

And now she really was laughing, but he sensed that merriment had turned into pity.

"It's your biggest problem Martin. You're a sweet guy. That's what I liked. You're dorky, unaware and totally endearing. I wanted to rescue you from yourself. Because you've dreamed up and built the most brilliant editorial concept for years and yet you're totally unaware of how brilliant you are. But it wears off, you know?"

"I guess. Do you really think it's brilliant?"

She sighed, frustrated. "Is there a girl Martin?"

"I don't know really."

"How can you not know?"

"I mean yes there is, but not in the traditional sense. I mean, she doesn't really feel the same way about me as I do about her, so it's not like it's mutual. She doesn't really know how I feel."

"She doesn't know, I take it because you haven't made any effort to tell her? Because you're hoping she'll do the work? You know, not everybody will chase you like I did Martin. Being the one doing the driving isn't as much fun for a girl as you may think it is, or even as girls make it out to be. It's funny you don't know this considering you're the king of advice. I suppose being in love is tricky when you consider love to be nothing more than cheaply dispensed advice."

A waiter appeared at their table. "May I take your order?"

Sarah didn't take her eyes off Martin as she declined. "I don't think I'll be staying. Why don't you come and take his order in five minutes?"

The waiter nodded and scurried off.

"I'm not in love. I hardly even know her," Martin said.

"And yet you called me, a girl you rejected, for advice on how to attract her? You're in love."

"Don't be stupid. I only met her, like, five days ago."

"And what of it? You should read some books instead of allowing the WAGs of the world to tell you what's great and what isn't. Literature will teach you that dancing around the issue of love until you've worn each other out before you dare declare it is a modern concept. Oscar Wilde wrote about love totally differently. Romeo and Juliet fell totally in love on their first meeting. Or watch a movie. Jane Fonda and Rod Taylor fell hopelessly in love on a single day in *Sunday in New York*. So did Martine McCutcheon and Hugh Grant in *Love Actually*. Love in Hollywood time is a lot more realistic than we give it credit for. Guys like you treat love like a game of who blinks first loses. You don't dare declare your love until it's long overdue and even then there's a competition not to be the first to do so. But you're not being honest with yourself. You're in love all right."

She leaned into him and motioned for him to give her his hands, squeezing them gently. "You'd better prepare to have your heart broken Martin, because you'll never put in enough effort to win *her* heart. And if you want to know the truth, that does actually make me a little bit sad for you."

## Chapter Twelve

Martin slumped into his office chair and threw his head back to stare at the ceiling. Sarah had been a turn for the books. He hadn't really anticipated how that might actually go, but on the walk down to Leicester Square, he'd at least entertained the notion that she might give him a top ten list of his most likeable attributes that he could bring back to the office to study.

He'd thought her explanations of love to be ludicrous, but on the way back to the office he had stopped in at one of the second hand book shops on the Charing Cross Road anyway to buy something by Oscar Wilde. *The Importance of Being Earnest* had turned up without too much hunting and he'd bought it for a Pound. A Polish phrasebook caught his eye, and he'd furtively bought that too.

His first action, before he even sat down was to stash them both in his desk drawer for fear that Drake the Robot would see them, and the thought flashed through his mind as he did, that it was evidence in support of Sarah's argument that he was a passenger in his own life.

He'd get to it. The book wasn't the problem; it just revealed the fact that there might be one.

He rolled his chair back from the desk and closed his eyes for a moment as the faint sound of an envelope landing, mingled even more delicately with the scent of violets. He opened his eyes as she stepped back out of his cubicle, cradling several other envelopes in her arms.

Instinct taking over, he shot out of his chair. "Kasia!"

She looked back over her shoulder.

"Congratulations on staying on your feet," he said, thinking off the cuff. Not a bad line. She actually almost smiled.

"Thank you for don't knocking me," she said in return.

He smiled and sat back down and then had a moment of panic that he'd blown an opportunity to really speak to her. He shot back to his feet, but she was moving away. He didn't know what he would even say if he called her back, so he let her go.

He was exhilarated. It was a start.

And then came the most lovely sound he thought he had ever heard. Laughter that he knew was hers. He stood again to see where it was coming from and his blood ran ice cold.

There it was, right before his eyes. Horror. She was happy. She was laughing. And what a laugh. But she wasn't laughing at him. Or with him. The object of her wonderful, melodic, rainbow kaleidoscope of a laugh was Rich. Rich the fink. Rich the asshole. The late Rich; the cold, dead motherfucker whose body the police are still looking for.

He watched as Kasia strolled off, still smiling, and hoped she would flash him some of those sunbeams. But nothing. She left. And he sat back down, winded.

Then Rich shoved his fat smug bastard face over Martin's cubicle wall. "I tell you what mate, that's the one you were talking about, isn't it?"

"Sorry? What?" said Martin.

"Oh right, you didn't see her? I've just met the girl you were on about. She's a bit of a bloody belter actually. And a really lovely smile and a laugh too. Really nice. I think I'm going to ask her out."

*"You're going to do what?"* Martin didn't realize he could hiss.

"Oh, steady on. What, do you really have your eye on her? Because she was just here and you didn't even notice."

"Rich, I saw her. We spoke. We shared a moment. Trust me, I have this one in hand, don't you worry about a thing."

"Oh. Good for you then mate. What did she say to you?"

"Well, what did she say to you?"

"She said she was pleased to meet me. And then I said something in Polish and got it totally wrong and she thought it was funny and we both had a laugh. I asked her if she had seen much of London and she said no, and I asked her if she wanted to see more and she said no, but I know she's being coy. I'll have that one on her back by Sunday, you mark my words. They're all goers, these Eastern Europeans."

"Rich, I'm asking you, as a friend, please don't do that. I really like her and I saw her first."

"Oh bravado!" Rich let out a belly laugh of pure, honest, appreciation. "I mean if you're genuinely serious, I'll wait for a bit. But I'm not about to allow a tasty little morsel like that to be snapped up by someone else and she won't be around for long. So you make your move or in a week, I will. There's your challenge. Go and get her."

He patted Martin on the shoulder and tipped him what he believed might honestly have been intended as an encouraging wink. It didn't encourage him much though.

He slumped in his chair, a little breathless to have had all control snatched from him; adrenaline coursing through his body at the realization that only his ability to get his act together and summon the courage to ask her out stood between Rich's foul, misguided, seedy lechery and Kasia's perfect, delicate, violet-scented body.

With the memory of her laughter at what was no doubt a torrent of Rich's most abundant charm, he knew he had his work cut out for him.

He hoped she might make the first move for him. He knew she didn't even yet know his name.

## Chapter Thirteen

At six, Martin slapped his MacBook shut and packing it into his satchel, he meerkatted over his cubicle walls to make sure nobody was around before he slipped Oscar Wilde out of the drawer and in with the rest of his things.

He stood, cast Drake the Robot a perfunctory mock salute and walked out. Drake the Robot would be wondering why he was leaving so early, but let him worry. On that evening, Martin needed to get away.

He headed onto the Tottenham Court Road and walked past the electronics stores, past the tube station and the Centre Point tower, coming across a Chipotle outlet and stopping to consider whether he should go in. Half of him said that he needed to eat. He hadn't ordered food once Sarah had left, paying for the water and receiving a surly dismissal from the waiter for blocking a table over the busiest time of the day.

On the other hand, he really wasn't in the mood.

He considered that maybe he *was* in love, and that if it was the case, it wasn't anything like how he had felt it before. With Charlotte, in his final year of university, he had finally, blissfully, been able to admit that he wanted nothing more than her, to verbalise what he had been feeling for over a year one night while leaning against the jukebox at The Saracen's Head. Her reaction wasn't what he expected, but she was enthusiastic enough about him to spend the next two weeks in a never-ending sexual release that had driven him to something far less complicated: unbridled, instinctive, pure lust.

He remembered the point at which she had told him, by phone, that she was moving on, and that it had been fun, but that she was getting back together with an ex-boyfriend.

He, already developing many of the isolationist tendencies he would perfect a few years later, had merely said "All right then," and put the phone down.

But that wasn't even close to where it ended. The feeling of abandonment, of desperate unhappiness, the swallowing, suffocating darkness of loneliness that consumed him in the weeks that followed even had a physiological effect, driving him to the point of chronic bronchitis which had him falling asleep at his desk during the day and waking up at night, drenched in sweat, burning like a furnace and crying out loud.

Only when one of his friends took him in hand and forced him to see a doctor did he begin the process of recovery.

Two months after that simple phone call, he had lost 11 kilograms as well as most of his confidence and a large part of his sense of humour to boot.

Martin had always denied the link, but he hadn't fooled anyone who knew him at the time.

And actually, it was worse than that. Far from being the man-eating mercenary that Martin wished her to be, and which description he allowed his female friends to use when speaking about her, Charlotte had settled down with the old flame and was still with him; a fact which highlighted that only he had interpreted their fling as more than it was.

Most guys would have regarded a short-term, all-sex, no-strings relationship as a score by which to win bragging rights for years afterwards. They would have had no problem with the notion of being a hot girl's fuck toy, doing to her, as Martin discovered to his shock, whatever the hell he damn well wanted, while she got her final inhibitions out of her system before seeking out the one she loved, as if she never expected rough sex again.

He remembered what she felt like, smelt like, tasted like, and though he had had to climb his way back from an abyss of bitterness about her, he had never forgotten the acid-trip mind-expansion of being in bed with her as they kept each other just at the point of climax for hours.

It had never been that good since and he had stopped even hoping he might find it again; stopped dreaming he might find a woman who would care about making him feel like that without demanding a fee first.

But before the sex, Martin had felt what he believed to be real love; beautiful, protective, gentle, affection.

He snapped back into the world briefly to realise that far from merely pacing on the pavement, he had apparently given a bravura performance of a tortured madman to the amusement of two young hoodie-wearing men sitting at the window and eating burritos.

His attention brought to the spectacle he was making of himself, he tried to pretend it was nothing and shuffled onwards. He made it no further than the corner however before deciding to just get dinner over with so he could settle the rising hunger inside of him. He went inside, ordered a burrito and a bottle of water and took a perch at the long aluminium counter that ran down the middle of the restaurant. It was busy and people sat to either side of him; a group of American teens sitting directly opposite.

This was the conundrum: if even speaking to Kasia required him to marshal all his courage and prepare what he would say rather than just going and saying hello and starting a conversation the way he did so easily with Jane and Shannon the Bombshell and Jenny Lucie Manette, then perhaps she wasn't for him. On the other hand, not speaking to her, not pursuing her, not gaining her approval ... well, he couldn't bear the thought of that. And if the alternative to swallowing his fear was leaving her to Rich, he was going to have to pull himself together.

But what was it? Pretty eyes? Really? Was that it? A nice smile? The scent of a happy memory from his childhood? Could that be enough to send him over the edge?

"Dude, you okay?"

Martin looked at the young man in the Red Sox baseball cap that had asked the question, and realised they were all regarding him with faint amusement.

"Sorry?"

"You're kind of staring into space there, and half your food has fallen out."

He looked down at the plastic basket into which almost the entire contents of his burrito had fallen while he had lost himself in his thoughts.

"Oh. Yep. I see that."

"You were gone dude," said Red Sox.

"Yep." Martin squeezed out a brief smile and headed for the door, binning his food. So much for dinner. So much for trying to work anything out too.

He pushed off down the road, his head still whirling, trying to think, trying not to, the traffic noise and the sounds of the pavement and those he shared it with all contributing to his deepening confusion.

He shoved his hands into his pockets as he walked, his eyes on the pavement just ahead of him, past Leicester Square, past the window where his non-lunch with Sarah had taken place or not taken place or whatever the hell, earlier that day.

His thoughts began to pick up speed, too many of them whirling in too small a space, creating friction, colliding, merging and breaking until he realised that for the previous several minutes the only things on his mind were the lyrics to the Bare Naked Ladies' theme to *The Big Bang Theory* which he had put to the rhythm of his footfalls between the cracks on the pavement.

He stopped abruptly and looked around. St. Martin-in-the-Fields off to his left, the National Portrait Gallery to his right. Kasia told Rich she hadn't seen much of London. Martin had lived in London almost his entire life save for his years at university and a gap year in South Africa, but he had never been inside either of those two buildings. In particular, places such as the National Portrait Gallery were a source of guilt to him. He knew that the sole reason many of the millions of visitors that swamped London during the summer even bothered, was because of the art galleries, and yet he'd never set foot through the doors of a single one of them.

It wasn't laziness or superiority. He simply knew it would just be fraud if he did so. Even if all he did was spend ten minutes looking at the simple stuff; the clear, full colour photographs of recognisable faces, he'd be committing an offense, since he earned his living by dismissing other people's art as little more than fad consumerism.

As he stood there however, he realised that fraud might be the only friend he had in casual conversation if his alternative was *"Hi, I'm Martin. I'm not really interested in anything."*

And there it was.

Nail on the head.

He couldn't talk to Kasia because he didn't have anything to say. Shallowness was protection. But shallowness was suffocating. It was limiting in any event.

He glanced around to see if anyone had noticed him examining the entrance, convinced there would be sharp looks of disapproval even from random passersby who would know he had no right thinking about stepping through that door.

Satisfied that nobody had worked out what he was up to yet, he crossed the road and made his way to the entrance, stopping to look around furtively once again, knowing all the while that he was being ridiculous.

Then he stepped inside.

A girl sat at a desk offering floor maps. She looked straight at him. He wondered what she was thinking. Was it obvious that he had no idea what to do? He hoped not. Feeling suddenly exposed, and fearful that she might be on the brink of asking him to leave, he ducked into the gift shop, grabbing a book off the shelf and starting to read in the middle, as if he had a specific purpose.

Safely out of sight, and fully aware of his idiocy, he did a brief scan of the tiny room, taking in the shelves of books, the posters and the various knick knacks, his eyes passing briefly over the other shoppers and stopping dead, with a near-heart attack as they captured the long, chestnut hair, reddish in the light.

*It couldn't be*. He shoved his nose back into his book, feigning interest while he wrestled with a realisation that closed his throat and made his heart race: standing next to Kasia ... was a man.

It didn't occur to him until later what a bitter twist it was that she would be there, in that gift shop, in that museum, at that time. To Martin it seemed closer to fate and he almost, for a moment, believed in it.

He looked up at them both, in equal parts wanting to see her lovely face and to get a look at the man who she had chosen.

Or who had chosen her.

The man who'd had the courage to go right up to her and ask her out and who'd had the good fortune that she said yes.

He cast his eyes up as casually as he could and realised to his horror that she was looking right at him as the fucker she was with negotiated change with the girl working the till.

Panic flooded through him once again and he tried to look casual as he diverted his eyes back down to the book, hoping he had carried off the desired intention of pretending he was staring into space as he thought about what he was reading.

And as he did it, the sheer stupidity of his action started to tap dance on his brain.

What was she thinking right then? Did she think he was a jerk? What if she took that as a sign that he wasn't interested? Because it sure as hell looked like he wasn't.

It suddenly hit him that he didn't even know what book he had ripped off the shelf. He hadn't looked and he hadn't read a word, just opening it to page 96 and pretending to read. What if it was something ridiculous? Or something perverted?

*But God she looked good.*

He saw movement. He tried not to look as if he had unwittingly arrived on a nudist beach, but the urge to resist was just as impossible. As they passed him, he turned to watch, drained and defeated. As they got to the door, he didn't even flinch as she turned around to look at him one last time before she disappeared. Unable to avoid the hopelessness, he raised a hand in greeting. And Kasia made everything right with the world once again by popping him the most beautiful smile he had seen yet.

*Everything right with the world for a moment anyway.*

As he placed the book back on the shelf, noting that it had been on nudes after all, though Martin doubted Kasia had noticed, he considered that no smile was beautiful enough to delete the existence of a boyfriend.

Or a husband perhaps.

He doubted that was the case, because she didn't wear a wedding band, nor, for that matter, an engagement ring.

But just because he hadn't dropped to one knee yet didn't change the fact that when the sun went down, she had someone to spend alone time with already, making Martin and the many shades of beige he could add to her existence, entirely uncompetitive.

On the other hand, she had looked back, to see if he had noticed her.

Looked back, that was, from beside the man she was with, and with whom she was leaving.

Yes, but she looked back anyway.

Did any of it matter?

## Chapter Fourteen

The following morning he rolled out of bed, did his 50 push ups, forced his way through 100 crunches, and stepped into the shower holding the single memory of the smile she had given exclusively to him, in his mind's eye.

His stomach roiled with a different image however. He'd beaten the boyfriend many times overnight, in the boxing ring, in a *Guitar Hero* play off, in every girl-impressing display of masculine awesomeness he could think of. Yet by the time he had woken up, the man had morphed in his mind, into Brad Pitt. *Fight Club* tough with *Oceans 11* cool. How could he compete with that?

Martin felt humiliated to have made such a vigorous mental play for her in light of this new story twist and though the real Kasia didn't know about any of it, he felt judged by the attention she gave him in the movies he had made in his mind.

Facing her was going to be tougher than ever.

His rounds that morning drew even more worried attention than they had the day before with Mama Mia Marigold, fiery-hot like deep molten ginger though her Spanish hair and compulsive dress sense were perfect black, coming close to crossing the line.

They exchanged envelopes, he dealt her a wan smile and an unremarkable line of chat.

"I think maybe it's flu," she said.

"I'll pop some pills," he said.

Drake the Robot may as well have been watching Martin's cubicle all morning because his eyes were on him the moment he entered the department area. He didn't look delighted that the previous evening's early exit had led to a second disastrous looking morning, but Martin sat down, not giving him the opportunity to try to initiate a pep talk.

He unpacked his things, including the Oscar Wilde book which he made no effort this time to hide, and he began vacantly, to open that morning's envelopes.

Stieg Larsson was continuing to dominate the lists, and he wondered, not for the first time, whether he should actually read *The Girl with the Dragon Tattoo*. Rule #3 precluded it however and the rules were everything.

The subtle scent of violets tugged him back into the world, and he spun around, on instinct.

Kasia was relatively tall, and in heels, she added another three inches. But she seemed to tower over him as she stood in his cubicle entrance.

His eyes crawled up her body from her feet to her face, noting the shapeliness of her calves, enhanced perhaps by the heels, her gentle curves that were just about perfect, her long, lovely unadorned neck and landing just briefly at her unflinching eyes before they overwhelmed him. He lacked the courage to engage her stare, and she gave away nothing of what she was thinking.

As always, she revealed just enough leg, and once again, she was protected just slightly against the arctic air conditioning chill of the lower floors by a thin purple cardigan.

Without a word, she handed him two big envelopes, obviously containing books that he would refuse to read, and he stole another glance at her eyes, half-smiling a thank you, while the image flashed before him of what he must look like, tired and pathetic in comparison to the Brad Pitt lookalike she had been staring at all night and perhaps even making love to.

"Thanks," he said, hardly getting the word out.

She frowned a little, but she moved on without saying anything as Martin sat holding his sealed books to his chest as if they were the last remaining memories of her.

The boys were in the break room again, prompting him to half consider abandoning his quest for tea which in any event was more of a means to avoid work rather than a real need.

No such luck though. Dave the Legend once again coaxed him inside.

"Martin, here's a new idea, and we need you to tell us if it has legs. A bacon magazine. Not made of bacon, but about bacon. Lady Gaga made raw meat cool and all the fashion and entertainment people say she's a trendsetter. If she says it is a go, then you have to assume that it is. In that world anyway."

Martin said nothing, but looked from one to the other.

Torpedo Steve stepped in, claiming ownership of the idea in doing so. "We can have bacon recipes, bacon art, interviews with celebrities about their favourite ways to eat bacon and we can run reviews of the stuff every month. I think it is genius, personally."

Martin realised he was at least partly serious. "Jesus."

"No good?" said Torpedo Steve.

*"Really?"* Martin was suddenly angry.

"Really."

"I take it, it's because you all believe the Shallow Review of Books is a load of worthless crap that I'm continually consulted as an expert on stupid shit like this, is it?"

Dave the Legend stepped forward. "Whoa, hold on Martin, what's got you?"

Martin flicked the switch on the kettle which had just been filled from the cold water tap. Frustrated, he grabbed a mug from the cupboard and slapped a tea bag into it, then turned his attention to Torpedo Steve.

"I'll tell you what, shall I? A bacon magazine probably would have legs among connoisseurs. There's a lot more required to review bacon than books because most people probably think more about their bacon. I couldn't ever do a Shallow Review of Bacon however because it would rely upon a celebrity eating bacon and no celebrity ever, *ever eats fucking bacon*."

He spat the last words out to the boys' undisguised alarm. Feeling suddenly awkward, he took a breath, conjured up patience he didn't feel and even managed a wink.

"Why don't you put it to the Pork Board or whatever the industry body is? They might even go for it, even only as a once off. You might even gain some notoriety for it."

He left them as they launched into an enthusiastic debate on the suggestion, but as he approached the pseudo-refuge of his cubicle, a loitering Rich assured him he would find no relief.

"So how's it going with the challenge?"

Martin sat down and Rich did the same. He looked substantially better than he did the last time he had sat in that chair, but Martin took momentary comfort that even Rich was outmatched by *Fight Club* Brad.

"I think the challenge can safely be considered over, to be honest, Rich" he said.

Rich's mouth fell open in genuine surprise. "What, are you going to tell me you've done the deed then?"

"No. And I'm not going to. She has a boyfriend."

"No she hasn't."

"She does mate. I've even seen him."

"Really? She told me she isn't seeing anyone."

"When?"

"The other day. She's only been here a couple of days Martin, so unless things have changed quickly, I'd be surprised."

"When did she tell you? How did that come up?"

"I asked her."

"When did you speak to her?"

"I speak to her every day mate. She's always around isn't she? You've obviously noticed that."

Martin bristled at the statement. Was she always around? Or was she always around Rich?

"Well Rich, regardless, I saw her with a bloke last night and she seemed to be pretty close to him. He looked like Brad ..." he stopped himself. *The world inside your head isn't the world.*

"He looks like *who*?"

"Nobody. Doesn't matter."

"It was probably her house mate. She lives with a friend and her boyfriend. Could've been him. Unless she went out on a date. She could've done that, I suppose. Is that what's holding you back then?"

Martin could sense his gloom lifting. "Yeah, but perhaps there's nothing to worry about there then," he said.

"So it's safe to say you haven't asked her out, is it?"

Martin attempted an admonishing glance. "I'm building up to it."

"Well, what conversations have you had?"

"This and that. Why?"

"Have you even actually spoken to her yet?"

"Yes."

"More than just hello?"

"We speak all the time, Rich."

"And yet you didn't know she doesn't have a boyfriend."

"Oh fuck off."

"Fine. But Martin let me reiterate that the clock is ticking and she isn't going to ask herself out. This is fair warning. I'm not leaving her out there when other blokes are bound to be circling."

## Chapter Fifteen

Martin stood to watch as Rich walked from the room, appalled that he considered what was always a fleeting infatuation for him, to be comparable to Martin's torment.

He recalled their first ever conversation in which Rich confided to being in a deep trough about the breakup of what he described as possibly the love of his life. "I tried to call her last night but I was too drunk to make any sense," he had said. "It's definitely all over. The best 13 days of my life."

That had been round one, and several others had followed, leading up to Miko Mikada the previous week.

He couldn't allow his Kasia to become another sleeper in Rich's train wreck.

That afternoon, as she came around again with a pile of envelopes for Drake the Robot, Martin stopped her.

"Hey Kasia." A legendary opening line.

Her mouth arched just slightly into a smile, but he saw her eyes come vividly alive as she turned her attention to him. Was that real, or did he just imagine it? Or did her eyes do that for everyone? He wished he could be Rich so he could see how she looked at him.

In the process of mental meandering, he lost all the lines he had practiced for this occasion.

"Did you enjoy the gallery last night?" was all he could manage.

"Yes. Did you see the exhibition also?" she said.

Her voice. To him. Exclusively to him. But why didn't he have a better answer to the question?

"Oh no, I was just in the gift shop."

"Oh. What were you buying?"

Time, he thought. I was buying time. Like I'm doing now. "Oh, a book. For a friend. An actual real gift. For his birthday."

"Okay," she said.

You could have won a world war in the second of silence that followed. A million thoughts collided in a splat of futility as he realised that she wasn't going to say any more than that. Beige. Beige conversation. Why would she care about anything he had to say when all he had to say was irrelevancy such as that? Sarah walked into his head and shook *her* head at him dolefully. *You'd better prepare to have your heart broken Martin, because you'll never put in enough effort to win her heart. Make the fucking effort ... say something!*

"It's a good shop," he said.

She cast her eyes aside briefly and it was obvious to Martin that she was thinking of her next task which, considering it was the delivery of envelopes to Drake the Robot, said everything there was to say about his conversation. She didn't move on though.

"Probably. I never really looked. The museum is great though," she said.

Back in the game boy. She's opening up another front. "Do you go to many museums? Is art your thing?"

A much better question. Insightful, thoughtful, politely curious, precisely the opposite of boring or intrusive.

"Yes," she said, her attention back. "This is the thing I like most about London is the quality of the art museums."

"Oh, I agree," Martin lied. "You should take a look at the Tate Modern or the Royal Academy."

"I've been to both. They're very great. So much to see you can never be done. Which one is your favourite?"

"Oh, I don't really know," he said. "I guess the Modern. I like the Warhols."

*And that's two lies in a row and you're not even seeing each other, you weedy little liar,* said in-his-head Sarah, hands on hips, revolted and mocking.

“Ah yes, I remember you are a big fan of celebrities,” Kasia nodded.

He almost missed it with the distraction of finding a justification imaginary-Sarah would buy, and it took him vital seconds to come up with a weak retort.

“I’m sorry? No I’m not,” he said.

But it was on lost ears. For the second time in his adult life, more or less, Drake the Robot was leaving his office and Kasia darted off towards him to hand him his documents with nothing more than an “Oops, sorry, I need to do this.”

Martin watched as she and Drake the Robot had a brief conversation and a little laugh. God knows what was so funny about some bloody envelopes. He sat, then stood, then sat again, half determined to wait for her as she came back, so he could keep talking to her; half aware that he couldn’t think of a single thing to say.

He was even a little angry at her. How could she cut straight through his work like that? Despite Isabel’s xenophobia, he thought the two of would get along famously. They’d certainly agree wholeheartedly about the Shallow Review of Books.

He hated that he always had to go to such pains to explain that his obsession with what Pixie Lott or Jude Law were reading did not imply an obsession with the actual people. And that his Shallow Review of Books was nothing less than a modern day literary guide with almost as much weight as the New York Times Book Review. Well, sort of anyway. To some of *his* readers, it was. And to deflect with as much energy as he could the embarrassing fact that he found himself in a position where he based his entire livelihood on publishing third party rumours about famous people like any other celebrity rag.

He squirmed. He felt his feet sweating into his socks a little as a flush of heat came over him. He’d seen on *CSI* one night that the feet sweat a cup and a half per day. Irrelevant. More anger, more frustration.

He had a bad afternoon and when he arrived home that evening, he didn’t even make an attempt to be silent, slamming his door behind him, and looking around to see if there was anything he could bear to break.

There wasn't. He hated that he was too stifled even to have an impulsive reaction.

## Chapter Sixteen

By the next morning, his rounds over, he knew he was going to have to scale the mountain he had built. Intellectually he knew he had it in him to downsize it to the molehill it probably was, but he couldn't wrap his mind around it. A mountain, it remained.

Overnight, he had run through a number of scenarios in his head for how it could play out, but knew he was lacking one key variable: Kasia. She may not use all the lines he had given her and he may end up having to think on his feet and that was a recipe for a total non-event.

In his imagination, where she fell for him and thought he was amazing, he was a funnier and better conversationalist than actually he was and he knew the reality was very substantially worse than even *he* cared to admit.

He procrastinated long past the point where he was able to convince himself he was prioritizing and finally assembled his mental crampons, hooks and ropes and pushed himself out into the hallway. *Just ask her out. Just ask her out. Just ask her out.*

He hadn't seen her all morning, so he took to the stairs to search the third floor. No Kasia.

Pulling the stairwell door open to head down to the second floor however, fate continued to toy with him. She was practically at the door, walking up the stairs towards him.

A sudden grip of panic tightened around him and he totally lost his nerve, blurting out instead a stupidly jolly "Good morning."

She smiled at him, but it was a smile beyond his powers of interpretation.

"Morning," she said, moving past him.

"Are you well today?" he said.

"Yes thank you. Are you?"

"Yes, top of the world," he said.

"Good," she said, smiling, but walking on.

*Fuck. Balls. Bollocks. Fuck, fuck, fuckity fuck!* He stepped into the stairwell as if everything had gone according to plan and walked back to his desk, determined to abandon it completely. There was no point. There was no sense in going through this kind of torture. She wasn't interested and there was nothing to be gained in going through the embarrassment.

He tore open his envelopes and read the tip sheets for that week. Kate Hudson was in town apparently, and was reading … oh really, who gives a shit about what Kate Hudson is reading? Why did anybody even care about shit like that?

He was angry. Angry at Kasia for not making a fuss of him. Angry at Rich for kicking him onto that path. Angry at Sarah for suggesting that he didn't have the drive to chase a girl like Kasia when he wanted nothing more than to do just that if he could only figure out how. *You'd better prepare to have your heart broken Martin, because you'll never put in enough effort to win her heart. And if you want to know the truth, that does actually make me a little bit sad for you.*

Sad for him. *Sad for him?*

He pushed away from his desk, and stood up. He knew he was pathetic. He just didn't know how not to be. What had he told Penny a week ago? *The secret is to do what you want, not what anyone else wants. That's the only thing that will make you happy.* In Martin's case, it was the only thing that was going to get the pounding, drumming, relentlessly ear-pulling, eye-poking, screech-making monkey off his back.

He headed once again for the stairwell, scouting the third floor when he got there. It was becoming a routine. No Kasia. He pulled the door open a little gingerly, but she wasn't there this time. Down to the second. A more complex floor, less open-plan, more compartmentalized. There were lots of people there he didn't know and their reactions told him he'd better take a moment to breathe and relax and lose whatever face he was making.

He took the stairwell to the first floor. She had to be there. Unless she had taken the lift. Shit, he never thought of the lift. He could spend the whole day running in one door and out another while she did the same, like a staged farce, while never actually seeing each other.

He walked along the hallway to the main office area and stood in the entrance, scanning the room. Like he was really going to speak to her in a crowded room anyway. He hoped she wasn't there because that would have given him only two choices: go and make a spectacle of himself in front of everyone, or loiter outside like a creep, waiting for her to come to him when her chores there were done. Considering his track record with that, she would have cause to call security.

It didn't matter. She wasn't there.

That left one place, assuming she was in the building at all. The break room on the first floor was two thirds of the way towards the end of the hallway; the only doorway between him and the window at the end which looked out onto an irrelevant side street below.

He would have no room to move if he didn't follow through with it. It was now or never. He assembled his troops, gave them a pep talk, and began to march.

As he slowed passed the break room entrance, she stood inside facing the door, in conversation with two other women he didn't recognize. They made full eye contact, and he completely lost his nerve. He nodded, casually, as if it was a surprise to see her, and just kept walking.

Towards nothing.

He wondered if she'd believe he specifically came down to the first floor so he could take a quick peek out of a window which enjoyed a view of the building's rubbish skips and a bicycle shed.

*Oh for God's sake.*

A few paces beyond the door he arrested his dive into total humiliation and turned to go back, hoping it would look casual when he passed the doorway again.

He didn't get the chance. Kasia stood in the hallway, watching him with faint amusement.

"Oh, hi. Kasia. Hey," he said, as if he was surprised to see her. Blathering moron.

"You were looking for something?" she asked.

"No. Nothing. Well, yes. Actually, I was. Would you like a cup of coffee?"

"You want to make me coffee?"

"Well, I was thinking of ... that maybe I could ... um."

"Thank you. That will be nice."

"Oh. Right, okay. Right, well why don't I do that?"

Though every instinct screamed at him to stop and think this through, he walked past her, into the kitchen, took a mug from a cupboard and poured her a cup of coffee from the percolator. He turned to hand it to her, aware that every eye in the place was on him. All but hers. She wasn't there.

He felt his stomach drop. He smiled weakly and walked past the ladies she'd been with moments before, to the hallway where he nearly crashed into Kasia again.

She was laughing. "I think maybe that isn't what you mean, right?"

He could feel his face burning. "No. Not really."

She held up her mug. "Well as you can see, I already have tea. Maybe you drink that one?"

"Yeah, okay. Thanks." He began to turn away.

"Maybe you drink it here. We have it together, that is the idea, I think?"

"Oh. Yes. That was the idea. I was thinking we could go somewhere else though. Would you like to go and get coffee somewhere?"

She bit her lip. "Why do you want to do this?"

"I don't know. For fun. For kicks. No good reason. I don't really have a plan. I just would like to know you better. It's just coffee."

"I don't think it is just coffee. When a strange man wants to have coffee with me even though we have said nothing to each other and so far all he has done is cause some bruises every day, I think it is something else."

"Like what?"

"Like what? Don't play games. I have a job and I need that job. I don't need a boyfriend. So I guess I don't need coffee. It's a mistake I think."

"Simple as that?"

"It isn't to be unkind. You seem very funny. Nice. I am sorry."

"Yes, me too. Sorry. Enjoy that coffee. At least we had that together." He smiled and oh Jesus, he winked. He replayed that last crap line in his head all the way back up the three floors to his office and all afternoon as he tried to work.

## Chapter Seventeen

Around three, Kasia stopped by and slipped gently onto his cubicle chair. He turned his own around to face her. She was smiling, reassuring. "Are you okay?"

He nodded, tried to make his face say *sure, why wouldn't I be,* but it wouldn't go there. "Yeah, I'm fine."

She seemed to be waiting for more. Finally, she shrugged. "Okay," she said and half stood.

He put his hand on her wrist. "Hold on."

She sat back down.

"Look, this isn't some heavy thing. I'm not trying to be weird or anything. I just think that I would really like to get to know you better and ... I don't know."

"Why do you want to do this?"

"Because I ... I don't know. There's something about you that I just really find interesting. Fascinating actually. And believe me, I'm not normally like this."

"Normally like what?"

"Oh I don't know ... like a blathering moron. Like a ... like a moron. I'm not normally the sort of guy who will pretend he hasn't seen you in a museum gift shop for fear that you'll think I'm following you."

Her face was suddenly serious. "Were you following me?"
"What? No. No, no, no, no, no."
She laughed. "I am teasing. I know you didn't follow me."
He was wrong about her laugh. It wasn't just a kaleidoscope of colour, it was a buttery, velvety, rich swirl of warmth and chocolate.
But then she bit her lip again, which he thought was maybe her thing when she was thinking. How wonderful to learn something intimate about her. "Martin, I hope this can be okay. I don't want to have a difficult relationship in the office. With you I mean."
"It'll be fine. Fine. No problem, I promise," he said, the air slowly bleeding out of him.
She smiled gently. "Okay. I hope so. I think you're very sweet."
As she got up and left, Martin's happiness took a solid punch in the solar plexus.

As the afternoon began to draw down and the after-work bustle began to slowly take life, Rich dropped down onto his cubicle chair, rather less gently than Kasia had done. Martin was slightly affronted, not only by the interruption but also by the fact that Rich had wiped out the memory of her being there, in his cubicle, in his chair, with him. Focusing on him. *Oh, and by the way Martin, telling you to get lost.*
"And?" said Rich.
"And what?"
"Don't be coy. You know what I want to know."
"Well, I asked her."
Rich grinned. *"And?"*
"She said no."
"She said *no?"*
"Yeah."
"What did she actually say?"
"She said I seemed nice but that she doesn't want a boyfriend."
"And what did you say?"
"Oh I don't know Rich. Something horribly embarrassing. And then she came here and sat right there and asked whether I was okay because she thinks I'm sweet and doesn't want to have a problem with me in the

office."

"What, she came here afterwards?"

"Yeah."

Rich broke out a broad grin and chuckled a little. "All I can say is bravo, Martin. That's the best story I've had today."

"Why? What's good about that?"

"Because Martin, you went up to a girl you're mad about and voluntarily asked her out. And I know this one means something to you, even though you'll deny it. So she said no, that doesn't mean she doesn't want to do it. She doesn't want to do it on the first invite perhaps. Maybe she wants to be chased. Or she needs to know that you're not just envisioning a casual shag."

He slapped Martin on the thigh, almost hard enough to snap his femur. "It looks like she'll be harder work than I thought she was; I was wrong about having her on her back, if you'll pardon me speaking about the centre of your universe like that. She isn't that bloody different though mate because none of them are. They all want you to put in some effort and not expect them to capitulate so easily. And if she came here afterwards she isn't exactly telling you to get out of her life is she?"

Martin rolled his chair back slightly from Rich to lessen the potential for further physical assault. "So what should I do?"

"Ask her out again. Take the threat out of it, but make it an evening event. Take her to a pub and tell her to bring a friend. That way she has a safety net, but you're still out together, after dark, very, very un-work-related and having drinks."

"Right. Why are you helping me here?"

"Because I can't go around and shaft the Baggage Handler mate, not when you're this far gone."

"I am not this far gone."

"No, of course you're not." Rich got up to leave. "I want a full report back Martin. And please don't tell me you've opted to ask her out for coffee again. Find a cocktail bar or a wine bar. Anything. But it has to be in the evening, got it?"

"Shall I take her to Tokyo perhaps?"

Rich smiled, a little taken aback and Martin knew it had been a cruel comment.

"I'm sorry, that was mistimed. The truth is I could use some of that Rich runaway freight train confidence."

"It isn't confidence mate. I don't have any of that. I'm just way more driven to get a shag than you are. On the odds, going to Tokyo seemed like a worthwhile gamble to me, believe it or not. It's about what you're prepared to do. This really isn't as hard as you're making it you know."

"That's what you think. In fact, it's the hardest thing in the world. I wasn't this bad when I was younger you know. Young girls tend to find me charming and interesting. As they become women, they become wiser, faster, and realise I'm intellectually a potato farmer. I don't know how old Kasia is . . ."

"... twenty six," Rich interrupted. Martin could see he was amusing him.

"Twenty six? Bollocks. That means she's already pulling away from me."

"That's because you're assuming what she wants is someone who is intellectually interesting. Maybe she likes potato farmers. You're assuming and you don't know that. Now do what I say, will you?

It hit him as he watched Rich leave that he didn't know whether he could trust the advice. Or even if it was well-intended. It sounded right, but it sounded simple. It sounded a little like advice for eating chicken wings when what he held in his hands was an oyster. Kasia wasn't a girl. She was Kasia. And Rich had lodged a formal notice of interest already so spinning Martin around a dozen times seemed a logical thing to do before he sent him off to pin a figurative tail on the figurative Polish donkey.

This was too big. And he'd seen too many people do ridiculous things like fly to Japan, or tattoo Gerome on their bodies by misunderstanding his advice to know that you're probably better off with a second opinion. But where was he going to get one of those? Where?

When the answer came to him, it made him laugh openly. No matter, there was nobody else about except for Drake the Robot who was separated from reality by his glass walls.

## Chapter Eighteen

Rupert answered the door quickly, though Martin could hear a fair amount of kerfuffle from inside before he did so. He was as surprised to see Martin as Martin was to be knocking on his door in the first place.

He pulled the door to behind him, but didn't close it. Leaning against the doorframe, his skinny body wore two thin jerseys over what Martin assumed was a t-shirt even on this warm summer's night and Martin wondered once again if he had some sort of illness.

"Hello Martin," he said; brief, but not discourteous.

"Hi Rupert. Sorry to bother you. Do you have a few minutes?"

Rupert folded his arms and extended his bottom lip. "I might have mate. What is it all about?"

"It's a little odd actually, but I need to run a scenario past you. I just need someone impartial to offer objective advice if you feel up to it."

"About what?"

"Girls."

Martin didn't seriously think the skinny little man he had long since discounted as a weirdo would have anything to offer, and was surprised when Rupert broke out into a grin.

"Ah, the feline members of our species. And how can I help you?"

"What, really?"

"Oh I would have thought I can help in this matter for certain. Tell me about it."

So Martin did. For reasons he couldn't have elaborated very well, he in fact told Rupert everything.

"So do the opposite," Rupert said. "Take all the advice a guy like Richard can offer and the do the opposite, because what works for a bloke like that is probably the complete opposite of what a bloke like you needs. Truthfully, whether you know it or not, girls, like cats in the wild, are the hunters. You either look like something they want to mate with or you look like prey. Don't think for a second they can't tell the difference and prey always looks like the bloke that is trying too hard. You can only be what you can be and you become much more mate-worthy when you're honest and up front."

Martin resisted a smirk. "Really?"

"Really."

"That's the weirdest advice I have ever received."

"And yet you're thinking that it seems surprisingly good, aren't you?"

He was. He said so.

"You any good at talking to girls Martin? Generally, I mean?"

"Generally, yeah. I suppose," said Martin.

"But not her."

"I really don't know why."

"It's because you like her."

"Which means what?"

"Which means you're putting too much weight on it," said Rupert, suddenly animated. "You're in the prey zone and you run the risk very quickly of becoming something worse. You become a cub she wants to take care of rather than a full-blooded male she wants to mate with."

"A wildcat's prey can become its cub?"

"Not in the wild. But there've been all sorts of instances all over the world where wildcats at zoos adopt piglets or puppies or something. It's weird, but it happens."

"Rupert, what the fuck are we talking about here?"

"You and your girl. Look, let's pretend she's human for a second ..."

"Which she is ..."

"Right. Well all right then, forget the wildcat metaphor for a moment because I may be stretching it. My point is that you like her so you're giving her too much power. She isn't asking for it, so she doesn't interpret it the way you do. Girls hate it when they see that sort of weakness in men. All she sees is that you're socially awkward, not that you're specifically awkward around her. She's got nothing to compare it to. In a casual situation, down a pub or something, that would make you prey. In a less casual situation, where you're seeing each other regularly, such as in an office situation, it makes you a potential cub. Someone she regards as non-threatening, slightly cute, perhaps a little sweet, but absolutely not someone she will ever consider mating with."

"She told me I was sweet today actually."

"Oh Christ, really? You'd better move fast then."

"And do what?"

"I've changed my mind. Do what Richard says. You're running out of time to create a new context for your relationship. If he knows her at all, the chances are he knows her better than you."

"I see."

"Well go home and think it through," said Rupert. "If there's anything else you need, I really do enjoy matters such as these. Call me a nosey bastard."

Martin thanked him and Rupert disappeared back into his flat.

As he closed his own door behind him, he wondered why it was that everyone seemed to think winning Kasia over should be a simple matter. Could it really be so?

## Chapter Nineteen

After several aborted starts, he marshalled every ounce of courage he could by mid-morning the next day and put his head through the door of the break room. Kasia was there with a colleague, leaning against the counter as they laughed about something in Polish. Several other people sat at the handful of tables within.

She wore a red and white striped sleeveless dress and sandals and her hair was up; the first time Martin had ever seen it that way. She left him in no doubt that his arrival was unexpected, but he could discern nothing about whether that was a good or a bad thing. He pushed it aside.

"Would you like coffee?" he asked her.

"I'm sorry?"

"I've come to make you coffee."

Her friend grinned at her and stepped away, leaving the matter to Kasia.

"When I spoke to you yesterday ..." Kasia began, but Martin cut her off.

"When you spoke to me yesterday you said you didn't want any strangeness. Well I guess this might qualify, I must admit I don't know how you would categorise something as broad as *strangeness*. But I have a need for caffeine and I guess if your schedule is the same every day, you're on break. So what do you say?"

She laughed a little, but cautiously.

"I don't know what to say to you," she said.

"Just tell me whether you take sugar."

She shrugged, the corners of her mouth twitching a little. "No sugar. No coffee either," she said, opening a cupboard and pulling out a box of green teabags. "This is what I drink."

He picked it up and inspected the box. "Okay. Tea it is."

The kettle was hot and boiled in a matter of seconds, to his delight. He made her tea, poured himself a cup of coffee from the percolator and ushered them to a table.

She sat down, still a little amused, but he could see she was starting to pull away. Again, he ignored it.

"So you said the other day that I'm a celebrity whore," he said.

Her face was suddenly serious. *"I said this word? Whore? When?"*

"No, you didn't say that word, but you said I was very interested in celebrities."

"Yes. It's the same thing as calling you a whore? I don't think it is."

"No, well never mind that. It sort of is the same thing, but that's because the word whore is misused. Oh look anyway, forget I said that.

That wasn't what I meant. You said I was interested in celebrities."

"Because of this report you do, yes."

"Have you read it?"

"No." She shrugged. "Once."

"And what did you think?"

"I didn't like it. It's a western idea, this, I think."

"What do you mean?"

"Ah, that you can become famous in so lazy a way. I always heard that in the west you get ahead and make money by being the best, but I think sometimes it is too easy to get this."

Martin laughed. The way he was feeling, she could have told him the whole English language was lousy and he might have considered a crash course in French. Or Polish.

"Wow. That's extremely honest. Too honest perhaps," he said with a forced chuckle to ensure she knew he wasn't offended.

"How can you be too honest?"

"Yeah, I guess. And in a way you're right. The Shallow Review of Books has an audience though and these things just have a habit of taking on a life of their own."

"What does this mean?"

I mean it's grown to be quite popular and I don't really have much power to change it right now."

"So you don't like doing it?"

"I don't know about that. I mean I built it from scratch so I'm quite fond of at least the basic idea. I suppose I could leave it all. But it surprises me how well it's done. I didn't expect it to do that."

"It is successful?"

"I guess. I don't know. It sounds a bit big headed to say that. It's doing very well, but I think you have to separate that from yourself if you know what I mean."

"No."

"I mean I can laugh about the Shallow Review of Books inside these walls, but out there I have to defend it no matter what. I have to take it seriously if it is going to be successful. I think the secret is to take the product seriously without taking myself too seriously. Does that make sense?"

Her mouth tilted upwards again, almost imperceptibly, but enough for Martin.

"That's me though, and I'm boring. Tell me something about you."

She shook her head slowly, but lit up a smile.

"Maybe some time," she said. "Right now, break is over."

As she started to get up, he shot to his feet.

She hesitated a moment. "Are you going to this roof party tonight?"

The roof. Martin remembered. The famous annual rooftop party for agency buyers and advertisers, which all staff were expected to attend. All except him. Drake the Robot had always exempted him from having to turn up.

He'd ignored the flyers and the buzz on the intranet, and had pretty much forgotten about the event altogether.

"I don't know. It's not really my thing to be honest," he said.

She nodded. "Okay. Thank you for my tea."

"No problem."

He beamed at her as she headed out the door, taking mental photographs of her. She turned to flash him a smile just before she disappeared out of view.

He was still on a high an hour later when Dave the Legend appeared over his cubicle wall with a grin almost broad enough to rip his face in two. "You all right?" he said.

"Yeah. Shouldn't I be?"

"What about the girl then?"

Martin pushed his chair back and swung around to face him. "Everybody's asking about the girl."

"Everybody's talking about the girl, mate."

"What do you mean?"

"The word's out. The Baggage Handler's in play."

"What?" Martin didn't disguise his pleasure. This was an exotic new twist to his reputation. "How?"

"Word travels fast. It just happens. So what's going on? Are you all set to do the wild monkey dance or what?"

"You mean sex?"

"If you want to give it a name," said Dave the Legend.

"No mate, we're not. I don't know if that's where this is heading."

"I see."

"You see what?"

"If I could offer some advice mate, it isn't going to head anywhere on its own. You ought to pick a direction."

"So I keep getting told."

"Anyway, the reason I'm here is to find out what time we can expect you on the roof this evening. Six o'clock is a good answer in case you need some assistance."

"It's not really my sort of gig to be honest Dave," he said.

With great flourish and a gunshot slap on the back that knocked the wind out of Dave the Legend, Rich arrived. "What isn't your gig?" he asked.

"He's not coming to the rooftop," said Dave the Legend, wincing at the sting.

"Yes you bloody are," said Rich. "Kasia's going to be there and so are you."

"She is?" said Martin.

Rich was unimpressed. "Am I going to have to do all your work for you mate?"

"No. I mean she asked earlier if I was going, but she didn't say that *she* was."

Rich and Dave the Legend looked at each other in disbelief.

"Martin, it is a source of amazement to me that I ended up on a plane to Japan by following your advice when you obviously know the sweet end of fuck all about the chase. Girls don't ask questions like that just to make general conversation. She was fishing," said Rich.

"Oh."

"Oh for fuck's sake can you do me a favour please and get out of the way because this glacial progress of yours is killing me," he said.

"Well all right, let's suppose I come to the rooftop ..."

"You're coming to the bloody rooftop," said Rich.

"All right, let's suppose I do. What am I supposed to do in such a public place with music thumping and clients all around and all that?"

Rich turned to Dave the Legend. "I'm going to leave you with this because if I stay here I'm going to drop him. I'm starting to get irritated."

Martin watched with genuine confusion as Rich walked away and then turned to Dave the Legend for an explanation.

Dave the Legend didn't look much more impressed. "I took advice from you once," he said.

"And did it work?"

"Remarkably, it did."

"What's your point?"

"Oh I don't know Martin. Let's see, we've got a warm summer's night on an open rooftop in the middle of London, with free alcohol and dancing and tipped into that mix, the beginning stages of a little romantic relationship. You're right. What the fuck could possibly go right between the two of you up there tonight?"

Martin dropped back into his chair. "Well when you put it like that ..."

Dave the Legend pointed at him with menace intended. "Six o'clock. Don't make me come and find you."

## Chapter Twenty

Very few people would regard a looming party as a chore. Very few people would describe an upcoming party as *looming*, for that matter. It was classic old school Martin. For the rest of the afternoon he had the sense that he was facing an obligation he'd rather just avoid, coupled with a suffocating sense of expectation. But unusually, the flutterbug of discomfort was forced to wage war with a pure-adrenaline sensation that he might have a real moment with Kasia.

He held on past six, staying at his desk and pretending to work though he couldn't focus on it. Finally, when he could put it off no longer, he pushed his MacBook closed, stood up and stretched. The office was deserted save for Drake the Robot, eternally in his glass cubicle.

Martin considered going to ask him if he was coming upstairs, but feared it would simply prolong the agony. He went to the lift, pressed the button for the sixth floor and sighed as it jerked gradually upwards.

Out on the roof, things were all abuzz. It was a warm evening with a clear sky and as much as he wanted to hate it, he was actually impressed as he took it in.

He'd never been on the roof before and was surprised to find a solid structure enclosing half of it, creating a break against the unpredictable London weather. Inside, there was long bar and another makeshift one. Outside, just evening sun lovers and a big potted tree.

There were more than a hundred people there; maybe even twice that many. Katy Perry blasted from the speakers and through the groups of throbbing people, some dancing, most just letting the alcohol do their talking for them, waiters swirled with trays of snacks.

He sneered a little at the small stage and microphone at the end of the balcony, hoping the speeches had already happened.

He scouted the room and caught sight of Rich, Dave the Legend and Michael Courtney-Hole, facing inwards from the edge of the bar, and checking the room for what Martin felt sure they would call *talent* or *totty* or something of that ilk.

"Hello chaps," he said.

Dave the Legend looked at his watch. "You're late."

"Got caught up."

"Bollocks. You just didn't want to come."

"Whatever."

Rich put his hand on Martin's arm. "Well you've come at the right time mate."

He pointed to his left, through a cluster of mini-crowds where a blue and black minidress-clad figure with chestnut hair, just slightly red where the light caught it, was in deep conversation with a man Martin had never seen before, but guessed was from one of the invited ad booking agencies.

"Is that her?" he asked.

Rich laughed. "Yes mate. It's her. Don't worry, we've been watching her for you in case you don't recognise her."

Martin gave Rich all of his venom in a single glance.

"Oh see it from my point of view," said Rich. "When have I ever had this much fun?"

"So what's the play here? What should I do? What would you do? Go over and speak to her?"

"Yes mate, and do it now," said Rich.

"Do this first," said Dave the Legend, passing him a bottle of Heineken. "All of it. In one. I want to see it all go down."

Martin took the bottle and chugged. He got it down in two.

"Good boy. That'll take the edge off. Now stand by for a second. I want a belch. A proper one."

Martin obliged.

"Good. You've now joined the party. About time. Now take these," Dave the Legend handed him a glass of white wine and another bottle of Heineken. "And don't stand around holding that thing. I want to see you drinking it. You're due for another one in twenty minutes so don't hang around."

Martin resisted. "What's the point in getting pissed here? I think I might need my wits tonight."

Dave the Legend shook his head. "No mate, you don't. Your wits suck. I've seen you when you drink and you're awesome between drinks two and four. You keep yourself in shape and don't get all deep and you're in for a good night."

Martin looked at the drinks in his hands.

"Which one is mine?" he said, with a grin.

"Fuck off. Go," said Dave the Legend.

The journey across the floor was the longest Martin had ever taken and though he covered the space in ten seconds, each one of them made him feel more self-conscious than the last.

Agency guy was a visible creep, at least to Martin's eyes. He had a goatee which Martin always thought suspect. Sporting a goatee was how the untalented recognised each other as members of a similar tribe.

As Martin got within earshot, he caught the middle part of a story involving a giant wave and a racing yacht. Presumably something agency guy either claimed to have been involved in or, give him credit, actually was.

He stopped mid-story to give Martin the full measure of his scorn in a bid to ward him off. Kasia turned to see who he was looking at and Martin chucked her a cheesy grin.

"Hey, how you doing?" he asked her giving an additional "Hey," to agency guy.

"I thought you weren't going to come," she said.

"Changed my mind. I got you this," Martin handed her the wine and took her nearly empty glass off her."

"Thanks," she said.

"You're welcome."

Kasia and agency guy exchanged glances and Martin could see agency guy wasn't rolling out the welcome mat. *Tough shit*, Martin thought. *My girl mate.*

Dave the Legend was right; even a single beer gave Martin's psyche a better voice.

"I've interrupted something. I'm sorry," he said.

"No worries," said agency guy. Goatee tribe code for *yes you have. Now piss off.*

Martin's apprehension with Kasia didn't extend to agency guy however. A miscalculation many people made with Martin was failing to realise that he really couldn't care for the most part whether they liked him or not.

"Then don't mind me. Please, continue. Unless this is private," he said, this last part exclusively to Kasia.

She shook her head, a smile spreading across her beautiful face that was unquestionably friendly.

"No, well, it is a little private actually mate," said agency guy.

Martin didn't acknowledge him, nor did he take his eyes off Kasia's for a second. The encouragement of her smile was the icing on the piss-agency-guy-off cake.

"In that case, I'll catch up with you a little later Kasia. I just needed to come over and tell you that's probably the sexiest dress I have ever seen and you look absolutely incredible tonight," he said.

There was no mistaking that her first instinct was surprise. But as she looked away, casting her eyes downwards, her smile turned to a grin. She was liking it. Bingo.

Martin didn't avert his gaze, and caught her again as her eyes returned to him.

Agency guy was feeling the squeeze to Martin's conquering delight. "You do look great," he said, the loser.

"So I'll catch you later?" Martin asked.

She nodded. "Okay."

"Good." He walked away without even acknowledging agency guy, hoping only that he wasn't the one responsible for signing off on the Unilever budget or something like that.

There was silence from the boys when he returned.

"Well, I did my thing."

Rich and Dave the Legend burst out laughing.

"Did your thing? Is that your thing?" said Rich.

"Actually, it went quite well," said Martin.

"I would say Martin, that contrary to all available evidence, you're something of a mighty fucking player actually," said Rich. "I can read body language mate and she was buying everything you were selling, whatever the hell it was. Unfortunately for our man over there, his line of chat apparently couldn't compete with the vision of you swaggering your way back here, because she looked back at you twice in about five seconds."

"Really?" said Martin. He turned and slotted himself between them against the bar, facing the room and specifically facing Kasia who was now visibly less engaged as agency guy once again held forth.

"Really," said Dave the Legend. "Run through it with us. I want to see if I can do what you just did this evening. There's that blonde over there from Carat."

Martin told them. Rich let out a loud bark of approval while Dave the Legend began a slow clap.

"You do understand what you did there, right?" said Rich.

"What?"

"You told her you've thought about having sex with her. You've been this timid, awkward disaster up until now and she's never thought of you like that before. In telling her she's sexy, you told her you think about her as more than someone you might have a cup of coffee with now and then. No wonder she looked surprised. But that smile is confirmation that you're okay to play that game with her. You play it right Mr White and you're in with a real chance of not sleeping alone tonight," said Rich.

"You think?" said Martin.

"I think you should go and find out," said Dave the Legend.

Kasia had extracted herself from agency guy and was making her way outside to a corner of the balcony, where she leaned against the railing, facing outwards, her face raised slightly into the bright summer night sky.

## Chapter Twenty-One

As Martin sidled up to her, she turned her face towards him.

"Hey," he said.

"Hey again."

"You having a good time?"

"Yeah."

"Good. It's not a bad party actually. I'm surprised. I never usually come to these things."

"Why?"

"I think they're dangerous. Work and pleasure are a bad combination. Either the work aspect prevents a party mood or the party aspect creates awkwardness in the office the next day."

She straightened up and ran her fingers through her hair, moving it back off her face. "So then why did you come this time?"

"Because you asked if I was coming. And I guessed that meant you were going to be here. And since you won't go out with me, this seemed like my best option."

"Uh huh," she said.

"Uh huh," he said.

"So you came to this party to see me. Why?"

"Why do you think?"

"I don't know. You tell me. To dance, maybe?" said Kasia.

"Do you want to dance?"

"Do *you* want to dance?"

"Not really. I just wanted to talk to you over a drink or two."

She took a tiny sip of her wine. "And why do you want to do this?"

"Wow. So many questions," he said.

"You don't like answering questions, do you?"

"Sorry. I'm not being evasive. My parents are both lawyers, so I've become great over the years at avoiding interrogation. I don't mean to be. It's a habit."

"Maybe you're too good at this habit," said Kasia. She winked, perhaps to show she wasn't being aggressive.

He didn't care anyway. They were talking. "So what about your parents? Are they in Poland? What do they do?"

"You want to talk about my parents?"

"I want to know, yeah."

She shrugged. "My mother died when I was seven. My father is a drunkard. They are both in Poland, yes."

"Oh. Sorry. I guess that's a sore point."

"Not for me."

"No?"

"It's just my life. What can I do?"

"Yeah, I suppose you're right."

"I suppose. You still don't answer my question though."

"Why do I want to get to know you?"

"Yeah."

"Is this unusual for you? For a guy to hit on you?"

"Is this what you're doing? Hitting on me?"

"Yeah. And in that dress, I'd be crazy not to."

"But I think we agree already, this mix of personal and work things is a bad idea, yes?"

"I'm willing to make an exception."

"Yeah, but you know my question."

"Why do I want to do this?"

She shrugged.

"See, I can't answer that. I don't have a solid intellectual answer for why I'm driven by an insane need to ask you out. I can tell you that this is extremely unusual for me because all I ever try to do is avoid relationships as if it is an obsession. Which I guess it is. But here you are and I think you're really exciting and I'm going to have to kill myself if you say no."

Kasia laughed. "I see."

"Anyway, we can talk about that later on. Right now, as far as I can tell, you're out and I'm out and you're looking incredible and we're both having a drink and I'm sorry I look like I just left my desk, but I actually did, so this is what you get. Better effort from me next time. For now, I'm going to call this a date."

She smiled again but then bit her lip.

"Okay," said Martin. "I know that look."

Kasia's surprise was undisguised. "What look?"

"There's something on your mind, and I'm guessing it's that you don't need a boyfriend, so you don't need to go out for a drink."

She shrugged, giving him a little *that's it in one, boy* look.

Agency guy reappeared. "Hey. I hope *I'm* not interrupting this time," he said, offering Kasia a fresh glass of wine.

She smiled at him, but declined the glass. "Sorry Jason, this time it really *is* private," she said.

Even Martin felt sorry for the poor guy. He stammered an acknowledgement, fell over an apology and tried to lace the whole lot with indifference, but it was obvious he was pissed off at the loss of her company. He moved away quickly like a dog had bitten him.

"How about I don't attempt to be your boyfriend until date number two?" Martin said.

She laughed again, but only at the absurdity. "How do you attempt to not be someone's boyfriend?"

"I don't know. How about I don't bring flowers, I don't open doors for you and I don't pull out your chair. And if you're chilly and haven't got a jacket, I don't offer you mine."

"Oh. You think this good?"

"Just come out with me."

She shook her head. "I can't Martin. I told you this. We can have a drink now."

"What is it? A boyfriend? A husband? A warrant from Interpol?"

"It's nothing. It's me. My life works the way it is."

"Jesus. You sound like I used to. Until a week ago, I mean."

"You understand, yeah?"

"I don't know. I think what we should do right now is change the subject because this one sounds like it's going to kill the whole evening."

"Okay. So what do you want to talk about?"

"Poland. Art. Errrr ... where you bought that dress."

"It's from Top Shop."

"It's fantastic."

"Thank you. I like it too."

He took a swig of his beer and she took a sip of her wine. He contemplated taking a chug. If there really had been a chance of sleeping with her that night, he had somehow managed to snatch a rejection out of the air without even asking for it, and he didn't know where else to take the conversation. Perhaps if he just kept chugging, she'd have to restart or stand there in silence.

He thought it, but blissfully, he didn't have to do it because Rich arrived.

"Hello Kasia," he said.

Her face lit up, to Martin's irritation. "Hello Rich."

"You're looking stunning tonight," he said, the inappropriately smooth bastard.

She smiled, but to his delight, it was aimed at Martin. "So I keep hearing."

"So what are you two locked in conversation about? From a distance it all looks a little flirty," said Rich.

"Oh, just things," said Martin, winking at her. No matter what, they'd certainly had a sort of a moment.

"Yeah, just things," she said with a smile. Maybe ... just maybe, she felt the same as him.

*Just things*. But as the evening wore on and Rich regaled them with war stories about his scandalous life and many love affairs, Martin wondered exactly what those things were. Had he been told to come back and try again or told to drop the matter once and for all?

He didn't know. He was on the edge of the dead zone where the signs and signals stop travelling or are no longer possible to interpret. She was warm and she was funny, but not exclusively to him. Rich was a far better story teller than he was and naturally gained much of Kasia's attention. But it was Rich she asked to hold her wine for her while she went to the ladies room, not Martin. Was she favouring him by showing him no favour? Was it a statement of neutrality: that he was neither her beau nor her bitch? Or was she just being a girl looking for a free hand to borrow? It was the worst place for an over-thinker like Martin to be.

He didn't leave with her that night, but neither did Rich and as Martin put her into a black cab and paid the driver up front, he made certain that neither did agency guy.

## Chapter Twenty Two

The next morning, he thought she would be expecting him to appear and he was knocked off his stride when her visible impatience told him he was wrong.

"Is this a mistake?" he asked.

"Why are you here?"

"Well since you won't go out with me, what other choice do I have?"

"But I keep telling you about this."

"But I thought after last night ..."

"I told you about this last night also. This is the kind of thing I want to avoid. Especially where I work. With you especially, you know?"

*"Why with me? What did I do?"*

"Martin, please. You're important around here. Everybody says it. This job I do I don't do it because I love it, I do it because I need to do it. I can't afford to lose it."

"I'm important here? Who says that?"

She shrugged with obvious impatience. "People say this. You know. These are the games I don't like."

"I *don't* know. Jesus. I wish someone would tell me that for a change. But anyway, it doesn't matter. Why would you lose your job by going out with me?"

"This is difficult for me, you know?"

"Difficult for you? You should be in my shoes."

"Why?"

"Because for reasons I don't understand, for the first time in years I'm reaching out to someone and I keep getting pushed away. By rights, with my head in the right place, I shouldn't even be trying. But here I am. And if you think this is some smooth pick up, you're wrong, because I'm as nervous as all hell here."

"I can see you're nervous."

"Just come out with me. It doesn't have to be a date, you can even bring a friend and I'll do the same and we can just be people enjoying a few drinks."

She sighed, shook her head, fidgeted, gave almost every single negative buying signal in the book. Martin was a particularly poor salesman however.

"If it'll make you comfortable, I won't even speak to you all evening. And I think I've already crossed the line into begging, which I swore I wouldn't do."

"It isn't that I find you uncomfortable."

"All right, then do this: I'm going to go out tonight with a friend to this bar called Secrets of the Beehive off Regent Street for a few drinks. If you and your friend happen to turn up, then we'll all have a fun evening together. If not, then I'll know that you really don't want me near you and I'll simply leave you alone."

"So it is go to this bar and have a drink with you or you don't speak to me anymore?"

"No, I'll speak to you. I'll even make you tea. I just won't chase after you like I've done all week."

"When did you chase after me this week?"

"Well it may not have looked like much because I'm really bad at this, but Kasia, I've done more to get your attention than I've done for any girl in like, a hundred years."

"This is what I am afraid of."

"I'm going to leave it to you," he said.

"Martin, please understand one thing. With me, words don't have two meanings. When I say I can't do something it isn't because I am playing ... what do you say ... hard to get?"

"I understand. But you please understand this: sometimes even the most determined plans can be wrong. This is new for me. Maybe you should try something new too."

She ran her fingers through her hair, stopping to clutch the top of her head as she studied his eyes like a police interrogator.

He breathed in, did a slight bow, and walked backwards a few paces towards the door. "I just hope you will," he said.

She didn't say another word as he turned and headed out into the hallway, but a few paces beyond the door, he shook his head, turned around and stuck his head back around the corner.

She was still looking his direction, her stance unchanged.

"It's off Regent Street," he said.

She broke into a smile and then a little laugh. "Yeah, you said that already."

"Oh. I wasn't sure. See how smooth I am?"

She was still laughing, but she didn't say anything else as he mock saluted and disappeared.

## Chapter Twenty Three

Martin sat down heavily. Time to reassess. She'd still said no, but he thought there was at least a chance that no could really be a maybe. On the other hand, he had not only spoken to her, he had done so eloquently. He didn't know where the hell he'd pulled most of that from, but he had both asked her out and made a compelling argument to support his request. He suddenly felt like a player, albeit a whiney, analytical one.

By allowing his mouth to run away however, he'd nailed himself into a corner which had first troubled him when Rich suggested this route of attack: Martin didn't have a friend. Not one he could call for this mission, in any event.

Rich was too close to it, and frankly wasn't to be trusted with Kasia, dressed to kill, in a social situation. *Like taking carrion to a pack of vultures and asking for advice on how to eat it. It isn't yours and it isn't safe.*

He didn't want to crash and burn in front of Dave the Legend and didn't want anyone from the office to know any more than they already did about this business in fact. He had already said and done too much and if it all went wrong, he didn't need his workmates to witness it. He knew there was a solid chance that Kasia simply wouldn't turn up at all. And then the brainwave hit him. If Rich had been largely the architect of the strategy that Martin was now pursuing, Rupert was at least the unwitting co-strategist. And since Rupert apparently had some girl advice worth sharing, he could be useful in making this date successful. He felt a little bad for adding that Rupert's emaciation and general screwiness were also sure to make Martin look great by comparison. Whoever Kasia brought along if she came, Rupert could keep her entertained, leaving him free to let rip his spectacular wit with her. He figured he'd probably have to buy all the drinks but that there was a good chance that having the opportunity to satisfy his nosiness might be incentive enough for Rupert. He just hoped that under the eccentricity, Rupert wouldn't turn out to be a lady killer and steal all his thunder.

"Tonight?"

"Yeah. In an hour."

Rupert looked a little like Martin had awoken him. He didn't have Rupert's number; had never had any use for it and had actively avoided giving him his. The only option he had was to leave the office as early as he thought he would get away with it without causing Drake the Robot any heartburn, and knock on Rupert's door.

"But it's Friday mate."

"You have plans?"

"No. No. Two women, eh?"

"One woman Rupert. The other one is Kasia. It's not a buffet."

"And what does she look like?"

Martin shook his head. "I don't know."

From Rupert's face, he should have lied.

"What does Kasia look like?"

"She's ... lovely. Really amazing."

"Balls. That means she'll be a hag then. That's always the rule with the really pretty ones. They never hang around with anyone who might be prettier than them."

Martin began to wonder if Rupert had been a mistake. *"Jesus."*

"No, I'm serious. The only saving grace is that she's from Poland which means she has Slavic bone structure and that's generally amazing."

"I don't know if she's Polish, Rupert. She could be anything."

Rupert stood back, folded his arms and fixed a stare on Martin. "Go on, keep trying to talk me into this."

"Oh Jesus, I don't know mate."

"All right, don't worry. I'll do it. Where are we going?"

Martin told him. Don't expect anything much. Don't get excited. Just a couple of drinks. He omitted that he was almost certain Kasia would be a no-show.

"Cool. Out of here in a half an hour; we'll be there by quarter past and I can get something to eat. I have an eating regimen and I'll be due for a meal then."

"Why don't you eat now? It's only drinks."

Rupert shook his head. "Don't worry, it'll be fine. See you in a bit."

## Chapter Twenty Four

Rupert was already waiting when Martin stepped into the hallway. Martin was pleased both that he was ready which made him less of a wild card, and that his being ready and waiting indicated an over-abundance of eagerness. By Rupert's own admission that made him prey, not mating material, which suited Martin.

Rupert wore a v-neck sweater over a shirt and had on a light jacket. Martin wore short sleeves.

"It's quite warm out, you know," he said.

"Not for me," said Rupert.

"Oh right. You don't feel the heat?"

"Not normally. I was in Mumbai in June and I felt it then all right. Had to lie around and sleep most of the day. Dreadful."

They set off down the hill to the Archway tube station, and Martin realised that Rupert wasn't going to keep pace with him. He usually found he walked faster than the people around him, but not enough to completely leave them behind.

He slowed down. "Rupert, I have to ask about you, you know."

"I've been waiting for you to. You're not one to acknowledge the dancing bear, are you?"

"No."

"So what you want to know is why is it that I'm a skinny motherfucker with no energy and no ability to regulate my own body heat, right? Or more specifically, what you want to know is whether it's catching?"

"I'm not worried about catching it."

"Well good. You can't."

"So tell me what it is."

"It's a lifestyle choice."

Martin could see he wasn't having his leg pulled. "Which, I take it, is a euphemism for an eating disorder. In the way that bulimia is a lifestyle choice or something?"

"No, no, this is controlled and careful and actually I'm in really good health."

Martin looked him up and down again. *Then why am I considering giving you a piggy back ride to save you a ten minute walk?* "I can see that."

"You're being sarcastic and that is the remit of an ignoramus."

"Okay, I'll buy a ticket. What is it you've discovered that proves being unable to move your own body down a hill is good for your health?"

"Fuck Martin, are you interested in the science or do you want to be a smart guy?"

"No, I'm interested. Tell me."

"Well, you're right about one thing. I don't have the physical prowess I should have as an adult male. That's a side-effect. Considering I'm not a prize fighter and have no designs on a title, that doesn't matter though. What I am is perfectly healthy. My nutritional regimen doesn't put my wellbeing at risk."

"Is that the good bit?"

"No, obviously not. The good bit is that I have the mental acuity of a snow leopard on a midnight hunt. I have so much mental clarity it is absurd. And since that's what I value most of all, my regimen obviously works."

Martin kept his thoughts to himself. He didn't mention that they were halfway down the hill and by now he would already have been seated on a train.

"And what is this regimen?"

"It's the same as a snow leopard on a midnight hunt."

"So what, once a week you devour a whole yak and then sleep up a tree for thirty hours?"

Rupert laughed. "You're close actually. The reason cats in the wild are such aggressive and successful hunters is because they're lean. They lie around a lot, asleep under trees because they don't have the energy to run around all day playing. They save their energy for a hunt and then pack all their awesome power into a single kill. But what makes them able to do that, ironically, is the fact that they don't have the opportunity to gorge themselves, you following me?"

"Sort of."

"Think of it like this: if lions or tigers or ... well, snow leopards ... had access to all-you-can-eat buffets and buy two, get two free pizza specials and bottles of fizzy cola with 65 tea spoons of sugar in each, they would be rubbish hunters. They'd be like us, fuzzy, dull and lethargic. Instead, they have one meal every couple of days, of almost one hundred percent protein, and it keeps them ticking without in any way compromising their ability to bring down the next antelope they come across."

They entered the tube station, through the gates and down to the platform.

"So you're saying you do have energy, you just don't use it?"

"Yeah. Though admittedly, the physiology of a human being is very different to that of a cat. I don't have any muscle because of how I am. But Martin, the clarity in my head is worth everything."

The place was still relatively quiet as they entered and walked over to the bar. There were a few suits who hadn't gone home yet and who would either head out to get something to eat or stagger home in a few hours.

Behind the bar, the walls ran with a golden-coloured liquid behind honeycomb-etched glass. A giant LCD screen revealed that the resident cocktail scientists had devised a dozen new ways to incorporate honey into alcoholic drinks.

"This is sweet," said Rupert.

Martin rolled his eyes. "I could have put money on you saying something like that."

"You're not eyeing up a cocktail are you?"

"I don't know," said Martin. He hadn't been, but now he wondered whether Kasia would think it sophisticated. Or maybe he should have a vodka martini instead; just James Bond enough to make a pretty hefty statement.

"You're having a pint," said Rupert. He ordered Martin an Estrella. "I can see you deliberating and it won't do. Remember the rule, be honest about who you are. You don't look like a martini drinking guy which means you're putting it on. What does that make you?"

"Prey?"

"Wow, I'm impressed. You listened."

"I do that sometimes."

"I'll have a sparkling water."

"What, you're not drinking?"

"What have I been saying? Anyway, you think with this body I should attempt alcohol? I'll pass out in ten seconds."

"No, perhaps not."

They sat on stools at a tall table and Martin checked himself out in the mirror behind the bar, making sure his hair looked okay. "Is there anything in my teeth?" he asked Rupert.

Rupert made a spectacle of checking, annoying Martin. "Nope, and you'll be pleased to know your nose is clear and you haven't suddenly had a volcano come up anywhere on your face in the past forty minutes."

"I was just asking."

"Look Martin, I don't know you, but even I can see you're nervous. Does this evening really mean that much to you?"

"No, it's just drinks."

"Nope, sorry, not buying a word of that."

"I don't even think she's going to come to be honest."

"Do yourself a favour and don't turn around just yet, but I think she just did," said Rupert.

Martin swung around to look. Kasia had come, with a friend. He could have died on the spot.

## Chapter Twenty Five

"Is yours the one that looks cheerful or the one that looks miserable to be here?" Rupert asked through a broad grin.

*Oh shit*, Martin thought. Kasia wasn't at her radiant best.

Martin and Rupert stood as the girls walked over to them. They exchanged pleasantries, did introductions and Kasia even warmed up a little.

The girls wanted white wine. Martin left them to Rupert and went to fetch it, looking back often during the two minute separation and noting with a sinking feeling that Kasia showered all her attention on Rupert. She had sat down opposite his empty seat however, leaving Rupert and her friend Ania, pretty, blonde, and also Polish as far as Martin could tell, to pair up.

From his body language, Martin could see Rupert thought he was a real winner with the ladies and began to wonder if he had miscalculated. He had a glint in his eye and had apparently decided this was the time to tap into a week's worth of digested antelope because he was considerably more animated than Martin had ever seen him. Ania was smiling. That was good. She was enjoying Rupert's small talk. Suddenly Kasia was smiling too. Not so good. Rupert was being engaging and brilliant and suave and accomplished and Kasia was beginning to take notice. Martin wondered if he should order the martini after all, to step up a gear and show he was a player.

And then Kasia turned his way, smiling. Was she looking for him or for her drink? Was she wondering when he would come back and sit with her or when he would come back and bring her some bloody alcohol so she didn't want to hack at her own throat any more at the thought of being there. He smiled back and picked up the two glasses.

"Here we go," he said, putting them down gently, as if the glasses were made of eggshells.

The girls thanked him.

And then he began to panic.

He had no conversation whatsoever.

He had Kasia, his Kasia, sitting with him, apparently voluntarily, and she had allowed him to buy her alcohol.

And she looked incredible in skinny jeans, heels and a pink t-shirt.

And he couldn't think of a single damn thing to say.

He picked up his beer. "Well, cheers," he said, wondering if he could keep sipping long enough to think of a bright conversation starter without necking the entire pint.

Kasia kept the smile on her face, the edges of her mouth quite definitely arching upwards, as she shifted in her seat a little.

And then the nightmare began.

"So is this your regular place?" she asked.

"Oh, no, never been here. It just seemed central though," he said.

Idiot. *It seemed central.* What a legendary reason for picking a place to go. How about *no, but the Rolling Stones first met here* or *they're world renowned for their wine list* or *Time Out rated it the number one bar in London* or something? *It seemed central?* What a beige answer.

"Ah," she said.

He wracked his brains. "So did it take you long to get here?"

Those bright, copper-coloured eyes mocked him. "About 30 minutes," she said, politely.

"Oh cool. Cool." A robust response, packed with wisdom and mystery.

"Yeah."

He realised he had to find something and fast. "Yeah. Oh fuck it, you know what, I picked this bar because it was recommended to me about three months ago by a Finnish guy and I couldn't think of anywhere else that had got a recommendation. And I didn't want to take you to a pool hall."

Her eyes lit up again and her perfect mouth slowly rolled into a grin. "By a *Finnish* guy?"

"By a *Finnish* guy."

"And who was this guy?"

"He was a telecoms billionaire or something that my mother was trying to represent and she has a habit of including me when she wants an informal client meeting. Something like, having a son means she's more in touch with family values or something."

"Sorry, I don't follow."

"My mother's a lawyer. In Paris. She's frightening. And when she doesn't want to be frightening, she asks me to go to dinner with her. I make her look less frightening."

"Are you frightened of her?"

Martin thought for a moment. "Yeah, actually, I am."

And Kasia laughed.

"I'm only partly kidding. She's hard core."

She looked around. "Well, it's interesting."

"You don't like it ..."

"It's okay. Is this your kind of place?"

He considered it for a moment. *The honest man is never prey.* "I don't have a kind of place really. But since you're wondering, dodgy theme bars aren't normally my sort of places, no."

"Ah, it's okay. It's very ... warm. The colours. I don't know why they make a bar all about bees though."

"Bees are great. Bees make honey. Their entire lives are dedicated to making the world a sweeter place. We should all be bees."

*Decent line. Where did that come from? Not bad at all. And she likes that a lot.*

Watching Kasia smile as she picked up her wine to sip it, he knew they heard Rupert's comment at the same time because her face transformed into shock.

He turned to Rupert. "What did you just say?"

"What? It's logical. I'm just being logical," said Rupert.

"But say it again."

Rupert sighed as if he was used to being misunderstood. "I have an eating regimen. It means I don't have a lot of energy. I merely suggested that if there was any chance we were going to have sex tonight that I ought to run out and get a couple of Snickers bars because otherwise I'll never have the stamina."

There was silence. Ania wore her disbelief like amusement. Kasia was more defensive; her barriers went up in the blink of an eye.

Rupert could feel the heat. "What? I'm not saying we need to have sex; I'm just saying that I'll need some prep time if we do."

Kasia's face said she was disappointed. "After all we've spoken about, is this what you expect from tonight?"

"No," Martin said. "I don't know what the hell he's talking about."

Ania picked up her bag and stood. She spoke Polish to Kasia, but her message was clear. *Let's get out of here. Let's go somewhere else. Whatever. Let's leave these two losers behind.*

Kasia stood too. She smiled at Martin, but it wasn't friendly. Even backpedalling as fast as he was then, he made a note to tell Dave the Legend on Monday that there was most certainly such a thing as an unfriendly smile. "This is what I was afraid of. And now we see how things are on Monday I guess," she said.

She thanked him for the wine, and the girls walked out of the bar without turning back.

Martin felt a helpless rage begin to rise up inside him and he swung on Rupert, a tirade of abuse locked and loaded, but Rupert had swallowed down the remainder of Martin's pint and was already beginning to sway.

## Chapter Twenty Six

Martin shuffled Rupert back onto the tube in autodrive. The walk down from the bar to the tube stop had been a humiliating experience of avoiding the judging eyes of passersby as Rupert, too drunk to walk properly, had to be supported. His lack of physical bulk took some of the challenge out of it, but his insistence on trying to speak, loudly and incoherently, drew an unending barrage of unwanted attention, it being far too early in the evening for even the many Londoners who had a drinking binge planned, to be drunk yet.

Martin kept his head down as he whisked Rupert roughly along, convinced that at least some of the scorn they attracted had to do with losing Kasia just when he almost had her.

He pushed Rupert up against the glass bulkhead inside the carriage and warned him not to throw up as the beeping sound chimed the doors closed.

He couldn't shut Rupert up, enduring what appeared to be a slurred stream of remorse as the train moved from station to station and he considered just pushing him into a seat and abandoning him for a while, even picking out an available slot.

A pretty girl with scarlet hair appeared to find them amusing and he realised he was holding Rupert up and against the bulkhead by the throat. He shrugged a mute explanation of annoyance.

Out of the tube station he attempted to board a bus but the driver refused to allow Rupert on board. The alternative, a long walk up one of the steepest hills in London, at least took the energy out of his anger.

The lift inside his apartment block opened to reveal the Spanish woman, on her way up from the basement where she had parked her black Mini Cooper which he had no doubt smelled like rich, exotic spices within. Vanilla and cinnamon and other things that only a perfumer would recognise. Biblical frankincense.

She almost snarled at Martin as he pushed Rupert inside and made a show of ignoring him as they rode up to his floor. For a moment, he felt defensive of Rupert; what the hell was so wrong with getting a little drunk now and then anyway? But the sting of Kasia's reprimand was the freshest thing under his skin and he yanked Rupert out by the shirt collar when the doors opened, ignoring the Spanish woman back.

"Where are your keys?" he asked, leaning Rupert up against the wall outside his flat.

Rupert responded with something incomprehensible.

"Oh for fuck's sake. Where are your fucking keys, Rupert?"

Rupert's head dropped forward, as if he had gone to sleep. Martin gave him an impatient pat down, realising before he did so that Rupert didn't have anything on him. If he had left home that evening with keys and a wallet, he didn't have them now.

"I don't believe this," he said. "I don't believe *you*. I really, truly do not fucking believe you."

He dragged the now sleeping Rupert down the hallway to his own flat and dropped him heavily onto the couch. He took off his shoes, fetched him a bottle of water from the fridge and got him a bucket in case what seemed to be the inevitable, happened. And then he went to bed.

It was probably the earliest night Martin had had for years, but he was wiped out and as he lay down he felt total weariness wash over him.

As he closed his eyes, Kasia looked at him. She looked half hurt, half angry. And half mocking. And half bored. And half pitying. If that was what amounted to a date; a half hour non-drink supported by a wingman he didn't even know, then he was precisely as pathetic as he thought he was.

He slept badly that night as tired as he was, partly because he couldn't get over an intense feeling of loss and partly because Rupert snored like a hibernating bear.

As the sun came up, he finally drifted off and when he awoke, Rupert was gone. He didn't leave the flat all weekend and switched his phone off.

He had to remind himself several times that it wasn't the end of the world, but every time he let the misery go, it was replaced with frustration. Finally, when it came, Monday morning was a relief.

Kasia fluttered into his cubicle chair as he sat down and gave him a reassuring smile. She was in red, the colour of war and he hoped she intended peace.

"I'm really sorry," he said. "I can't tell you how stupid that whole thing was."

"It's okay Martin. My friend actually thought it was quite funny. But I think we maybe are making a big mistake if we do anything like this again."

"You do?"

"Yes. I am sorry. I like you. I think you're nice. But you know, I told you before, it's better to have no involvements like these. For you too."

"I see."

"It's okay?"

"Is this because the idiot I was with asked a stupid question? Because it seemed to be going fine until then."

"You call your friend an idiot?"

"He's not my friend."

Kasia frowned. Once again Martin realised he wasn't connecting at all. "So why did you bring him?"

"He lives in my building. I mean, I know him. I just don't know him, if you know what I mean."

"No. Please explain this."

"He lives on the same floor as me. I just didn't realise what he was like until Friday night."

"This is the friend you brought? Someone you don't know?"

There was no sparkle in her eyes.

"Yeah. It was a mistake, obviously."

"Okay. Well, I must go."

Kasia stood up with a whoosh. Martin leapt to his feet as if he'd been ordered to.

"Is something wrong?" he said.

"You don't think so?"

"I'm really not following."

"You know Martin, Ania is a good friend of mine. I know her for many years. This is who I came with. I think your choice of friend says something you don't realise."

## Chapter Twenty Seven

"So you're giving up then mate?"

Rich put two pints down on the small, worn, round table at the back of The George. He'd been surprised when Martin had asked him to go for a drink, but Rich never passed up an opportunity for mischief or scandal.

Martin ran his finger down the moisture on the glass, then picked it up and took a big gulp. He put it down again and shrugged.

"Well what's the point if she went out with you? Why give up now?"

"She's not interested Rich. I mean, she is, but she isn't."

"But she said she brought her friend along. That's sort of an important little detail, isn't it?"

"The only reason she came to see me this morning was to say, give it up and walk away. She didn't come for any other reason."

"And so you're going to?"

"I think she's just telling it like it is. She seems to do that. And maybe it's better anyway."

"How is it better?"

"I mean, the way we are now, there's a sort of sexual tension which is actually pretty great. Sexual tension in the office is always great. It's almost worth never acting on it, even if the opportunity arises because when it all goes wrong, it is gone forever. And I reckon even the faintest hint of possibility makes the days more interesting, even if there is no chance of you ever turning it into anything. How boring would the office be without it?"

"Bollocks."

"It isn't bollocks."

"So you're going to look me in the eye and tell me you'd prefer to leave her out there than take a risk because you don't want to ruin the sexual tension that you've just this second invented? You're talking bollocks."

"I don't think I'm the one doing the leaving out there, Rich."

Rich picked up his beer and took a swig, keeping his eyes on Martin as he did so, sizing him up. "Well I'm all for breaking the tension mate, so do you mind if I ask her out?" he said.

"Why?"

"I mean, if you don't intend to follow this up."

"We've had this chat."

"We had it when you placed dibs on her. If you're not interested, what difference does it make?"

"She'll never go out with you anyway, so why bother?"

"How do you know she won't?"

"She said so."

"She said she wouldn't go out with me?"

"No, she said she didn't want to go out with anyone."

"But if I can convince her?"

"You can't."

"But if I can?"

Martin shook his head in disbelief. "You can't."

"So what's the harm in trying then?"

Martin threw up his hands. "Fine. Ask her. Fuck it."

"Steady on, mate. If you're worried about it ..."

"I'm not worried Rich. She'll tell you to get lost, I'm sure, so what difference does it make?"

Except that Martin wasn't sure at all. He endured another half an hour of miserable beer while Rich killed two triumphant pints, and then walked quickly away in the opposite direction to put as much distance between he and Rich as possible.

As he approached the entrance to the Tottenham Court Road tube station, his mobile phone rang. It was Rupert.

"I tried to call you over the weekend. Several times," he said.

"How did you get my number anyway?" Martin asked.

"One of your business cards was on your coffee table."

Martin grunted.

Rupert released a torrent of apologies and oaths that he had never been in that state before and would make it up to him, but Martin hardly listened. Between the noise of the street and the noise in his head, he didn't much care for anything Rupert had to say and in the face of the new threat from Rich, he had forgiven him anyway.

Martin had hardly sat down with a cup of coffee the next morning when two books flew over his head from behind him, narrowly missing him, but sending his cup flying. Coffee splashed everywhere, and ran off the desk into his lap, onto his MacBook keyboard and all over his desk.

He spun around to see Kasia, standing, hands on hips, her eyes aglow with brilliant fury.

*"What the hell?"*

Her eyes narrowed. "If you're not going to respect me at all, then don't expect me to respect you. And stay the hell away from me."

"What are you talking about?"

*"You know,"* she sneered. "Don't send your friends to chat me up."

*Rich*, he thought. The bastard did it.

Kasia sucked the air out of his cubicle as she left and he leapt to his feet to try to protest. It wouldn't have done any good anyway since she was gone, but as he did so, the office erupted into laughter and applause.

He looked at the mess of his desk and realised it was a metaphor for what he was doing to his life. He picked up his MacBook which was still working, and tipped it upside down. Coffee poured into the puddle on his desk which was already pouring over the side and onto the floor.

And then he began to laugh.

He ignored Drake the Robot throughout the mop up operation and took longer with it than it required in order to avoid talking to him. Ultimately however he couldn't ignore him any longer. He went to his glass fish tank office and closed the door.

"That's not like you Martin."

"No, it isn't. Although to be honest Drake, I'm starting to question what's like me and what isn't these days."

Drake the Robot motioned for him to sit.

"Should I have her sacked?"

"No, why? Why would you do that?"

"Oh dear."

"Oh dear what?"

"Martin, I hate to say I told you so, but I told you so, you know. I take it that wasn't an attack out of the blue? You did something to deserve that, didn't you?"

"Yeah."

"And she's reacting to it because that's what women do. They react to things that men do. And in so doing, they slowly begin to control our lives, and God help you if you step out of line."

"Huh?"

"I'm talking about women Martin."

"Well you're not talking about Kasia."

"No? How so?"

"She's not like that."

"Oh good. You found the outlier. How is she not like that? When I've just witnessed you spend half an hour cleaning up tea from your desk that she spilled by throwing something that from my angle looked like it was aimed at your head?"

"It was coffee. And anyway, I did something stupid and she was angry. That's all."

"Oh dear God, you're gone aren't you?"

"Oh, not you too. Will you all just give me a break with the bloody love advice?"

"Does she even know how far gone you are?"

Martin crossed his arms defiantly sat back, fixing Drake the Robot with whatever contempt he could muster. It was pointless however. "No."

"I see." Drake the Robot leaned forward. "Martin, don't screw everything we have up over an office flirtation. Keep your head clear for me. For us. For everything."

## Chapter Twenty Eight

Martin wasn't home for sixty seconds before Rupert came knocking. He tiptoed to the door to see who it was, silently he thought, but no sooner was he there than Rupert told him he could hear him and insisted he opened up.

Martin obeyed without enthusiasm.

"Ah, there you are," said Rupert.

"Yep, here I am. At home. In my flat. Amazing, eh?"

"You're being ratty and sarcastic, but it's okay, I deserve it. I've come to apologise."

"Oh don't even bother. It doesn't matter." Martin stepped aside and waved Rupert in.

"It does matter. I was a complete asshole and I've gone and messed up your entire evening. And as I recall, you were doing quite well."

"Can you remember anything of the evening at all?"

"Yeah, of course. I can even remember thinking that my suggestion was a good one. I still do to be honest, but I think the timing and the exact wording may not have been optimal."

"No, perhaps not. Although I have to hand it to you Rupert, setting ground rules the way you do, you must either get blown off a lot or laid a lot. One or the other."

"Mmm. Well, anyway, did you manage to put it right with your lady?"

"She isn't my lady, and no I didn't. In fact, I've really fucked it all up good and proper way beyond anything you did."

Martin told the story and was archly offended that Rupert found it amusing.

"It's because she's scared of you Martin."

"Scared of me? Why?"

"Look, there's this girl where I work and we've got a pretty well-defined relationship. There's a chance she'd sleep with me if I had tattoos, long hair, a Repsol Honda and was a member of a rock band. And if she didn't already have a husband who did most of that and two kids that she dotes on. And assuming she was the sort of girl, which I don't think she is, to jeopardise all that on a tryst. Assuming all that, there would always be the chance, if we weren't already too good friends for it not to be weird, because we've worked closely together for almost a year already."

"So?"

"Despite all that, I'd get into bed with her in a flash."

"What's this got to do with anything?"

"Even though it might ruin everything we have. In the cold light of day, I'd have to say there's probably too much to lose. By mid-way through any evening however, I would wreck everything we've got for a night of meaningless sex. Probably. For a weekend of it, there wouldn't even be a contest."

"Okay. That's because you're a rat."

"Well actually Martin, it's because I'm a fairly average bloke. And girls know that and it takes ones like your friend a long time to get beyond it. I mean there are plenty of slappers about who'd do you for the laugh of it after a few drinks. But that isn't what your friend is about and so she's being guarded. And every time you demonstrate that you're not serious, she backs off a little more."

"I don't know how much further back she can go. She's been in reverse since I met her."

"And what you've done to counter that is bring a stranger to meet her best friend and send a colleague around who she knows wants nothing more than to shag her as if she's your property to hand out. You're not exactly playing a champion's game here Martin."

"Yeah well, it doesn't matter. I'm out."

"Oh the hell you are. She's nervous of you mate, but she still turned up the other night and the last I remember there wasn't a gun at her back. And she brought her best friend along which means something. You have to be able to see that, you can't be as thick as you're making out."

"Maybe I just wore her down."

"No mate, you didn't. Walk away if you want to, but you'll be a moron. And anyway, you're nuts over her so how is it going to get better for you if you don't keep chiselling away?"

That night, Martin hardly slept at all. By morning he still hadn't come up with a good way to approach her, to apologise or to show her that he wasn't actually a complete jerk.

He didn't have to in the end. She did it for him. He forced good cheer into his performance on his rounds that morning, collecting envelopes from Red Stella, Nelsinho The Grave Digger and Shannon the Bombshell who gave him a lift by overtly mentally undressing him.

It hadn't lasted however and by the time he got to the office he was in no position to handle the battering that was to come.

The lift was empty as he stepped into it on the ground floor, but as he turned around, Kasia stepped in behind him, her face once again registering nothing whatsoever. She turned to the doors, her back to Martin, and prevented a man in a red tie from entering.

"Sorry, it's full," she said.

"What?" he said, as the doors began to close in front of him.

"The lift is full," she said. It wasn't a tone of voice you argued with.

As the lift began to move upwards, she swung around to face him.

"Kasia, I'm so sorry, I really am," said Martin.

"You don't know what you're talking about. You don't give people permission to go out with me. What the hell is wrong with you?"

"I didn't mean it like that."

"Is it all you want to do to fuck me around?"

"No. I didn't mean to do anything at all."

But the doors began to open on the first floor and Kasia just shook her head then turned and walked out. She didn't look back.

Martin rode the next three floors alone, but the rising car had nothing on his suddenly lifted spirits.

As he sat down, he realised two things: that trying to think of a clever entrance was pathetic in the face of Kasia's honest directness ... and that he was getting to her. Martin knew from years of handling baggage that anger was deepest and most confrontational when there was genuine emotion.

He realised the absurdity of being thrilled to have disappointed her so thoroughly, but he revelled in it anyway.

He stood to go and speak to her, to take it to her the way she had taken it to him several times now, but stopped himself, remembering that she very specifically didn't want drama in the office and knowing it could just send her over the edge.

As he powered up his MacBook and organised that week's *goods*, he decided he'd wait until she came around and then just tell it to her like it was. It was enough to smear a smile across his face as he sat alone in his cubicle.

But then Rich stopped by.

"Bloody hell mate, I don't know what's up with Kasia, but she's just asked me out."

Martin's whole body surged with adrenaline. "What?"

"Yeah. God knows. Maybe she's just thought about it a bit more. We're going to have dinner this evening. I'm hoping it'll lead to other things."

Rich raised his eyebrows at the last statement as if he was expecting a congratulatory fist bump.

## Chapter Twenty Nine

Martin felt like his plug had been pulled. As the energy surged out of him, the office got hotter and the normal buzz of office banter seemed like an affront to him personally; pleasant chatter about matters of excruciating banality in the face of a war. He knew his time was up if he didn't go into battle.

When Hernando Cortez invaded Mexico, he allegedly ordered his ships burnt once they were offloaded to snuff out the option of escape. He suddenly hated that his own boats remained unburned and mentally kicked himself, screamed at himself, tarred and feathered and eviscerated himself to rid himself of the indecisiveness that was fast becoming catastrophic.

And it felt powerful.

For the first time in a good long while, he began to contemplate a real challenge not in terms of how to avoid it, but how to wrestle it to the ground.

He knew Kasia wouldn't shy away from such a challenge; she'd proved that from the start. He'd have to do the same, and he'd have to do it that day, before Rich could make his plans a reality.

True to form, she appeared on the floor with her head at a defiant angle and walked with intent, though she did so down the opposite side of the floor.

Martin didn't even hesitate. He silenced the dissenting voices in his head and took off after her, matching her pace and meeting her head on as she rounded the cubicle farm at the end of the floor.

Her face said *don't even bother*, but it was too late for that now.

"I know the last thing you need is a scene so I'm not going to make one. But can I at least apologise to you?" he said.

She stopped, but didn't respond. He might have felt chilly if his heart wasn't racing.

"Can we step outside for a second?" he asked.

"If you mean it, just do it," she said.

He noted with considerable irritation that much of the office buzz had come to a dead stop. Clearly he offered the promise of unmissable entertainment.

"All right," he said, ignoring everything but her. "I'm sorry. I was trying to keep Rich away from you. I've no doubt you can take care of yourself, but he was intent on chasing you and no matter how much I tried to stop him, he was determined to ask you out. In the end I guessed that if I just said go for it, you'd say no and that would be the end of it."

Her face didn't display any reaction whatsoever.

"But you've actually gone and said yes, I hear," he said.

Kasia didn't flinch.

"Thank you for the apology," was all she said before she brushed past him to continue on her mission.

But Martin could smell the creosote and burning timber; could hear the crackle of the flames as they devoured the masts, the wheelhouse and every plank of decking.

As Kasia moved out of the department and called the lift, he followed after her, stepping into the car just behind her.

The same man with the red tie they had denied access to that morning was already inside and frowned his recognition.

"I need this lift," said Martin.

Kasia turned around, surprised and as far as he could tell, a little alarmed.

Red tie's face dropped in surprise.

"Out," said Martin, holding the door open with his right hand, while pointing the way out with his left.

"What do you mean?" said red tie.

Martin noted that Kasia's whole body language had shifted quickly from shock to fascination, she was seeing something undiscovered and unexpected.

“This is your floor,” said Martin.

“No it isn’t.”

*“Mate, it’s your floor*. I need this lift for an intensely personal discussion and I need you to get the hell out. Now.”

Red tie looked from Martin to Kasia and back to Martin, his shock increasingly apparent.

“Oh, you know what, fuck this. You two need to sort your lives out,” he said, and stepped out of the lift.

Martin didn’t thank him; his attention was now fully on Kasia. He reached behind him and hit the button for the first floor and as the car started heading downwards, he tried to keep his voice from trembling.

“Okay, listen. I don’t know you and you don’t know me, but we seem to have packed a lot of anxiety into a very short space of time and I take responsibility for that. I came down to invite you out for coffee last week because I like you and I thought it would be exciting to get to know you. The Rupert business with the Snickers bar was unfortunate. You’re smiling. That’s good. The simple truth is that for whatever reason I probably like you one hell of a lot more than you like me, assuming you like me at all and believe me when I tell you, I can do a little better than this.”

Kasia’s smile was all about her eyes which livened up as he spoke.

“This is the first time I actually believe you’re not just playing games,” she said.

“Good. Because I’m not.”

“What I don’t know is what you want. What you expect.”

“Nothing. Not really. Well one thing. Not what I expect as such, but what I would like: don’t go out with Rich. Let me start again instead.”

“I told you I don’t need complication. I already did things here that I regret.”

“Cool, then let’s keep it uncomplicated.”

He realised he was wrong. There was a big difference between the way Kasia looked when she was happy and when she was not.

“I’ll think about it,” she said.

“Thank you. I can’t ask for more than that. But staying on topic, if you're looking for a lack of complication, Rich is not your man. If there is only one person on this planet who's a worse bet than me, it's Rich."

The lift stopped and the doors opened and Kasia stepped out, turning as she did to face him. Martin thought she was trying not to smile outright; trying to play it hard for a while longer. She was bad at faking.

"I'll think about it," she said again, but as the lift doors began to close, the smile broke into a little laugh.

## Chapter Thirty

Rupert answered his door almost as soon as Martin knocked, as if he had been waiting for him.

"Well, you're certainly changing," he said.

"What do you mean?"

"I mean you've been my neighbour for over a year and you almost completely ignored me for the first year of that. Now you won't leave me alone," he grinned.

He stepped aside and ushered Martin in. Rupert's flat was full of piles of National Geographic magazine and camera equipment with framed pictures on all the walls of feline predators: cheetahs and tigers and others. There was an expensive LCD TV, but the only other furniture was a multitude of black and yellow beanbags. One had a blanket and a pillow.

"You sleep there?" Martin asked.

"Like cats in the wild," he said.

"Cats sleep on beanbags?"

"You know what I mean."

"Well anyway, I just thought I'd tell you that I think I've patched things up with Kasia. Your advice turned out to be good again."

"You really *are* changing. It's amazing what love can do."

Martin shrugged. "Yeah. Things are finally looking up."

He hadn't stopped looking around the room, taking it all in, and noticed finally, the six packs of Snickers bars on the kitchen counter in the corner by the door.

Rupert followed his gaze and then chuckled gently. "I met her again mate. Ania I mean. At the supermarket. It turns out she had time to reflect and thought my indiscretion to be the funniest thing she's ever heard. So we've sort of hooked up."

"Oh right. I see. That was easy."

"Girls are easy mate, that's what I keep telling you."

"And have you required Snickers power yet?"

"I shouldn't talk about such things. It's ungentlemanly. But yes, I have as it happens."

"Oh wow. Well done," said Martin, not really meaning it.

*How the hell can a guy as fucked up as Rupert nail a girl like Ania and I have to fight for every inch of ground with Kasia?* he thought as he unlocked his front door. *What the hell is the matter with me that I can't even get a girl to go out with me and he can get one into bed with a stupid, crass comment like that? Is that the secret?*

He hadn't felt real anger for a long time. Repressed and constrained, he'd held back his feelings for years, keeping things shallow. That wasn't going to wash tonight. He lashed out at the air, shadow boxing at nothing, while only just holding back a furious roar from deep within his belly. He was pathetic. And finally, he was drained. He leaned against the window frame and looked out onto the street below but his eyes were immediately drawn to Polly. She stood at her window, unmistakable concern across her face.

She gave him a thumbs-up and he shrugged. He was in no mood for games. He rolled over the back of his couch and flopped into its cushions, staring at the ceiling and decided to yell out loud anyway. It felt good.

But then the buzzer rang, and he yelled again. This time not so good. Whoever it was could fuck off, he thought, only vaguely bothering to wonder who it actually might be.

But it rang again.

He shouted at it.

It didn't help. The third time it rang, he dragged himself to his feet and pressed the intercom button alongside the front door.

"It's me."

"Who?"

"Who do you think?"

"I'm sorry? Oh wow. From across the road?"

"Yes."

In retrospect, he didn't know why he let her in except that she was Polly and it seemed like a perfectly natural thing to do.

He opened his front door and leaned his back against the door frame, facing the lift and waiting for it to arrive.

When the doors opened, she didn't avert her eyes all the way down the hallway. She had on little red shorts, flip flops and something that only barely deserved to be called a tank top.

He said nothing as she approached, more than a little bemused that she was there and bowed in apprehension.

"You look down," she said, finally with him, an Australian twang adding an unexpectedly exotic extra dimension to her.

Up close, Polly was even more beautiful than he had realised. She had perfect, long, sun browned legs and pert little breasts that pressed up hard against her top so the outline of her nipples were clearly visible. He had never seen her closely enough to see that her eyes were sky blue.

"I am a little," he said, trying to disguise that he was aroused.

Polly smelled expensive, and though it was subtle, he guessed that she'd given herself a squirt of something only moments ago.

"Well, I'm good at cheering up if you want me to," she said.

As he stepped aside to let her in, warning lights started to flash inside his head.

He closed the door and as she turned around, he pulled her close and kissed her. She responded with enthusiasm, letting her tongue dance around playfully against his. He moved her slowly over to the couch, hardly loosening his embrace and gently lowered her down, kicking off his shoes as he moved on top of her. She didn't resist, but she wasn't entirely at the game either, he noticed.

"Should I stop?" he asked.

"Do you want to?" she asked.

"No. I don't."

"Could we maybe have a little less anger?"

"Oh God. Sorry."

"Don't apologise. I guess we're getting straight to it. So let's get straight to it."

"Did you want to talk first?"

She laughed, surprised, perhaps sarcastic. "That's the normal convention. It doesn't matter. You're in no state for conversation and I don't feel much like forcing it. I need this too. Just maybe calm down a little?"

He nodded. He smiled. He pushed her top up and began to kiss her nipples, her neck and then her mouth again.

She responded this time, sitting up a little to allow him to pull her top off while she unbuttoned his shirt, and helping him to slide her shorts down so she lay naked beneath him. She was beautiful, he had to admit, with a little tattoo of a seagull on the left side of her soft, smooth tummy. Her eyes gave no doubt that she was eager for a night of fun.

She tasted wonderful. She felt incredible. But ultimately, *a night of fun* turned into twenty minutes of *it's all about me*, as Martin systematically rebuilt his machismo at her expense.

He hoped she didn't mind, but it was all he could do to even care.

He rolled over and she sat up, turned around and kissed him on the cheek as she reached for her top.

"Sorry," he said.

"It's okay."

"Is it?"

"It's fine."

"But not what you expected?"

"What do you think?"

"Mmmm."

"You know, if I'm honest, I thought you'd be a lot softer. A lot more sensitive. I thought we'd got to a place where I might not be a quick fuck."

"Oh shit, I'm sorry. It's been really weird lately."

"It's fine. I didn't expect Don Juan DeMarco, I just, if you'll pardon me, feel a little like a whore at the moment."

Martin sat up sharply. "Oh God, I didn't mean to make you feel like that. I really didn't. My head's a total mess. I'm really sorry."

She waved her hand, dismissively. She wasn't interested in sob stories. "Don't stress about it."

"I don't even know your name," he said.

"I don't know yours. I have a name for you though and I prefer it to your normal one."

"How do you know?"

She shrugged.

"Well what is it?"

"Not telling you. Your reaction on hearing it might ruin it. It isn't like it matters."

She pulled on her shorts and turned around again to face him, brushing her hand against his face.

"Cheer up," she said.

"I have a name for you too."

"Well don't tell me. Keep it to yourself. It'll be our thing."

She got up and slipped on her flip flops again. As she pulled the front door open, he stood, still naked and followed her to the door.

He put his hand on her arm to stop her. "Can I ask you something?"

She shrugged again as if she was a silent, sullen teenager.

"Why did you come here?"

"What do you mean?"

"I mean why would you come over here just for sex?"

"Oh, you know what? Fuck you."

"No, I don't mean anything by that. Only that I don't understand the motivation."

"I didn't think it would be like that," she said, waving her hand in the direction of the couch.

"I didn't have any control over that."

“Tell me about it.

“Look, I really think you’re great. Even though it may not seem like it, I enjoyed the sex. I just ... oh fuck!”

Over her shoulder, he watched Ania step out of Rupert’s flat.

He probably had the time to yank Polly back inside before she noticed, but instead he froze so solidly that even the lava flow of contempt she spewed in his direction as she caught sight of him, naked, with a scantily clad girl leaving his flat, couldn’t thaw him.

Polly turned to look as Ania shook her head in disbelief and marched towards the lifts.

Without thinking, he took off after her. “Ania, Ania, stop, stop, stop,” he said.

She stopped dead and turned around to face him, immediately casting her eyes from side to side to find somewhere else to look.

“You’re naked.”

He’d forgotten. “Fuck.”

She turned back around and walked away.

“It’s not what it looks like,” he said.

She didn’t respond. He turned around with his hands on his head as Polly pushed past him, her face red with anger or embarrassment. Probably both.

“Polly, I’m sorry,” he said, desperately.

The only acknowledgement he received was the middle finger, over her shoulder as she pushed open the door to the stairwell.

## Chapter Thirty-One

By the next morning, his despair had turned back into anger. Though he knew he was entirely to blame, he pushed it away, lashing out instead at his Peepers who kept him shallow, at the pinstriped banker on the tube who irritated him just by his gold cuff linked presence and finally at Rich who had forced him onto a runaway train and uncoupled the caboose.

"I'm out," he said.

Rich jumped a little at the sharpness of his tone and stood to face him, dropping the receiver on a freshly dialled phone call, carelessly into its cradle.

"Hello," he said.

"I'm out."

"Out of what?"

"Out of the challenge. Out of the whole bloody mess I've got myself into. *You've* got me into. You're as much to blame as I am."

"What are you talking about?"

"Kasia. My life. Everything. I'm out."

"Do you want to have a seat?"

"No, I don't want a seat. I don't want anything. I just want to be left alone. I'm over all this Rich. I don't want it."

"Kasia?"

"Kasia. The challenge. This competition. Any of it. It's all been a mistake and I want out."

"Well mate, as far as I can tell, the competition is over anyway. Not that I was competing. I just wanted *you* to."

"Why?"

"Because you need to get a life."

"Why is it over?"

Rich broke out a grin. "Will you relax? She told me yesterday she wasn't going to go out with me after all and I knew what was going on. I asked her if it was about you and you should have seen her smile. She's falling for you mate."

"*Was* falling for me."

"What do you mean?"

"Nothing," said Martin, turning and leaving.

Martin found Kasia on the first floor, walking down the hallway.

"Hey, Kasia," he said.

She stopped and turned to face him, her eyes dull, her stance weary.

She looked like she hadn't slept.

"Well at least you stopped," he said.

She gave him full eye contact, but the brightness was gone.

"Why wouldn't I stop?"

"Have you spoken to Ania?"

"Yes. She's my best friend. We speak all the time."

"Oh. You never mentioned she and Rupert were together."

Kasia didn't react to the statement.

"Anyway," Martin pressed on. "If you've spoken to her, I may have some explaining to do."

"Why would you have to explain anything?"

"Well something happened last night that I'm not proud of at all and I ought to confess it to you I think. Or rather, I know I need to. But it was a mistake and it wasn't at all planned, I really need for you to know that."

"Oh?"

"Yeah. Well, has Ania told you about it?"

Kasia rolled her eyes. "Oh stop the bullshit Martin. You had sex with a girl. Last time I check you are adult and free to do whatever the hell you feel like doing. Why would this have anything to do with me?"

"No, look, you're right to be upset, but you should know I don't have any interest at all in that girl. I really don't. It's just something that happened and I didn't intend it."

"What difference does it make to me?"

"I want it to make a difference," he said.

Her eyebrows revealed a full appreciation of the effrontery of his statement.

"No, that's not what I mean. Look, all I do is think about you. I swear it. I don't even know that other girl's name. She just knocked on my door and we had sex and ..."

Kasia's mouth fell open in perfect shock.

"No, that isn't what I mean either."

She smiled, another cold smile he'd have to tell Dave the Legend about and placed a hand on his shoulder.

She shook her head. "Poor Martin. So full of bullshit you don't even know it."

Her sarcasm released the anger that Martin had managed to push just below the surface. "I'm trying to apologise here."

"For what? What are we to each other that you need to apologise? Since when do we have anything to do with each other's lives?"

"You know how I feel about that. About you."

"Yes, I know what you say. And now I know what you do. And I told you I don't need a boyfriend, so why not stop this being so stupid and stay away from each other."

## Chapter Thirty Two

He fell into his cubicle chair and was very lucky not to miss it altogether.

His satchel still over his shoulder, he threw his head back and stared at the ceiling. Suddenly, his view was full of Penny.

"Martin ...," she said.

"Not now Pen."

"I really need some advice."

He tensed and her face said she noticed. He leapt to his feet and turned on her.

*"Advice?"* again with the hiss.

"Sorry, this is a bad time, I can tell."

*"A bad time?"*

"I'll come back."

"Back when? Back why? *Why?"*

"Martin, what's wrong?"

A few heads began to meerkat above the walls of the cubicles all around him and he turned a full three-sixty to see them all. He caught sight of Drake the Robot, about to bite into his sandwich but transfixed instead on Martin. He realised he was making a spectacle of himself, but he could no longer bring himself to care.

"I'll tell you what's wrong. What's wrong is every piece of advice in this building is total crap. All the advice I've received in the past few weeks and frankly, all the advice I've ever given. What makes you think I've got any bloody idea how to fix your problems? Have you seen the ones I make for myself? I can't help you Penny. I can't help anyone. I can't even help myself, and you're seriously better off just doing the opposite of everything I've ever advised. Just ignore everything I've ever told you and do the opposite."

Penny looked frightened, so Martin tried to regain some control.

"I can't help you Penny. Not this time. You're better off ignoring me," he said quietly.

"Okay Martin. Thanks," she said, stepping away from him backwards and then walking swiftly away from his cubicle. The other meerkats began to pop back down once the meltdown was completed, and he was left only with Dave the Legend's head in view.

Martin gave him the thumbs up, but Dave the Legend gave him a frown. He didn't believe a word of it.

He sat down and leaned forward, resting his head on his desk, waiting for him to turn up. It took less than ten seconds.

"Martin?" said Dave the Legend.

"Daaaaaave! Heyyyyyy!" said Martin, not lifting his head from his desk.

"Anything you want to talk about, or are you just taking a new personality for a spin? Because I have to tell you mate, this new one sucks."

"Thanks Dave."

"You want to face me mate?"

"No."

"Martin, sit up. I'm bigger than you. We can do this with or without pain."

Martin sighed. He sat up and spun his chair around to face Dave the Legend.

"Better?"

"Yeah mate, better. Now what the hell's going on?"

"Girls."

"Oh."

"Well, girl. Singular."

"Right. I take it things aren't going well then?"

"It's fucking my life up and I don't know what to do about it."

"May I offer some advice?"

"No."

"Oh right. Because it'll be shit."

"It all is."

"You're not going to kill yourself or anything are you?"

"No Dave, I can assure you I couldn't be remotely bothered to go to that trouble."

"Right. Well if you want to talk ..."

"Thank you."

"Right," said Dave.

"Quick question."

"Yep?"

"Is Drake the Robot looking this way still, and has he taken a bite out of his sandwich yet?"

"Errrr. Yes he's looking, don't know about the sandwich. Hard to tell. Oh, no, it looks intact."

"Then will you excuse me? I'll save him the trouble of ordering me in for a pep talk."

He stood and pushed past Dave the Legend who obligingly stepped back. "Keep your head up Martin. You of all people should know love's full of complication."

Drake the Robot didn't take his eyes off Martin all through his approach, as if he was using them as a tractor beam. Martin returned the favour, keeping his eyes fixed on Drake the Robot like it was a game of freak out. It occurred to him that Ennio Morricone's *The Good, the Bad and The Ugly* theme would work perfectly for the scene.

He didn't knock. There would be no point.

"Drake? May we speak?" said Martin, continuing his psychological game. Drake the Robot knew perfectly well that Martin never wanted to speak to him.

“Sit,” he said, pointing to a chair. A redundant gesture, Martin thought; he was hardly going to sit on the floor.

“So I suppose you’re wondering what that was?” said Martin.

“No.”

“No?”

“She threw a book at your head. I expect this one is a tough cookie. What you two are getting yourselves into now is entirely your business. I don’t care about it to be honest. Go all Mickey and Mallory if you need to.”

“Really?”

“Yeah. I’m tired of telling you what’s best for you and you ignoring me. I want a good column. I’m narrowing my list of expectations when it comes to you Martin.”

“This will not affect the Shallow Review of Books, Drake.”

“Well let me be clear once again that I won’t let it. Come up with the goods this week and don’t forget the first word in the title is *Shallow*.”

“Why would you think you need to tell me that?”

“Christ Martin, I knew you the moment you walked in the door last year. You’re struggling. Don’t let it affect your work.”

## Chapter Thirty Three

He tiptoed past Rupert’s flat that evening, unlocked his door silently and then decided to slam it shut with as much force as he could muster in a sudden urge to regain control.

If Kasia was gone, he was an idiot. He knew it. He went to the window to draw the curtains so he could block Polly out, but then realised that would be about as insensitive as he had ever been and so he stood by the window instead, waiting to see her.

It took a minute or two, but finally she appeared and noticed him out of the corner of her eye, the way she stopped and twirled around.

He smiled and gave her a thumbs up. She nodded. No smile. Then she pulled her curtains shut.

## Chapter Thirty Four

He was in bed earlier than normal, when it hit him that he should send flowers. It was another pain au chocolat opportunity and he didn't want to miss it. He climbed online and searched for flower retailers. The first one on Google was a national giant called Nuts about Flowers, which offered next day delivery and gifts as well. It would do. He began to trawl. This one looked like it was for old people. That one looked like it was for an obscure office colleague who was recovering from a bunion operation. The fresh cut flowers were even more confusing. Stuffed bears and puppies and boxes of chocolates in a never-ending spread of colours and shapes only added to his indecision.

Finally he selected a dozen red roses with long stems in a wrapped box. Card details in, he paid and checked out. Then he cancelled it.

"What the hell am I thinking?" he said, quietly. Talk about overkill.

He clicked back to the start, weary, but now determined. Yellow roses, also in a box came up slightly cheaper, but looked like they would be perfect. He paid again and checked out.

And then he cancelled it.

Yellow roses symbolise friendship, or at least he thought he had read that somewhere. And also, they were cheaper than the red ones and he worried she would know that and think he was cheap which would ruin everything.

*Chocolates!* He looked for something unusual and finally settled on champagne truffles in a fancy box. Once again he paid and checked out.

And once again, he cancelled.

*Chocolates? Really? Who said she even ate them? Her perfect, shapely legs said she was probably a jogger. Or a tennis player. She'd look incredible in a little tennis skirt. Okay, focus. This isn't about sports. It is about her diet however. And her legs. Those legs. And those eyes. And that mouth. Those lips. Oh sweet Jesus, do not send chocolates. Ever.*

The sudden sound of the phone ringing yanked him away from his thoughts with a start. He always ignored the phone as a rule and that was one habit he wasn't in the mood for changing. *On the other hand, the phone doesn't usually ring at ... what is it? Eleven thirty! Shit!*

He picked it up.

"Hello?"

A voice with a heavy Indian accent came flooding down the line.

"Hello, am I speaking to Mr Martin White?"

"Speaking."

"Ah, hello sir. I am Mike from Nuts About Flowers. How are you this fine evening sir?"

"Um. Fine."

"Very good. Yes, we are seeing that you are placing three cancellations in less than one hour. We are wondering is there something that you are having a problem with in our system?"

Martin made no attempt to hide his irritation. "No, it's all fine."

"Three cancellations Mr Martin."

"I'm just trying to decide what to buy."

"Roses and then roses and then chocolates. What did you do to the lady sir?"

This was a step over the line. *"What?"*

"Sir you can tell me and then I am certain to be able to help."

"What did you say your name was?"

"Mike, sir."

*"Mike?"*

"That is correct sir, Mike."

"What's that short for?"

"I am sorry?"

"What is Mike short for? Michael?"

"Yes sir, it is short for that very same name."

"You're no Mike. What's your real name?"

"Please sir, this is my name."

"And where are you calling from?"

"Sir, I am from Nuts About Flowers."

"Yeah, but where in the world?"

"From Watford."

"No you're not."

"Yes I am sir."

"Tell you what Mike, you tell me your real name and where you're from, and I'll tell you what I did, is that a deal?"

"Sir, I am Mike and I am from Watford."

"So what's the weather like in Watford right now?"

"Sir, I am sorry, I am inside of the building so I cannot see the weather."

"Bollocks. Then I'm not telling you anything."

"Sir, I am only trying to help."

"Then tell me the truth."

"Sir? All right. I am Satishkumar."

"And what do your friends call you?"

"Mike sir."

"Oh the hell with it. All right. And where are you Mike? Don't say Watford."

"Today I am in Bangalore sir."

"Jesus."

"All right sir. But now tell me what you need all these flowers and chocolates for."

"What are you, the love doctor or something?"

"Sir, we have a deal I think. I am telling you the truth, now you tell me."

"What did I do?"

"Yes sir."

Martin sighed, but took a little comfort that Mike was nothing but a voice. He told him everything.

There was silence.

"Mike?"

"Sir, so let me understand. You had sexual relations with another woman after the woman you love forgave you for doing her wrong?"

"Yes. And it sounds even worse when you put it so succinctly."

"Mr Martin, may I recommend a loyalty pack sir, with a discount card for bulk orders, spread out over a month with free delivery as long as the total amount exceeds £500?"

"£500? You're joking aren't you?"

"Well believe me when I say, it's going to be a long time before you're off the hook for that one. I think you're going to be buying lots of flowers."

"Shit."

"That is correct Mr Martin."

"Well what are the details?"

By the time Mike and he ended their conversation, he had purchased the whole package including eleven white and one red long-stemmed rose to be delivered the next day.

## Chapter Thirty Five

If a clear indication was needed that Martin was way out of his depth, it was that he honestly thought roses might mend fences with Kasia. When he awoke the next morning he was hopeful and played out in his head the way he would win her over once and for all and then continue to lavish gifts upon her that would delight her.

It came as a shock to him therefore when a box of roses landed on his desk mid-morning. He turned to look. She didn't bother with pleasantries.

"These seem to come from you. I don't want them. Perhaps the no name girl who knocks on your door at midnight will want them, but I never, ever, will."

He didn't see Kasia again, but the rectangular box which sat on his desk all day was a subtle reminder that she was a long way from being his. As the day wore down and the after-work buzz began to pick up energy; something which until just a few weeks before had marked the start of his real work day, Martin grabbed his mobile phone.

He scrolled through the recently received calls and found Rupert's number.

"You want to come out for a drink?" he asked.

Rupert snorted. It wasn't overt; wasn't obviously a snort at all, but Martin knew he heard it.

"Perhaps I should," he said.

An hour later they were at The Angel where Rupert found them a table at a window while Martin fetched a pint for him and a sparkling water for Rupert.

"I'm retiring from baggage handling," he said as he sat down, anxious to set the topic for the evening's conversation, and determined the topic would be him.

"Why?" Rupert asked.

"Because I have a renewed appreciation for how complex relationships are."

"Isn't that a good thing?"

"I'm bad at them."

"Well you're not the smoothest guy on the planet. But you're not bad. You just seem to be unusually keen on self-sabotage. Anyway though you're nuts to give it up when you're discovering how much there is to say. You were the Baggage Handler before Martin, you're like the super handler now."

Martin dismissed it with a wave of his hand.

"And anyway, Kasia likes you so cheer up," said Rupert.

"She thinks I'm an asshole."

"Right. Which means you're getting to her."

"Oh what the fuck Rupert?"

"I mean it. And she keeps telling you to get lost and leave her alone, but she keeps coming to you to say it. She could just ignore you and avoid you like the plague and be totally inaccessible, but instead she comes to you. To tell you personally. You can see that, right?"

Martin shrugged, but the observation was one he wanted to be true.

"Ania tells me she was very upset when she discovered you were shagging someone else. Ania thinks you're an asshole too by the way but only because you upset her friend. Women mate. So feline, I keep saying it. You think they're fragile and soft but you'd be genuinely surprised to discover how tough they actually are and how self-sufficient. They don't flake the way men do. But you get them purring and you have to do a lot to switch that off. Once they like you, they generally like you," said Rupert.

"Well I'm sorry Rupert but Ania didn't bloody need to tell her," said Martin.

Rupert's eyes told Martin that his timing was as bad as his luck lately. He didn't need to turn around to know Ania was there.

"Hello Martin," said Ania.

Martin turned to face her. "Hello Ania. Are you well?"

"Yes, I am well."

"Good."

"Okay."

Rupert leapt to his feet to get her a drink leaving Martin to think of something to say to Ania who had sat down. The silence was long enough to be embarrassing as Rupert struggled for attention at the now busy bar.

"It's not what you think," he said finally.

"What I think is that you had sex with a girl the night before last, is that right?"

"Yeah . . ."

"Then it is what I think."

"Yes, but it wasn't like that."

"Martin, do you think I care? I don't care. I don't care at all. You did what you wanted to do and that is fine. So what?"

"Because you told Kasia."

"Yes, because Kasia is my friend and I don't want to see her making a mistake."

"Well, she isn't going to make one because she's been as difficult as anyone I have ever met. She's standoffish and truculent and just difficult."

"I don't know all these words, but obviously you are an idiot if I can say that."

"Oh great. Keep it constructive, won't you?"

"You're not that great you know? A great girl like Kasia should be hard work. You shouldn't fuck other girls the same day that you make a big deal of her. It means you're not serious and then you're just looking to have some fun. And she told you that she doesn't like this right at the start."

Martin turned his eyes away, uncomfortable looking at her.

She leaned in, as if she didn't want anyone else to hear. "You know, I tell you something which I don't know why I tell you, but yesterday Kasia was in the best mood after work and I think it is because of you. After that she felt even worse than ever once I tell her about this other girl."

"Well why did you tell her then?"

She sniffed. "I'm going to just ignore this stupid question."

Rupert arrived back with a glass of wine for Ania and as he sat down he mock shivered. "Wow, it's frosty here. Perhaps we should break this up?"

Martin sat upright. He knew Rupert meant him but by then he was feeling thoroughly confrontational. "What do you mean?"

If Martin was threatening, Rupert didn't seem to care. "Martin, look, to be honest, you need to go and have a think about some things. Getting drunk isn't going to make it better. Go home. Go to sleep. Decide what it is you want."

Ania raised her eyebrows in challenge.

"Fine. Fuck it. Fuck it. I'll see you guys around," Martin got to his feet and charged out the door.

## Chapter Thirty Six

Martin had never had much of a relationship with his father and only really recalled some of the most extreme things he used to say. As he raced up Highgate Hill he recalled a conversation when he was no more than ten years old, when his father had advised him that a solid gold rule for winning was to never step down from anything, no matter that the evidence said you were wrong.

"Son, it's a sign of power if you're never magnanimous in victory. Don't ever let them tell you that a good winner is anything other than someone who punches the sky the way a heavy weight boxer does. It's all or nothing. You brag when you've taken it all. But let me tell you something even more important: it's a sign of your willingness to use that power when you act that way even when you know you're wrong. They'll tell you to knuckle under when you're losing. I say go on the attack. It's like poker. Confidence is often enough to make you a winner, even when you've got nothing."

As he had come to realise of course, it was all crap. Or at least, it was all useless advice. He didn't have *nothing*. He didn't specifically have *something* either. What he had was a form of suspension in an ice cold vacuum. What the hell was he supposed to do with this *now*?

At home, he ordered a pizza and cracked a beer. He sat in the dark, the only light coming from the TV, muted on a news channel showing non-news updates on a slow day.

When he finally went to bed, a day of anger had wiped him out. For the first time in weeks, he slept well.

## Chapter Thirty Seven

He abandoned his workout routine all weekend and on Monday morning. Push ups and crunches were the last things on his mind and he grabbed a slice of the previous evening's pizza before he headed through the door.

Jenny Lucie Manette was top of the agenda for the day and he got to St. Pancras earlier at her request so she could make her train without rushing.

"Should I be worried about you?" she asked him, sizing him up. "I mean, I know we're not supposed to talk about such things."

"No," he said. "Here's the thing: for the first time in years, I think I'm moving my life forward again, and it is a cruel irony that the first thing I think I'm going to have to do is stop moving at all."

"I'm sorry?" she said.

Martin had the feeling that Jenny Lucie Manette had only asked because she didn't think she'd actually get an explanation. Rule #1 of Shallowness meant such questions were safe when they were aimed at Martin. He didn't really know himself why he was giving her any detail.

He shook his head, adding a smile as he did so. She was right. "It doesn't matter. I'm in a holding pattern and I think it might be a long one."

"I don't know what that means Martin," said Jenny Lucie Manette.

Maybe she was interested after all, Martin thought.

"I mean I think I'm in for a long wait for someone and I think I need her to help me move my life forward. I mean that the first thing I'm going to have to do in order to move forward is begin a long wait. It's complicated."

"You're seeing someone?"

"I don't know."

"Wow."

"Tell me about it."

"All right, good luck. I have to run. But Martin, do me a favour if you will: don't do a Tom Cruise couch flameout thing. I mean, if you're actually going to allow yourself to fall for someone, try to keep your head."

He was genuinely shocked. Had he just had his ego slapped? "Why wouldn't I?" he asked.

"Because there is none so zealous as a convert. And I've always thought of you as the loneliest man I know. If you're reaching out to someone, just remember that you're probably the worst equipped man on the planet to do that without making a hash up of it. I mean that as a friend."

"The loneliest man you know?"

Jenny Lucie Manette looked at her watch.

"Look, I have to go. I'll see you next week. If you want to chat, we can get here earlier, though that's probably going to ruin your whole morning. Your choice. Text me. And good luck."

He was still reeling when he approached Mama Mia Marigold, so it stung doubly when she didn't change the message.

She was out of sequence, but since she was leaving for three weeks in Valencia, it was get her goods now or not at all.

"It's not flu still?" she asked.

"I don't have flu, Mia."

"You have what then?"

"Nothing. Love problems."

"Oh. Really? You?"

"Yes me. Why not me?"

"Hey, these are your rules, not mine. Don't get excited about my words. But I think if you're going to fall in love, I'm not very surprised to see you look so like you want to confíe el suicidio, you know?"

"Why does everyone say that?"

"It's too much change. She's English?"

"Polish."

Mama Ma Marigold let out a long, steady whistle.

Martin bristled. "What?"

"This is heat for you Martin. I hope you know what you're doing."

"I can handle it."

"You look like you want to kill yourself or someone."

"It's an illusion."

"Hey, I say this as your friend, okay?"

Marina Triple Platinum fixed him with her North Sea eyes as he came towards her. She said nothing. She didn't have to.

"It's just a girl thing and I'm working it out," Martin blurted out, exasperated under her gaze.

"We talking about our personal lives now?" she asked.

"No."

"Okay. So this thing ... you want me to care or you don't?"

"No, I don't want you to."

"So why did you tell me? I think this is breaking the rules, right?"

"Yes. And God bless you Marina, thank you for being at least one person who doesn't feel the need to ask me a load of questions."

"Why should I ask when you just tell me all the answers anyway?"

Martin shrugged. He handed her the pay off. "Right. As you say."

"Thanks," she took it from him. "Just don't go and kill yourself okay? Because if you ask me, you're thinking about it."

"I'm not going to kill myself. I'm not. Why does everyone keep saying that?"

"Everyone is saying it?"

"Pretty much."

"And you don't think you should listen?"

Shannon the Bombshell was last. He'd left her for last because she always put him on a high. As he shuffled towards her that morning however, the mental undressing he usually enjoyed from her was replaced with ... *what ... with compassion?* What the hell was that look on her face?

"Hey lover," she said, a cigarette between her scarlet-tipped fingers.

"Hey yourself."

"You want to talk about it?"

"There's nothing to talk about Shannon."

"Right. Sure there isn't."

"I'm just having a bad day."

"But you know what you look like, right? Or you wouldn't have raised it before I did."

"I know because everyone else has told me this morning."

"Who's everyone?"

"More Peepers."

"Girls?"

"Yes. All of them."

"Girls are smart about these things. It's one of the reasons I like girls from time-to-time if you know what I mean. You should listen."

"Can't I have a bad day now and then?"

She flicked her cigarette aside, not looking where it went. "Sure you can. But this ...," she pointed a long, slender finger and drew a circle in the air in front of his face. "This is not a bad day. This looks more like all the troubles in the world, crushing your shoulders."

He sighed. "Shannon, just this once, I'm going to ask you not to make me the centre of your attention."

"Aaaah, you noticed."

"I always notice."

"So when are we going to do something about it? I can make all of this go away," she said, tracing her finger in front of his face again.

"What am I going to say?"

"Some bullshit about a restaurant?"

"I just can't do it."

"I see. Well, you know where to find me if she doesn't work out. Just don't take your time Marty."

## Chapter Thirty Eight

As far as mornings went, he'd had better. He tried to perk himself up on the tube ride back to Goodge Street, focusing on Shannon the Bombshell and her continued interest rather than the certainty Mama Mia Marigold and Marina Triple Platinum shared that he was one step away from sucking down on both barrels of a shotgun.

As he rounded the corner outside his office, he was vaguely aware that he recognised the large man in the denim jacket that leaned against the wall. He'd had enough conversation for one day and was already regretting his decision to initiate it with his Peepers, but as he attempted to pass the man by, he felt a hard shove that took him by surprise, tipped him off balance and sent him to the pavement.

"Get up," said the man.

Martin looked up. Who was he? He knew the face, but couldn't recall from where. "Have you got the right person?" he said.

"Have I got the what? Are you being a funny man now then?"

The voice triggered a new memory and suddenly he put the two together. It was Gerome, Penny's boyfriend who just weeks ago was thanking him for saving his relationship.

"Gerome?"

"Get up."

"What the hell are you doing?"

"I don't want to chat princess. I want to break your fucking head. Now get up or I'll just start with my feet. You want that or would you like to try to be a man?"

"What the hell's going on?" said Martin, getting to his feet.

He shouldn't have bothered. Gerome unloaded a right hook that toppled him over again and temporarily blinded him while a sharp pain burst out from the middle of his brain.

Martin was aware of a scuffle, but it was a minute or two before he was fully able to comprehend that Jane had witnessed the assault and had called security. She had also called Penny apparently because the predominant noise in the shouting match that ensued, was her.

A crowd had begun to form, and he looked up to survey the faces. No Kasia. Good. He didn't want her to see him on the floor, the loser in a one-sided fight.

Eventually he fixed his attention on Gerome and Penny right about the time his name began to bounce.

"Martin's a good friend. He just wants what's best. And you can be sure I'm getting rid of the tattoo," said Penny.

"Good, because it's shit," said Gerome.

"You're such a cock. No wonder he told me to leave you."

"I'm a cock? *I'm a cock?* That cock's lucky these security blokes are here ..."

It was too much for him to handle, even with a badly throbbing eye and a splitting head.

"Wait one second," he shouted.

Both Gerome and Penny stopped and turned their disbelieving attention on him.

Martin didn't wait for an objection. "When the hell did I tell you to leave him? When the hell did we have any sort of discussion about this at all?"

Gerome switched his attention to Penny.

Penny put her hands to her hips. "You need to make up your mind Martin. You said last week to do the opposite of your previous advice. You said before I should stay with him, so I know what you meant."

Martin got to his feet again, light headed, but now more angry than dismayed. "Penny, listen to me. And listen carefully. What I said was, stop asking for my advice. Whatever you heard, that was my message. Nothing else."

He turned to Gerome. "And you. Fuck you. Fuck you for making your problems my problems. If she's leaving you it's because she thinks you're a cock mate, not because of something I said. You have to wonder what kind of relationship you have when she's constantly looking for outside advice rather than coming to you."

The two security men stepped forward, but Gerome waved them down. "S'all right. I get it now."

He turned to Martin and extended his hand. "Sorry mate. No hard feelings?"

Martin looked down at his hand in disbelief. "Oh for Christ's sake," he said as he pushed it aside and walked into the building.

And then, just inside the entrance, he stopped and turned to the crowd, such as it was. "Let me just say, to everyone here, that I'm out of the baggage handling business. Out. Please tell others. And Gerome, thanks for the shiner."

## Chapter Thirty Nine

As he looked back over the previous few weeks, Martin had to admit he'd been the only one jinxing his love life. Sarah had spurred him to action, Rich had forced him out of his comfort zone and Rupert had been the image of the dedicated cheerleader. Kasia herself had taken what appeared to be big steps to overcome a natural fear which Martin had in a lunatic frenzy of self-destruction, done almost everything he could to confirm.

Even Mike from Bangalore had seemed to understand what Martin needed to do better than Martin had himself and ultimately his recommendations were all Martin had left.

He tried to speak to her, fighting through the futility as Kasia continued to play an unforgiving game.

"Can I help you?" she had asked, her face blank but her stance defiant.

"Can we talk at least?"

He had begun to spend a noticeable amount of time in the first floor break room, waiting for her to make an appearance. Her response had been to simply spend more time out on the floor as a means of avoiding him.

"Why can't you just leave me alone?"

"I can't. I'm crazy about you."

"How can I ask you nicely enough? What will it take?"

"I can't Kasia. I just can't. And I can't stand you being like this with me."

"That's *your* problem."

"Yes. And I accept it. This is me trying to solve the problem though and I'm not going to stop trying."

"You should. It will not change."

But he didn't. Mike had a standing order to send the same flowers every day, gradually increasing the number of red ones to *increase the heat* as Mike put it.

"The more chillies you add to a curry, the more entertaining it is Mr Martin. The more irresistible it is. Trust me. Throw in some more red ones because I bet you she's looking in the boxes."

"They're coming back to me sealed every day."

"They're still sealed every day?"

"Most days."

"Right. The others, she's taking a look. Maybe she's trying to disguise it by declaring to her affiliates how irritated she is, but she's taking a look anyway. Trust me, add some more chillies to your mix."

But still she returned them every day, personally placing them on his desk, usually without eye contact or even a single word. He allowed the boxes to accumulate until they took up a sizeable part of his desk, to show her that they were hers or nobody's. Finally, 23 days after that first delivery, on a day way past the point when Martin had accepted he could have to grimly hang on forever, she didn't immediately move on.

"When is this going to stop?" she asked.

"When you stop giving them back," he said.

"You're going to bankrupt yourself."

He almost let it all out how he had bought a bulk discount order off

Mike from Bangalore and felt like punching himself in the head for the thought. *You put a cost on romance, dickhead. You certainly don't merrily explain how thrifty you've been.*

"I think it's the least I can do," he said.

She almost smiled and his heart leapt. For Kasia, almost smiling was turning out to be code for secretly delighted. Or perhaps that was overstating the case. She was certainly warming up however.

"How is your midnight friend?"

"I don't know. I haven't seen her since. I doubt I'll ever see her again."

Kasia nodded and turned to leave.

"When is *this* going to stop?" he threw her question back at her.

She took him on, full eye contact, her eyes just faintly aglow but the faintest smile from a second before, almost gone.

"Not yet."

"Okay. One day then."

"Don't hold your breath."

"It could very well come to that," he said.

Once again, just the faintest hint of a smile.

If Martin had been asked to identify the best days of his life, he thought the day when Kasia switched *never, ever* for *not yet* would have to rank among them.

He didn't pursue her at all that day, fearful of ruining the tiny promise of sweetness that had suddenly reignited.

That night, he tried to call Mike from Bangalore but couldn't track him down. He left a message on the website and sent an email to the info@ email address.

Mike called at midnight.

"My apologies Mr Martin for the late telephone call. I am just now coming on shift."

"It's okay," Martin said. It was too. He was delighted to hear Mike's voice.

"What is it that I can do for you Mr Martin? And what progress with Kasia?"

"Progress is good actually. Today she returned the flowers as usual, but she stopped to talk."

"This is excellent news sir. And what did she say in this talk you had?"

"She said she wasn't ready to forgive me yet. Previously she had said she would never forgive me. The word *yet* seems to be incredibly positive by comparison."

"Yes Mr Martin. It is sounding like she is getting ready to let you off the hook."

"So what do I do now?"

"Sir, may I make a recommendation?"

"Yeah, that's what I need."

"Please hang up the telephone."

"I'm sorry?"

"Because I am obliged if we are on a call, to try and sell you something. My advice at this juncture however would be that throwing money at your problem is no longer what is needed. Now you must throw yourself into it."

"I thought I was."

"No Mr Martin, we have together facilitated a charm offensive from a distance. But does someone as special as Kasia not deserve the best of you?"

"Which is what?"

"*You* sir. Your personality. Your honesty. Flowers in boxes are only evidence of how you feel, not proof. What is needed now is proof. Now you must close the distance and put yourself in front of her. She needs to be feeling what you're feeling because that is what is important here. Anyone can send her flowers."

Martin sent her some more anyway. And even though he had exhausted his £500 limit, he extended it in order to earn Mike some more commission, buying flowers for everyone he could think of, his mother to surprise her, Rupert and Sarah as an apology for his behaviour and Rich because he wanted to show there were no really hard feelings while also rubbing a little salt in any wound Martin hoped he had.

That night he had his best sleep since he had first knocked Kasia onto her backside that random Thursday afternoon.

## Chapter Forty

The next day all she delivered to his desk was books.

He turned to study her, realising he was being handed another chance. The only things that gave her away were her eyes which were smiling even as the rest of her face denied her emotion.

“Is this all I’m getting?” he said, picking up the books.

“You were expecting something else?” she asked.

“No, I’m pleased with just these.”

“Good.”

“Thank you.”

“For delivering your mail?”

“No.”

She nodded, once. She left. He sat back with enormous satisfaction.

His phone rang and he picked it up immediately.

“Are you being sarcastic?” said the voice he knew perhaps best of all voices.

“Isabel. Nice to hear from you.”

“I’m running between meetings. I’ve got one of Sarkozy’s ex-people on the ropes. I don’t have time for games.”

“I take it you got my flowers.”

“I got them.”

“And do you like them?”

“What difference does that make? What’s this about?”

“Well, when a son sends his mother flowers, there usually isn’t an alternative agenda.”

“So what, have you got the Russian girl pregnant?”

“Polish girl.”

"Semantics."

"Not really. And Sarkozy is Hungarian himself isn't he?"

"Precisely why I don't trust him."

"Anyway, she's not pregnant. She's as far from pregnant as she could possibly be. To the best of my knowledge anyway."

"Which means what?"

"It doesn't mean anything. The flowers are just a message of affection from me to you."

"Well you picked a fine time to do it."

"Christ Isabel, tell you what, next time I'll book some time in your diary in order to send you flowers will I?"

"Oh don't be melodramatic."

"Do you at least like them?"

She sighed and he knew her eyes were rolling. Basic questions always bored her.

"Yes Martin, I like them very much."

"Really?"

"Asked and answered."

"You're welcome."

"Okay. Well done."

The constant tone said she had disconnected. Whatever *well done* meant, he decided to take it as a thank you.

At lunch time Martin found Kasia in the first floor break room.

"Have you eaten?" he asked.

She smiled the first open smile he had seen for the best part of a month. It was stunning and it was aimed at him. He understood what victory felt like but he was surprised at how quickly she had warmed up. Kasia didn't attempt to hide anything; he had been forgiven and she had moved on.

"No. But I have something here. You want to share with me?" she said.

"Yeah," he said. He lifted his lunchbox. "I brought something too. We can have a picnic."

They sat on the countertops and ate, not actually sharing anything at all.

"Tell me something new and interesting about you. Something I don't know," she said.

His standard line for years had been "there's nothing interesting about me really," just to deflect attention. He nearly rolled that out this time too, but caught himself before he blew yet another chance.

"Well, are you aware that they call me the Baggage Handler?" he said instead.

"Who?"

"Lots of people. People in this building."

"Why?"

"Because everyone comes to me to offload their baggage."

She shook her head.

"You know, not their actual baggage. I mean not physical stuff. All the other sort of baggage though. Their problems. Their complaints and their worries and all the neuroses they have piled up. They come to me to offload them."

"Why?" He could see his explanation hadn't made matters any clearer.

"Because I'm good at it, I guess. I have a way of seeing things that other people can't sometimes. I don't know, it is just something I'm good at. Or something I used to think I was good at anyway. I'm not so sure anymore."

"You? You're the worst at creating problems for yourself. You even got hit in the face for it."

She was teasing, she even winked, but they both knew she was right.

"How sweet that you noticed."

"Your face was twice as big with this black eye."

"Yeah, it was. We're you at least worried about me?"

She shrugged. "I was thinking you were an asshole. I don't feel sorry for assholes."

He laughed with real appreciation. "Ah, there's that honesty again."

She winked. "Of course I didn't like you getting hit like that. But I also felt like doing it myself, so I was a little bit happy."

Martin couldn't remember the last time he had laughed as hard. "Words don't have two meanings, right?"

"Exactly," she said, her delight obvious.

"Well, believe it or not, this round of screw ups is a new thing. Until recently you could ask anyone here and they'd tell you I'm the go-to guy when you feel like complaining about your life."

"That sounds depressing."

"Ah, but the important thing about me is that I've always had a habit of avoiding gathering any baggage of my own. I mean, I don't have any problems, really."

"You don't have problems? You're lucky. Or maybe you're ignoring them."

"No. No, look, I'm not being clear here. What I mean is that I listen to other peoples' troubles so often; they hate their wives and their husbands and their boyfriends and girlfriends and flatmates and landlords. They hate their jobs and the weather and they don't earn enough and they have too much debt and they don't want to go to their parents-in-law for bloody Boxing Day and so on. I hear all this stuff and I drew a conclusion many years ago that I don't want to be like them at all. So I avoid anything that might lead to those sorts of problems."

"I don't follow exactly. How do you avoid having problems, I want to know."

"Because I don't have relationships that are anything more than superficial. Or at least mostly-superficial. I don't like getting involved, you know? And I don't ever spend more than I have. I work hard so that I don't have to. I mean, half the guys here don't have the option of leaving their jobs because they're so in debt on their cars and their flats that they need their paychecks. I don't have that problem because I'm careful with money."

"You're cheap?"

"No, I'm not cheap. Do you think I'm cheap?"

"I don't know. You never took me anywhere."

"I've tried to. You won't bloody go."

She winked at him to show she was kidding. "But tell me this Martin, why then if you don't want any problems, do you bother with someone like me? Believe me, I have problems. I can take up hours of every day with my problems if I decide to unpack my suitcases."

Martin laughed. "Kasia, I've already made such a mess of my life because of you, I almost don't recognize myself any more. But honestly, I understand why everyone else seeks out these sorts of complications. Why they put themselves through it. I've been wrong. I'm finally starting to get it."

"So what's changed?"

"You."

"But why though?"

"You've become like an addiction for me and I can't put you down. I haven't felt like I could care less about anyone for a long time, but you're just different."

"I'm not different. There are a thousand girls who are a better idea for you. Believe me, you don't want to get involved with me."

"I think I do."

"I know you don't."

"I'll take my chances."

"I'm warning you, you'll find more suitcases than you have ever imagined."

"Baggage. The term is baggage. And I don't think I mind."

She bit her bottom lip.

"I mean, this time you didn't return the flowers, so you can't back out now," he said.

"Maybe I just liked the box they came in this time."

"Was it a different box?"

She shook her head, her beautiful mouth spreading to a smile again. "No."

"Kasia, listen to me if this goes somewhere then great. If it doesn't, then that's okay too. Except that it'll be a real pity."

She was still smiling, but it faded just a little. "The problem is that it will go somewhere. I can promise you that."

"And I promise you that isn't a problem."

"Mmmm. We'll see." She looked at her watch and realised she was late, she leapt off the counter. “Oh, I have to go.”

He slipped off the counter too. “Nice lunch,” he said.

She touched his hand, lightly, but deliberately and he felt like she examined rather than looked at his eyes. It was just a second, but it sent Martin’s pulse racing.

“Okay, well, see you around,” she said.

“Yeah,” said Martin.

And she was gone.

## Chapter Forty-One

Something was missing all afternoon and Martin couldn’t put his finger on it.

Around four, Rich popped into his cubicle chair with a relaxed smile. He was holding a bouquet of long-stemmed roses.

Martin swung his chair around to face him and rolled his eyes at the sight of him.

“Thank you Martin, they’re lovely.”

“Fuck off.”

“You really shouldn’t have. A back rub would have done.”

“No, but really though, fuck right off.”

“Flowers mate?”

“You weren’t the only one.”

“Why then?”

“Because you’ve been one of those instrumental in helping me win her over.”

Rich looked at the twenty-odd other boxes on Martin’s desk. “How many did she cost you in the end?”

“I don’t even care to count them. It’s been worth it.”

“So you’re sorted then?”

“Yeah.”

“And what does that feel like?”

"Rich, I don't know when last I felt this alive."

Rich grinned. "I'm really pleased to hear it mate. So what are you doing with her tonight?"

"Tonight?"

"You're taking her out aren't you?"

"Oh shit. That's what's been missing."

"What?"

"I need to go and find her."

But she was already gone and as Martin settled back into his cubicle, he realised he didn't have her number.

In a scurry of panic, he tried Rupert's number but it went straight to voice mail. He grabbed his things, slapped his MacBook shut and shot to his feet, but it wasn't worth much. Drake the Robot spotted him as soon as his head appeared above the cubicle wall and beckoned to him.

"My apologies Drake, I'm just in a bit of a rush this evening," he said, only half-entering the office.

"Come in, sit down."

"Can we do this tomorrow?"

"Won't be a few minutes," said Drake the Robot, waving Martin into a seat.

It was unmistakeably an order and Martin followed it. He said nothing, but raised his eyebrows and hooked his fingers together impatiently.

Drake the Robot wouldn't be hurried.

"So I see the lady didn't return your flowers this morning."

"No she didn't. Are we going to have *this* discussion?"

"*Which* discussion?"

"The usual one. You disapprove and so on."

"I don't actually."

"That surprises me."

"Are you aware Martin that over the past three weeks with this whole flower business, you've done your best work yet? I've never seen you so focused and frankly, the Shallow Review has been as good as it ever has."

"Oh. That really does surprise me. So are you going to wish me good luck then?"

"With what?"

"With Kasia."

"No Martin. I'm going to tell you not to mess things up, same as I always do. You're right, we're going to have *that* discussion."

Martin sat back, his frustration evident.

"You have to be somewhere?" said Drake the Robot.

"I need to find her," said Martin.

"Then out of courtesy I'll be brief, believe it or not," said Drake the Robot, leaning in. "You're in the danger zone. Don't allow some love affair to soften you up or change your outlook. I'll tell you straight that the new, motivated you is one of the best versions of you I've seen yet. Compared to the near-suicidal self-pitying you of a few weeks back, this is a revelation. But I know what women can do to you Martin and the next thing you know she'll be influencing everything you do."

"Okay Drake. I'll watch out for that," said Martin.

"So will I."

"Easy peasy Drake."

Drake the Robot grunted.

Martin knocked on Rupert's door, but there was no answer. Inside his own flat, he put his things down, and wondered what to do. He peeked around the corner to see if Polly was there. She wasn't; though her curtains were open that evening, her lights were all off.

He realised he was starving and went scouring through the fridge, whipping together a sandwich and then flicking on the TV at a total loose end for anything to do. It was absurd. Kasia was out there somewhere, no doubt wondering what the hell he was up to. He tried Rupert's number and then went up the hallway to knock on his door again.

He was wound up and frustrated with himself so that when Rupert came knocking at ten o'clock, he practically charged the door.

"Where have you been?" said Rupert.

Martin stepped aside to let him inside. "I've been here mate. Actually I've been trying to reach you. Your phone is off."

"No battery," said Rupert, fishing his BlackBerry out of his pocket and waving it at Martin for proof. "But didn't you get my message?"

"Message?" said Martin.

"On your voice mail. I left it at five."

"I never check voice mail."

"Well *fuck*, Martin."

"What did you say?"

"Come and join us. I just had a great night with Ania and Kasia actually. Brilliant evening. You should have been there."

"Where?"

"Out. A couple of places."

"Shit."

"Yes. Well apparently you had a nice time with Kasia today. She was really cheered up by it all. You're back in the winning seat I think. So why is it that you've gone to all this trouble and just at the time when you broke through the chill you didn't think to ask her out?"

"You're the second one to ask that. So did you say you left a voice message?"

"Yes I did. And if others are asking this, it's an obvious question, yeah?"

"I don't know. I thought I was taking it slow."

"Do you want to take it slow?"

"No."

"Then why did you choose to?"

"I don't know. I thought that was what she wanted."

"Based on what?"

"Based on that she's a girl. And she's a particularly cautious one."

"Then I'll have to base all future advice on that you're an idiot. Taking it slow doesn't mean don't spend time with her. That's called not taking it at all. Taking it slow means don't shove your hands up her top the first time you go out. Kasia had a nice time mate. She was good company. I can't help thinking she'd have been *great* company with you if you had taken her somewhere. Wake up," said Rupert.

He patted Martin on the shoulder as he turned towards the door. "Oh, and Kasia got hit on a lot of times and believe me she can take care of herself. She knows what she wants Martin. She's capable of telling you to take it slow if she wants to. If you've ever taken any of my advice before, take this: stop assuming things."

## Chapter Forty Two

Martin was in the office early the next morning. Kasia was already there. He found her putting her things away in one of the storage cupboards on the first floor.

"So I understand I missed a good evening last night," he said.

She beamed at him. "Why didn't you come?"

"I didn't even know Rupert left a message until he came to my place after it was all over."

"Oh."

"That's not the real reason though. I didn't come because like a moron I don't have your number. I don't even know your surname or whatever you guys call it … your family name? How impressive is that? I don't know if I really know anything about you."

She laughed. "What do you want to know?"

"Your surname and your phone number."

"That's easy. Anything else?"

"Yeah. I want to know if you're doing anything tonight and if not, whether we can get away somewhere where there isn't a lot of noise and actually properly talk for the first time ever."

"You know Martin, I have only been here two months. You make it sound like years."

"It's felt like years. Shall we have dinner?"

"I may have a better idea."

"Since when is it for you to make the decision when I'm the one doing the asking?" he winked.

She laughed. "Ah, okay. Let's do it your way then."

"Fantastic," said Martin.

Kasia bit her bottom lip. He took her hands in his and inclined his head towards hers a little.

"What's the matter?"

She smiled. "Just . . . is this you being for real?"

"Yes," said Martin. "Oh look, I'd be lying if I said I wasn't on my best behaviour because I'm trying not to screw this up again, but that doesn't make this false in any way. I don't know if I can be the guy on the white charger, but I can't think of anything I want more right now than to make you happy. And I really, really care about what you think of me."

She nodded, but her smile was replaced with a face so serious Martin wondered if it masked something else.

"I don't know what this white charger is. It's a horse I guess. But okay, I like the answer. You know what else? I believe you," said Kasia.

His mobile phone started ringing as he stepped out of the lift and he charged the 30 metres or so to his cubicle so he could offload all his stuff and get it from his pocket. It was a number he didn't recognise. He hated those. He ignored it.

Two minutes later it rang again. We watched it ring with irritation, willing it to stop and waiting for it to do so before he continued getting himself organised for the day.

He realised with alarm that for only the second time in more than a year he had forgotten his Peepers; the first time being a morning when he had the worst flu of his life and simply slept straight through the morning.

They'd have to live with it. He'd simply had better priorities that morning.

The mobile phone rang again. He ignored it again.

Despite what he thought about Drake the Robot and the nickname his work habits had earned him, he was surprised to see he was already in the office as well, looking like he'd had a perfectly good night's sleep.

Then his desk phone rang. He had so many screening rules with Jane downstairs that he knew the call would be safe. Even so, he picked it up with some trepidation.

It was Jane.

"You're there. I didn't even see you come in."

"Nope, I beat you to it this morning."

"My my, aren't you the early bird?

He chuckled. He realised he was in a great mood. "I *was* this morning."

"Well look Martin, I've been fending off this woman for you for the last couple of days who says she has written a love story which has been picked up by ... by ... um ... oh, Harper Collins, and she finally made me promise that I'd give you the message. I know you don't want it so don't start stomping around up there. But I promised and now I've kept my promise. Okay?"

"What's her name?"

"Who?"

"*Who.* The woman who left the message."

"Really?"

"Yes."

"I never wrote it down. I didn't think it was important. Angela something. Knight, I think."

"Angela Knight?"

"Yeah. You don't want her number do you?"

"Yes."

"Oh. Shit."

"You didn't write it down, did you?"

"Why would I?"

Martin's mobile phone began to ring again, on his desk. Irritated, he flicked it to silent.

"Okay, well if she phones again, please take the number. Maybe I should call Ms. Knight and see what she'd like."

"Did you find God or something Martin?"

"Something like that."

The subtle sent of violets grabbed all his attention. She slipped into his office chair and handed him some mail.

"Hope there's money in here," he said.

Her face was suddenly serious. "Can there be money in there?"

He laughed. "No, I'm joking. You really don't get jokes do you?"

She smiled. "I don't know."

"So tell me, is there anything you don't eat? I really ought to know that by now."

"I don't know. Some things. I always love sunfood."

"Sunfood? What's that?"

"You know. Like it's got the sun in it."

"Like, what, like Italian food?"

"It can be."

"Wow, that's like a whole category I don't understand."

"You know. You do. Like if I pick fruit from the supermarket, I like cherries or peaches or this sort of thing."

"Right, but since we're not eating fruit, should I find an Italian restaurant?"

"Or an Asian one."

"An Asian one. Now that's a good idea. Is Asian food big in Poland?"

"Not so much I don't think. But it's big in London. You want to know a nice place?"

"No. Let me pick it. Let me surprise you."

She grinned, full of life and warmth, he almost had to slap himself that it was for him.

"Okay," she said. She stood up, not taking her eyes off him. "Tell me later."

He spent an hour searching Google for the perfect Thai restaurant. When he finally settled on a choice, called and secured a reservation, Martin was starting to feel very pleased with himself indeed.

## Chapter Forty Three

His mobile phone rang again. Four times now. He couldn't remember how to get to his voice mail so he went to his provider's website and looked it up. He dialled, but the only message was from Rupert, exuberant and cheerful.

*"Martin, not sure if you have something on this evening, but I'm at the Rose and Crown with Ania and she's brought Kasia along who is looking as fit as you like. I don't know if you're aware but you two are well over the hump. Ania says you've worked everything out. Get your ass down here. Come and be with your wild kitten."*

He laughed at the last part. Rupert was almost indescribably weird, but he couldn't believe it had taken him as long as it did to give the guy a break.

Whoever his mystery caller was, they didn't leave any messages of their own.

It didn't matter. He practically skipped to the break room to make coffee. But as he turned to leave, mug in hand, having snaffled a fist full of wafers from one of the jars he usually ignored, his path was blocked by a face so gloomy, he almost couldn't help laughing.

"I know you're out of the business," said Jake the IT Bastard. "But I could really use your help."

If there was anyone in need of help in that building, it probably *was* Jake the IT Bastard. So named for his ability to make any computer error the user's fault and somehow make the fix so complicated that nothing ever worked quite the same once he had left. His only saving grace was that he was needed and that he was the least bad of the group of technology nerds who had given themselves license to torture the entire staff complement.

He wore a Ramones t-shirt, but Martin doubted if he could name a single song. He suspected Ramones t-shirts were worn more in hope of being considered *awesome* by people such as Jake the IT Bastard than out of any affinity with the music.

"If you mean baggage handling, yeah. I'm out."

"I don't know what else to do. I don't know who else to turn to."

"How about someone that knows you. I don't know you."

"I need an objective opinion."

Martin waved him to a chair with a smile. "Take a pew. Let me tell you something important. Maybe the most important thing I know."

Jake the IT Bastard sat down and Martin sat opposite, leaning in so he could speak privately though there was nobody else in the room.

"I've found a girl, Jake. Are you aware of this?"

"I heard you've started seeing someone. Everyone was surprised you'd managed to pull it off."

"Yeah. You're right. Not only have I found a girl, I no longer doubt that she's into me. She's amazing. I'm really happy right now."

"Thanks for that. Let's talk about how well your life's going, shall we?"

"Yes, let's. Because a sidebar to all of this is how I've got here. You say everyone's surprised? I'm not surprised they are. I wouldn't have initiated this in a trillion years. And every time I did something off my own bat, it was a terrible, embarrassing balls up. You wouldn't believe how I've got in my own way here and what a mess I've nearly made of this about half a dozen times now. If your intention is to show me contempt openly, Jake, then please continue with the eye-rolling and the sighing. If you want my help however, pay attention, because here comes the good bit. I don't have the faintest idea how to help you. You think I have the answers because I have some sort of a reputation for it, but actually all that I know has been insufficient to save me from screwing up my own life again and again like it's a bad comedy. I can give you a load of pretty words if you want and maybe we'll hit upon something that will work. But as likely as I am to help you solve your problems with some random bits of advice, I'm just as likely to send you down the wrong path and mess everything up for you. Because there is no good advice. It's all bullshit. Except for this one thing. One thing that I know to be true. You want to know what it is?"

"Yeah."

"Do whatever the hell you want."

"Sorry?"

*"Whatever the hell you want."*

"How is that helpful?"

"Actually, it's the most helpful thing you'll ever know."

"How do I know if what I want is the right thing?"

"You don't. It may not be. But it doesn't matter. I've come to the conclusion we're all spending our lives looking for yes or no answers to existential questions. We want a right or wrong response where none is appropriate. What you want is probably entirely different to what I want, but both of those responses are absolutely right."

"So do what I want? What if what I want is to walk in here and spray the lot of you with a TEC-9? Would that make me right?"

"No, that would make you a murdering fuckhead. It would also make you someone who clearly plays far too many shoot-em-up video games. But at least it would be you acting on instinct rather than dragging yourself in here hoping to find some elixir piece of advice that will make all your problems go away."

"You don't even know what my problems are."

"I'm telling you that I can't help."

As Jake the IT Bastard left, Martin felt sure that he'd both done the right thing, and that he'd better not have any problems with his MacBook anytime soon.

## Chapter Forty Four

He had another missed call on his mobile when he got back to his desk. The same number. He was beginning to think he should return it when his office phone rang.

"Jane?"

"Martin I've got that woman on the line for you. Angela Knight."

"Oh great. Let's speak to her."

*"Really though?"*

"Really though."

"All right. I suppose it'll stop her from sending you boxes of scorpions to demonstrate her hatred of you. You wouldn't want your Kasia handling those, would you?"

"You know about that?"

"Are you joking? What, did you think it was a secret?"

"I don't know."

"I think it's cute Martin. She seems very nice."

"You think so?"

"Does it matter?"

"It sort of does, yes."

"That's sweet."

"You can never tell where it's going to come from, you know?"

"Well, anyway, if we can prevent the new love of your life from having to cart around crates of hate aimed at you, that's a good thing. Take this call. I'm putting her through now," said Jane.

The phone clicked and he could hear a voice in the background.

"Hello?" he said.

"Martin White?"

"Yeah."

"Angela Knight. I believe you're the go-to guy for the Shallow Review of Books."

His mobile phone began to ring. Same number. He flicked it to silent but realised it was probably more important than a call centre trying to sell him something.

"Yes," he said, pretty much automatically.

"Have lunch with me," she said.

"I can't do that," said Martin.

"Can't is bullshit. You can. You just won't from what I hear. But what if I tell you I have the most extraordinary love story on my hands that even you'll be able to take lessons from."

"What do you mean?" said Martin. If ever there was a perfectly-timed sales pitch.

"Have lunch with me."

He was tempted for the first time ever.

"What can it hurt?" she said.

"It's not what I do Angela."

"So why did you take the call? They tell me you're impossible to get hold of and your switchboard lady has been putting me off for a week. And yet you took it."

"I don't know," he said. It was a good question, but he knew the answer.

"So?"

"When and where?"

He found Kasia on the second floor and waited for her to finish what she was doing. She smiled all the way over to him. "You really are following me," she said.

"No no, this is pure coincidence," he said.

She laughed.

"Listen, I'm going to meet an author for lunch."

"Why?"

"Well this woman called with a book that sounds interesting and so I thought I'd find out more about it."

"I thought you said you never do that for this report of yours."

"I don't. This will be a first."

"Okay."

"Yeah. But anyway, it means I'm not going to be around to join you for lunch."

She took his hand and looked around quickly to make sure they weren't being watched. "Don't feel like you have to come and tell me these things Martin. This is work. You need to do your job. If I see you around we can eat together, but it doesn't matter."

"Oh. Right. I wasn't really doing that," he said.

"Yes you were. It's okay, but you don't need to."

Lunch was a revelation. Though it was a blatant violation of Rule #1, he quickly got into the spirit of it. Angela Knight turned out to be younger than he'd expected her to be, far prettier than he'd assumed and altogether more exciting. By the time lunch ended, he had agreed to read her book and to give her a fair review in the Shallow Review of Books. She gave him an autographed copy.

As lunch ended, his mobile phone rang again. He ignored it once more, but decided to dial the number back when he was done. He was back at the office before he remembered however and as he got to his cubicle, he had the dual demands of a ringing mobile once again and a fiercely demanding Drake the Robot who had this time come all the way to his office door.

"Martin," he commanded.

Martin was alarmed. If Drake the Robot had abandoned his normal, simpering tone, it was unlikely to be good. He elected to answer the mobile instead, waving his hand at Drake the Robot and indicating he'd be in as soon as he'd taken the call.

He looked up the number he had ignored 11 times now and dialled it. It was Sarah.

"Are you playing games Martin?" came the voice.

"Sarah?"

"You're sending me flowers and then ignoring my phone calls. What are you playing at?"

"I'm not ignoring you."

"I've called eleven times."

"I was ignoring the unknown number, but I wasn't ignoring *you*. I mean I didn't know it was you."

"It's my work BlackBerry."

"And how am I supposed to know that?"

"But you didn't call either."

"I ... why would I?"

"You're a fucker, you know that?"

"Sarah, what's the matter? Don't you like the flowers?"

"Why did you even send them? That's what I want to know. Why bother even sending them if you're just going to play games."

"I'm not playing games. They're thank you flowers. For helping get me out of my normal torpor and making some effort with Kasia."

"Who?"

"The girl I spoke to you about."

"Oh fuck you Martin."

"What? What's the matter?"

"I've sent them back to you. I don't want flowers from you if you're just going to use them to hurt me."

"I thought it would be a nice thing to do. I wasn't trying to do anything of the sort."

"Well you did, okay? And I've sent them back. And you can shove them for all I care. Just leave me alone."

The phone went dead. Martin was stunned. He hadn't predicted that. He looked over at Drake the Robot who was practically pressed against his office window with his hands on his hips. His stare alone was sufficient to tell Martin he had better move his ass.

"Sit down," he said as Martin got to the door.

Martin did.

"I got a nice message from a publicist at Harper Collins."

"Oh shit," said Martin, under his breath, but perfectly audible in the enclosed space.

"Am I not getting through to you Martin?"

"It doesn't change anything Drake. But Angela has put so much effort into writing it, the least I can do is read it."

*"Angela?"*

"Angela Knight."

Drake the Robot sat down heavily, keeping his eyes on Martin. He picked up something on his desk and fidgeted with it for a second, eventually banging it down with a sharp crack which apparently wasn't intended.

"Fine. Read it. But it has no place in the review. People don't care what the books are about. They don't care about the writing. Nobody does. Don't forget that. And don't think for a second this is anything less than a massive compromise on my part."

Martin flushed with irritation. "I don't know how much I agree anymore Drake. Perhaps there is a little more depth to ... well ... everything."

"Trust me, there isn't. You think superficiality is shit? Here, take my car for a spin." He tossed a set of keys to Martin. "It's an AMG C55. It's superficial. Metal and paint. But I tell you what, it's as good if not better than anything meaningful you can care to suggest. Philosophy my friend is whatever you want it to be. Don't go rejecting everything you know to be right just because you think you're in love."

"You know what Drake? You really need to get laid."

"Are you getting laid, Martin?"

Martin allowed his defiance to take over. "Yes I am as it happens."

Drake looked over Martin's shoulder, at the door. "Yes?" he said.

Martin turned around to see who was there, but his stomach confirmed what he knew before he even knew it.

The fresh face of happiness that she'd worn all day was gone. It was clear Kasia was wounded.

She walked across to Drake the Robot's desk, placed two packages down, and walked out, avoiding Martin's gaze entirely. Martin leapt to his feet and followed her out, through the office to the hallway. Drake the Robot apparently knew better than to try to stop him.

He caught up with her and spun her around.

"Ignore everything you heard there," he said.

"Martin, really, what is wrong with you?"

"Look, he just pushes my buttons and he does it deliberately and I'm too bloody stupid to just ignore him."

"And the flowers?"

"Sorry?"

"Oh, I put them on your desk. I guess I forgot to mention that. They're from a girl that you sent them to."

Martin put his hands to his head and grabbed fists full of hair. "Kasia, this isn't what you think it is."

"Why do those words always come out of your mouth?"

"I mean it. These weren't sent to a girl for any romantic reasons. They were for a totally different reason."

"They're the same flowers you sent me. In the same box. From the same place. How many other girls get the same flowers?"

"I'm telling you, none. Just this one, just this once. Because she helped me with you."

"How did she help you with me?"

"I mean, she helped me with advice. When I wasn't sure what to do. She basically told me what an asshole I had been to her when she worked here and told me why I was an asshole and opened my eyes and now I'm trying not to be that kind of asshole."

"You bought the same flowers you bought me for another girl who used to work here?"

"Yeah, but it isn't even close to the same."

"Tell me how it is then. I want to know."

"She was years ago and nothing happened."

"Which is why you gave her exactly the same flowers you gave me. Go see. The box fits perfectly with all of mine. It makes mine look stupid."

She turned and was gone. There was no stopping her.

Remarkably, Drake the Robot had his head down as Martin got to his cubicle.

The rest of the afternoon was a waste and when Angela Knight called to thank him, Jane accused him of schizophrenia.

"I thought she was your new best friend."
"I categorically do not want to talk to her."
"Jesus, Martin."

## Chapter Forty Five

As Martin passed Rupert's door, it opened. He had a bottle of Heineken and a bottle opener. Martin stopped to size them up and Rupert packed out laughing.

"What's funny?" Martin asked.

"God, you're such a fucking disaster. You couldn't write a book about this stuff. Really it is hysterical," said Rupert.

"Fuck off."

"No, stop. Get over here and drink this beer."

"I don't want it."

"Come on. It's for Dutch Courage."

"What?"

Rupert produced a slip of paper between his fingers and offered it to Martin. "This is where Kasia lives. You need to go there and say you're sorry."

"I have said I'm sorry. I've done it daily since I met her. I'm worn out mate. It doesn't seem to matter what I do, it's one step forward, two steps back."

"God, you know, talking to you is like talking to a child. That's the cost of love. That's what it's like winning the one you love. What, did you think you were just going to sweep her off her feet? That doesn't happen. Especially not when, let's face it, you're a bloody disaster with women."

Rupert slid the paper into Martin's pocket, opened the beer and hooking Martin's arm, pulled him inside.

"Listen Martin, and listen carefully, it doesn't matter what *she said.* What matters is what *you want.* We've been through this. And don't tell me you want anything more right now than to go and see Kasia."

"Oh that's where I heard that. That's a pity. I thought I'd come up with it myself."

"Have this beer."

"Actually Rupert, I think what I want is to go home."

"If you go home now, all you'll do is wallow in the agony. If you go and see her, you'll feel better even if you feel worse. And so will she. And the difference between the two is probably two beers to get you out of this morbidity of yours. Now come on, and start with this one."

The road that Kasia lived on was unremarkable, save for the fact that she lived on it. The summer sun was starting to dim at a little after eight as he turned onto it, but it was still functionally daylight as he passed the lines of cars along the kerb, dusty because of the near total lack of rain over the previous two weeks.

Number three was almost at the opposite end. It was a fairly unremarkable house too. Semi-detached with a pebble dashed exterior and a red front door. There was a light on in the front room and in the upstairs windows and he could hear music as he walked up the short path from the open gate.

He almost lost his nerve, but Rupert was right about the two beers. He'd allowed Martin no more than two before he sent him on his way, but the effects were still with him.

He rang the doorbell and then stepped back from the door as if he expected it to open outwards.

A shadow appeared and then the door was pulled open. It was a man. The same one he'd seen at the National Portrait Gallery he thought, though he couldn't be completely sure. The man had a serious face as he leaned against the doorframe and folded his arms. "Yes?"

"Hello. Nice to see you again. I think. Anyway, I'd like to see Kasia if she's in."

"Who are you?" asked the man.

Martin extended his hand and forced a smile. "I'm the wanker that keeps fucking things up with her every time we make some progress."

The man's eyebrows shot up and he dropped his arms, perhaps

readying himself for a scrap. “Excuse me?”

“Please just tell her that will you?”

“Does she know you?”

“Oh, she knows me all right.”

“What’s your name?”

“It doesn’t matter. If I tell you that you won’t introduce me the way I asked you to and that will negate half the impact of my being here.”

“What are you talking about? Are you drunk or something?”

“Please tell her.”

The man shrugged and went inside, pushing the door closed behind him. Martin stopped it from closing completely, with his foot.

Inside, he could hear a conversation and all at once, the door was pulled open all the way again.

Her hair was up and she was wearing shorts and a t-shirt, relaxing at home on what remained a warm evening. She didn’t bother to disguise her amusement.

“I suppose Ania gave you the address?”

“She gave it to Rupert.”

“Ah”

“I want to apologise Kasia. I want to tell you that I know I’m a wanker and that I deserve your anger and so on but the truth is there has just been a stupid misunderstanding here. You’re right, there are a lot of those with me but I’m telling you they’ve got everything to do with the fact that I’m totally out of practice here. You think I’m playing around, sending flowers all over, and I assure you the only thing I’m doing is trying to get your attention and hope that you don’t think I’m a constant walking disaster. That’s all I want.”

She maintained the slightest of smiles throughout, the corners of her mouth creeping just slightly upwards.

“Thank you. Martin, I accept this apology like I always do because I can see you’re trying and I still believe you. But you really need to get yourself together. I mean it. This newness and this ... this excitement I guess, is starting to run out. And so are all these clever speeches you can make so easily. You write a column you know? Clever words are what you do, so it’s not a surprise you are good with them. You also need to be better with actions, you know?"

"Yes," he said, eagerly.

"I mean it. When you send me flowers, it is nice. When you send me flowers every day for three weeks, I know you are trying hard. I only stopped you because I felt bad that I really believe you would keep going for the next year. But when you send the same flowers to another girl who doesn't mean anything to you, it cheapens everything. It makes it like the flowers you sent to me weren't special and everyone gets the same."

"I get it. I do. I don't think enough sometimes, but that doesn't mean my intentions aren't the very best."

"I know. I wouldn't be talking to you if I didn't think so."

"Can we please go and get a cup of coffee?" he said. "We're supposed to be out eating sunfood as we speak, not standing on your front doorstep."

She shook her head, but the smile spread out across her face. "Listen, I really appreciate you coming around. And it is good that now you know where I live, I think. But it is getting close to nine and I think you're a little bit drunk. Also I am going away for tomorrow and the whole weekend so I have to pack my bag."

"Oh. Where are you going?"

"Krakow. My friend is getting married."

"Oh. So I'm not going to see you tomorrow?"

She smiled. She laughed a little. "I'll be back on Monday."

"Okay. But are we okay?"

"What does *okay* mean Martin?"

"I don't want you to think I'm a wanker."

"Well, that's in your hands, you know?"

"All right," Martin said. He worked up a smile.

Kasia laughed. "You're pathetic sometimes, you know that? But you do a lot more right than you think you do. Just believe in yourself some more, will you?"

She leaned forward, placed her hand on his left cheek and pressed her lips against the right.

It was very likely the best kiss Martin had ever had.

## Chapter Forty Six

He was buoyed by the kiss through Friday and finally cut himself some slack over the weekend, even spending most of Sunday in a pub and food crawl through Camden with Dave the Legend and his gang of legendary scoundrels. Dave the Legend had been almost floored when Martin called him to find out what he was up to, and even more astonished when Martin actually met them at the Camden Arms. He could have killed, gutted, stuffed and mounted Martin on a plinth of gold when Martin turned out to be the one to topple Monica, the cute Italian barmaid finally into Dave the Legend's corner. "I've been chatting her up for weeks mate. I should have just called you in, in the first place," he said.

Martin laughed. He was pleased to have helped, and considering all it took was an independent observation that Dave the Legend was actually one of the greatest guys he knew, to earn a relenting shrug, it was the least he could do.

"Where are you gonna be?" she asked.

"In the market. Not sure. Foraging for something strange and different to eat," said Dave the Legend.

"I'll see you there after three. We should go to the ethnic food area. There's nice stuff there," she said.

"Whoop Whoop," Dave the Legend said. Sometimes even the eloquent are lost for words.

The whole day reminded Martin what fun used to look like and he wondered several times what the hell had happened to lead him so far up the path of isolation he'd set himself to so firmly.

Strong habits die hard however and by Sunday evening he was exhausted just from having other people in his immediate space.

The next morning, Martin's rounds were splendid. Though it was raining when he woke up and continued to rain all morning, he was in a good mood. Suede shoes were a bad call, and squelching feet all day were an unwelcome reminder of that, but even that didn't matter to him.

Jenny Lucie Manette glimmered in the sun streaming through the glass ceiling at St. Pancras. "Big day last Wednesday," she said. "Two A-listers. Two remarkable books. I even got comments from one, but you'll have to keep those to yourself or they'll know where their spy is."

She winked and Martin winked back. "Gotcha. Bond of secrecy and all that."

Jenny Lucie Manette laughed. "Okay, well gotta run. Paris calls. See you next week."

And so it went. The uncomplicated, un-detailed interactions he had demanded of his Peepers were so routine now that they were actually better at it than he was.

He hopped from tube to tube across London until he got to the office, stamping his feet in the doorway to try to shake the water out.

Kasia sat down, wafting beautiful violet before he even had a chance to unpack his MacBook.

"Good morning," she said, beaming.

"Good morning yourself. How was Poland?"

"Still the same."

"Weather?"

She blinked. "You want to talk about the weather?"

"Well, it was a wedding."

"Ah. Ah, you're right. It was okay. It didn't rain. Not like here it seems. You're soaked."

"Have you been outside?"

She laughed.

"Do you want tea?"

"No. I have to go or I'll be in trouble. I just want you to think about something. Do you like art or just museum gift shops?"

He laughed. "I like them both. I also like museum cafeterias and car parks."

"You're an idiot. That's okay. There is this place called the Dale Gallery on Poland street in Soho, you know?"

"I know the street, yeah."

"Okay, so tonight there is a show of an artist from Poland that is really great. It would be nice to see it and it would be better if it was with someone."

"*It would be better if it was with someone* is hands down the vaguest way anyone has ever asked me out ever."

"What is vaguest?"

"Never mind. Of course. Polish art on Poland street. What could be better?"

"That's the name of the show."

"Is it?"

She laughed. "No. It's Polish humour."

He laughed too. "It's brilliant."

"You're sarcastic."

"You're brilliant anyway."

"Yeah? Okay. I'll take it. So you can come?"

"Kasia, if I had to cancel my mother's birthday to finally spend an evening out with you, I would do so."

"No you wouldn't. She frightens you, remember?"

"Which makes my point all the more, doesn't it?"

They both laughed. This was getting easy. At last, Martin thought.

"So should I pick you up?" he asked.

"No, it's ridiculous. You'll travel all the way across town and the gallery is here. I'll see you there at seven. Meet me there and we can look at the paintings together."

"Great. That sounds great."

"Good," she smiled and touched his hand. It was all Martin could do not to try and steal a kiss right there and then.

He leapt to his feet and walked her to the lift, making a big show of pressing the button to call it but she just laughed at him and pulled open the door to the stairwell instead showering him with sunshine as the door closed behind her.

He got back to his cubicle and took off his shoes, wringing his socks out and grimacing as he put them back on. It no longer mattered to him in the least.

## Chapter Forty Seven

That evening, he arrived at the Dale Gallery at seven, pleased with himself for keeping things in check and not being there an hour early.

She was already there, stunning in jeans, heels and a black jacket. She smiled as he came in.

"Are you ready?" she said.

"You're joking. I love Polish art. I wouldn't miss it for the world." He winked.

She laughed. "I see. You're still sarcastic I think."

"Not at all."

"Mmmmm."

They took two glasses of chardonnay from a passing tray and she led the way to the first painting.

It was abstract and he suppressed an inner groan. If he had to pinpoint art that he liked, it wouldn't be this. The images on the website hadn't prepared him for the sheer scale of the artistic vacancy of the exhibition in real life. He didn't say anything however; even a social novice like Martin knew better than to express an opinion about art when he had nothing of value to offer.

They stood in front of it and both slightly cocked their heads. "It's red," he said.

"Yes. It is. But there is more there than just red. Do you see it?"

"What? No."

"There is a small girl there."

"Where?"

"In the fabric of the painting. She is lonely. Her mother is in a cancer ward, in and out of hospital where she is too sick even to speak to her or to hug her. Her father is giving up, hiding his misery with cheap vodka. She stands there, holding Elek, this old brown bear with one worn out ear where she has chewed on it as a small child and watches her mother sleep. She feels afraid and hopeless and totally alone."

He looked at her, and suddenly understood. "I see. How old is she?"

"Six. Near her seventh birthday." Her eyes were sad.

"Oh wow. That's … Jesus. That's dreadful."

"Tell me what you see. You must see more than red."

"Maybe we should move to the next one. Perhaps I'll see something more in that."

She turned and walked, not looking at him as she moved to the next painting, two metres away.

It was blue.

"Do you see only blue?" she asked him.

"Actually, there is something in this one," he played along. "I see a young boy, around 11, the product of a privileged middle class background, who took to shoplifting. Little things. Bars of chocolate and toy cars, just because he could."

"This child stole things?"

"Yeah. He was bored perhaps. Or just wanted the thrill. I've never really thought it through."

"Why would you tell a story like this? I tell you something sad and you tell me how you're spoiled. It isn't the same."

"It's the first thing that came to mind. I guess that if you know all the bad things about me and like me anyway, that will make our relationship stronger."

"I see. Is stealing chocolate the worst thing about you?"

"No. It isn't."

"What is?"

"I think it's your turn."

"But I don't have stealing stories. Or crimes I have committed or anything like that."

"You've been squeaky clean your whole life?"

"Clean? I don't know about this. But in Poland with communism, you didn't take things that weren't yours. Not that there was anything to take."

"Mmmm. Next painting?"

They moved on. The next one was yellow.

"This one I see only yellow," she said.

"You have to look deeper."

"You want another story about me? How about this one: it isn't in the painting. When I am 17, my uncle arranged for me to go to the university in Paris. Nice for me, eh? And there I go to the place where they are going to give me transport and I have my passport in hand, and then I realize that all the other people there, they are all girls like me. Young. Pretty. Something is wrong, I think. I turn around and I ran and I went to a friend's house. There I stayed for a few days and on one of those days my uncle came looking for me, angry and frightened. He took money from the men who were supposed to be providing transport. I guess I am expected to go and be a prostitute somewhere. So then, at 17, I am alone again. But the second time, I'm just angry, not sad."

"Jesus. So what did you do?"

"I went to Torun. It's not far, but it's far enough. I went to the university there. I did some jobs. I did some things I shouldn't have done also which I think is what you call irony. But I made the payments and I did my studies. Then, when Poland joined the European Union, here I am."

"What sorts of things?"

"*You know*. I won't talk about this. A girl can earn money when she needs to."

"Wow. Shit, you've really been out there alone, haven't you?"

"You make your life or you have to let someone else decide for you. I don't like this."

"Right. God, that's a big story. And your uncle?"

"Fuck my uncle."

"Right. Fair enough."

They exchanged a glance, his uncertain, hers suddenly defiant.

"Do you want to know what I see?" he asked.

"In this painting there is nothing. Only yellow."

"Not true actually. I see a guy working in a publishing company, bored and fed up when suddenly this beautiful girl comes into his life and changes the way he thinks about his life."

She smiled, but her eyes didn't join in.

"Have I offended you with that story?" he asked.

"I'm not offended. And it isn't the story."

"Then what?"

"Tell me something about you. I know your work. I know that you like to steal things. I know you're afraid of your mother. What about you though?"

"*Used* to steal things. And only a couple of times."

"It's not important."

"It's not the same thing."

"But you don't tell big stories about your life."

"Kasia, when have I had the chance?"

"You have the chance now. I made the chance with a big story and you came back with something stupid."

"I thought we were just talking."

"You see, this is where I am afraid also. Because I still struggle to speak English and I can tell you stories but you are the expert and you don't want to tell me anything."

"You want a story?"

"I don't want anything you don't want to tell me. No. I don't want a story anymore."

"Let me tell you one."

"No. It isn't the same now."

"No let me think of one."

"Yah, think of one. You're so closed, Martin. You think you're the one that is afraid here?"

"Are you afraid?"

"I don't know. Maybe I should go," she said.

"Don't. Let me tell you a story."

"It isn't the same."

"Let me do it anyway."

She shrugged. "If that's what you want, go ahead."

"Do you want me to?"

She rolled her eyes. "Why is it for me to decide?"

"Well let's look at something else then. There are other paintings here. Maybe something will inspire us both."

She shook her head. "No. Forget it. I need to go. I have an early morning."

"Don't. Please. Don't go. Not again."

"Not again? Is it my fault things end like this between us?"

"That's not what I mean."

"Tell me this then Martin. I keep asking you but you don't ever answer. Why do you want to be with me?"

"Because you're not like anyone else. I've never felt this way about anyone else."

"Which way?"

"Just ... I don't know. You're different."

She shook her head, her disdain plain to see. "What you mean is that you find me beautiful and that's a stupid way to look at things."

"It's not just about that."

"How is it then? I want to know. Really."

"Why are you like this? You're not like this with anyone else."

"Because nobody else means anything," she said, shoving her glass into his hand. He watched as she grabbed her coat and left. As she passed the glass façade of the gallery, she didn't look back.

## Chapter Forty Eight

Martin drank both glasses of wine, quickly and considered a third. He realised as he left the gallery that the most important statement of the evening had been Kasia's last. On the walk and tube and walk home, he thought it through and by the time he got there, he knew what he needed to do.

Rupert came through his front door as Martin stepped out of the lift.

"I thought you were on a date," he said.

"Stop knowing everything about my life, will you?" said Martin.

"Fine, but ... I thought you were on a date."

"I was."

"Well what happened?"

"It was a disaster."

"Oh. Shit Martin, I'm sorry."

"It doesn't matter. It's a hurdle. She went out with me. She's not getting off the hook again."

Rupert was impressed. "Oh, listen to the fighting talk. Very good. Well done. And quite right."

"Too bloody right," said Martin. He patted Rupert on the shoulder and continued down the hallway.

Inside, he fell onto his couch face first and just lay there for a moment. Then he rolled over, fished out his BlackBerry and began typing.

*A story. When I was four or five years old, old enough to remember, but perhaps not old enough to understand, I was very sick. A very bad bronchitis. I was in bed for weeks and I discovered later on that it was actually potentially life threatening. Of course I didn't know that at the time. I used to sleep in a room where the door was always left ajar because I was afraid of the dark, and there was a light on, on the landing just outside so that there was a rectangle of light on the wall on the opposite side of the room. I was lying there on one of those long nights, looking at the light, when two angels walked past. I know that may sound strange, but there were two people, with wings. A large one, perhaps an adult, holding hands with a little one, perhaps a child. I can see them as clearly today as I saw them that night. It is an image that is embedded in my mind. When I feel a little frightened to this day ... and no, I don't mean frightened of my mother ;-) ... I think of those two angels and they make me feel ... safe, I guess. I have never told anyone that story. That's just for you.*

He dropped his BlackBerry onto his chest and put his hands behind his head, lying, staring at the ceiling, and listened to his breathing. It was a moment, he knew, when he had done all that he could.

Five minutes later, his BlackBerry buzzed. He picked it up. He smiled in relaxed satisfaction.

*:-) Beautiful. Thank you x x x. It's all I ask. Sleep well.*

The following morning wasn't like any Martin could ever remember experiencing. He woke up relaxed, feeling rested and strong. He revelled in the hot water from his shower and found only comedy in his pathetically stocked fridge; the result of weeks of neglect. It was all turning out to have been worth it.

The morning was fresh though dry and the day promised to turn into a warm one. The Peepers were on form. Shannon the Bombshell lavished him with tacit sexual disrespect and he lapped it up without encouraging it further.

When he got to the office, he saluted Drake the Robot as he dropped his bag onto his desk. Drake the Robot waved back and actually appeared to be amused.

He unpacked, sat down and realised with a start that he wasn't alone. He almost yelped, stopping himself quickly before the sound was out.

Kasia, seated in his chair, laughed out loud, almost spilling the cup of coffee she extended towards him.

"God," said Martin.

"I'm sorry," she said, still laughing.

"You'll give me a heart attack."

"Good morning. I've been waiting for you."

He took the coffee. "Thank you. And good morning back."

"Thank you also. For taking me seriously."

Maybe it was the mood he was in. He'd never seen Kasia look so untroubled. Her eyes glowed bright copper and smiled their own smile in an already delighted face.

"I've got lots of stories to share Kasia."

"I know."

"Can I tell you another one?"

"No. They're something special, these stories. I don't want to hear them here. But there is something else. Today is Tuesday."

"Yes it is."

"Ah. Well on Tuesday I have some friends and we go out to a restaurant. It's Polish, so the food is what we eat. But me and these friends we go every week and I want you to come with me."

"Are they all Polish?"

"Yes. Why?"

"I mean, will they mind?"

"No. They'll like to meet you. And anyway, I want them to."

"Great. I'd love to meet your friends."

"You're sure?"

"Wild horses couldn't stop me."

"This is like that white charger?"

"Sort of the same thing. It's a good thing."

"Okay."

She stood up to leave.

"You realise though this is the second time in a row you've asked me out," he said.

"Well since it never works out when you do it, maybe we should keep it that way for now," she winked.

"Nice."

"You can suggest the next one."

For Martin, at that moment, life had rarely been sweeter, and against his instincts, he decided to react to it, fully.

He cracked open his MacBook and began to write. That week's Shallow Review of Books was a triumph of his spirit over the demands of the boys upstairs. He hoped that Drake the Robot would adapt, but he didn't really care. He centred that week's edition on the Angela Knight book, reviewing it though he hadn't read it, basing his comments on the enthusiasm of the author herself. It was good enough. It was about love, and he felt lifted just spreading the word.

He found her for lunch. She ate a peach and drank tea while he had a sandwich. It was all easy. It was the best lunch he'd ever had, he was certain of it.

When he got back to his desk, he wrote the last part for her, as a declaration of love and as a footnote, he apologised to John Stevens for the trouble he had caused. It was the deepest, most thoughtful edition of the Shallow Review of Books he had yet produced. He was proud of it and of himself, and he felt certain that Kasia would agree that this edition at least was worthwhile.

He called John Stevens' publisher to get his phone number so he could tell him what he had done personally, certain that otherwise Stevens would miss it entirely.

"What did you say your name was?"

"Martin White. From the Shallow Review of Books."

"And what is it you want?"

"I told you this already. I want to contact John Stevens."

*"To apologise?"*

"Yes."

"Hold on please."

Martin did. For two minutes. Then the voice came back.

"Hi there, sorry to keep you holding. We're having a little bit of difficulty believing this is Martin White to be honest. I've been told to extend apologies if it is, but we're going to need you to send a signed letter. Just scan it in and email if you like."

"A letter saying what"

"Oh, who you are really. It's just that Martin White has never apologised for anything he's done and there are a fair few axes to grind around here, let me tell you."

Martin got the details and started to scribble out a letter on a company letterhead when he realised he was way over-compensating.

As he prepared to leave at the end of the day, he could see Drake the Robot in his office, toying once again with his one boot, like he was contemplating making love to it.

## Chapter Forty Nine

Martin could do no wrong that evening. He changed, grabbed a taxi and went to collect Kasia, and from the moment she sidled up to him on the back seat, she was singularly attentive. She laughed at his jokes, hung on his every word, and her eyes never stopped seducing him.

Martin wondered throughout whether she could really be as interested as she openly displayed, but he didn't challenge it. She was hotter in that moment than anyone had ever been and he wondered what it would be like to get naked with her; wondered what she would look like, what it would be like to play with her properly.

The restaurant was named The Patio and it was buzzing when they arrived, and Martin suspected he was the only non-Pole there. Kasia looked around, saw her group and took his hand. She grinned at him. "Are you okay?"

"Yeah." At that moment, he would have happily done anything she asked.

"Good. come on. I want them to meet you."

It was a table of sixteen and Martin was an instant object of fascination. Through broken English, he began to piece together bits of her life which only a couple of months back he'd have done anything not to learn about in defence of Rule #1.

And as pork cutlets made way for cheese cake, the conversation finally turned entirely to him, starting as it so often does for a man out with a beautiful woman: with a challenge.

The enemy combatant was Marek, and he was considerably bigger than Martin, substantially more drunk and Martin suspected, naturally aggressive.

"So you think you know Polish women?" he slurred, pointing a fat finger awkwardly.

Martin didn't get it at first. His raised eyebrows, intended as a mute request for a repeat, were badly misinterpreted as Marek's fist came down hard onto the table, rattling the dishes.

"Did I miss something?" said Martin.

"Marek, stop your shit," said one of the guys. Red shirt. A name Martin had no chance of remembering first time out.

"You think this is okay?" said Marek. "And this fucking guy is okay?"

More protests. Martin suspected this wasn't new behaviour and that the group knew where it normally ended up. He supposed Marek had a thing for Kasia too, and that his presence was a terrible affront.

"It's okay, I'll take the question," said Martin. He'd never have done that two months before.

"Take the fucking question," said Marek.

"What do you want to know?"

"You don't tell me nothing. Fuck you."

"Oh. I see." Martin laughed slightly. That was a mistake.

Marek climbed to his feet, albeit wobbly, with a menacing glare. He was too drunk to be properly threatening, but the challenge was nevertheless impressive.

It was Kasia that took it up. To Martin's amazement, she stood up, faced him down and rattled off in Polish what Martin could only assume was a severe verbal kick in the balls.

Then the other men were on their feet and though he didn't know what he was doing, Martin leapt to his.

But what could have amounted to legendary after-dinner entertainment ultimately came to naught. As Marek was helped out by some of the guys, everyone else sat down.

"Sorry. He's a Stalinist," said Red Shirt.

"Really?" Martin had never met a live Stalinist before. He didn't realise there were still any of them about.

"No. But he thinks like one."

"What does a Stalinist think like?"

"You know Stalin, yeah?"

"Yeah. I painted him once."

"Huh?"

"I painted Stalin. And Lenin. And Trotsky and Mao and Castro. In black and white. Well, shades of grey anyway."

"Please explain."

"I mean it just like that. I got paints and an easel when I was young and I didn't know what to paint, so I decided to paint black and white canvasses of the worst dictators in the world."

"Why?"

"I don't know. It seemed like a cool thing to do."

"You think dictatorship is cool?"

"No. It has its place, I guess."

"Only someone who never had to live with one can say that."

"No, that's not really true. I mean, there's a time and a place for everything. Even dictatorship."

"How is there time for dictatorship? Except when there is a crisis."

"Well, maybe only and precisely then. When there is a crisis. Like when the ship is sinking, you don't vote about whether to get into the lifeboats. The captain of the ship becomes the dictator and you should be grateful to have him there."

"Poland was a dictatorship and nobody had a reason to like the government."

"I guess. But here's the thing about you guys. Whether it is Lech Walesa or Wladyslaw Gomulka, or whether it is your army riding on horseback against invading German tanks in 1939, or the uprising in 1956, you've always had the balls to stand up for what you demand.

It's just what you do. And it is rare that you meet a Pole that isn't defiant. I know I met one of the most defiant people I have ever met," said Martin, winking at Kasia.

There was silence.

Martin looked around the table. "What?"

"Have you been learning Polish history?"

"No. Why?"

"And yet you know Gomulka? You know about 1956? Amazing. Maybe someone should go and call Marek again. He'd feel like a big asshole for this."

"It's just stuff."

"Just stuff? I don't think so."

"Yeah it is."

"No, really."

"Well, okay, perhaps it's more than that. Let's say I have a renewed interest in your country and all its things."

"Did you ever go there?"

"No. But actually, even before I met Kasia I thought I should. I read somewhere once that of the ten coolest bars in Europe, five are in Warsaw. Forget history; that sounds cool."

Martin could see that the table was coming towards him at that point. It was a little like the break room and he was being asked to consult on some Dave the Legend lunacy. He liked it, and it was heightened by the look in Kasia's eyes.

Red shirt continued to lead the probe.

"We always are a country with problems though. Even before communism. Even before the Nazis. I don't think Poland can ever be fixed properly. It's not in our nature."

"That isn't true. You keep getting closer, don't you?"

"No. Our politicians are always more corrupt than the last ones."

"Yeah, on the surface, they might be. Ours aren't a lot better. But it's a fundamental fact of government that the country keeps ticking over because in the background there are intelligent and well-educated people in the art of government who keep chipping away. It's not the stuff that makes the newspapers because they prefer the scandals and the corruption that you're talking about. None of those guys matter though because they don't have much to do with the irreversible move forward which is going on in the background. I bet your guys are making better progress than you think they are."

"You think?"

"Yeah."

"Wow."

"What?"

"The biggest Polish fan on the table is the only guy that isn't Polish."

"Well, sometimes you have to be apart from the problem to be able to see it for all its nuances, I guess. But you're in the EU now. That has to count for a lot."

"Yeah. It means we can come here."

"But are you here because this is where you want to be, or are you just waiting for the day you can go back? I mean you're all Polish, so you obviously like each other. And you speak it to each other so you're still big on your own language. And this is a Polish restaurant. I even went to see some Polish art not that long ago."

"And do you like it?"

"Let's say I have a renewed interest in it," Martin squeezed Kasia's hand. She squeezed back.

It was a good evening. When Martin helped Kasia put her jacket on, she leaned into his ear.

"I think I want this evening to go on a little longer," she said.

Martin couldn't suppress a grin. "Good," he said.

## Chapter Fifty

The taxi driver did well to ignore them on the way to her place. Inane, pre-sex conversation that didn't go anywhere because Martin was long since out of practice and Kasia continued to cede control of the evening to him. He had her laughing endlessly which he knew was a good sign, but if he had been the driver, he'd have been rolling his eyes in despair.

He imagined him simply running the wheel over hard to the left and ramping the cab onto the kerb, turning to them and saying "for God's sake, take a few minutes while I go for a walk. Just do her, will you?"

Mercifully, it didn't happen.

Instead, he gave Martin a wink as he paid the fare, while Kasia almost skipped to her front door. When Martin got to her, she was searching for her key and he suddenly faced an awkward situation he had thus far been able to avoid. The time for meaningless small talk was over, and he felt ineloquent in the art of warm teasing.

"This going to take long?" he said.

She smiled, but didn't take her eyes off her bag. "It's here somewhere."

"Did you forget it?" *Stupid question. Come on, do better than that. Say something funny.* "Maybe it's inside."

She fished it out, with a flourish. "Here. I'll never forget it. If I do, I can't get in. The other two sleep too much," she said, laughing.

In that moment, Martin had never seen her more beautiful. Her eyes danced in the orange glow of the light over the doorstep and where the corners of her mouth could tilt playfully upwards at the suggestion she was amused, right then, they even seemed to quiver slightly. Martin realised she was nervous and that could only mean she was contemplating the next step. It was art. It was lovely art, like a perfect sequence of time slowed down so you could see every moment unfold in splendid detail. She was nervous, but she didn't hesitate for a second. As the key hit the lock, and she turned around to see him, quickly flicking her eyes from his feet to his face, Martin handed control back over to her. It was too magical to see her shed the final layers of self-protection for him to intervene. It was too magnificent to watch her silent declaration of readiness to let herself go, completely. In that moment, Martin realised that he no longer had a choice but to completely adore her.

She pushed the door open and he followed her inside. She put her finger to her lips for silence and pointed to a table Martin couldn't see in the darkened hallway. Naturally, it having been pointed out, he bumped it as he walked past, knocking a pile of books off it and onto the floor. Naturally, the sound boomed through the house, though it probably wasn't really as gunshot loud as his mind made it out to be.

Kasia laughed quietly, but quickly pulled his hand to lead him into the living room, pushing him into the couch which faced a TV which was absurdly large for the room.

He reached out for her, but she danced quickly away.

"Ah! Wine."

"Wine?"

"You don't want wine?"

"Yeah. Wine would be good."

She grinned as she kicked off her shoes. "Back in a second."

"Quickly."

"You got somewhere you have to be?"

"No, I have someone I have to be with."

"Hah!"

As she headed off to the kitchen, almost as an afterthought, she grabbed a remote control from the couch arm and pressed play on a CD. *Love Story* by Taylor Swift began to play and Martin didn't even try to suppress a smile. He couldn't take his eyes off her perfect legs, her perfect ass and the way it moved poetically from side to side as she walked.

He heard her open the fridge and open and close cupboard doors, probably looking for glasses. He put his head back and smiled. *Life, at this moment, is perfect.*

He sensed movement. He smiled again, his eyes still closed, waiting for a touch he felt sure would come and which would mark the beginning of an entirely new chapter for him. For them. But the touch didn't come. And the next voice he heard wasn't hers. And it also wasn't happy.

He sat up and turned to the kitchen as a woman disappeared into it. The flat mate. And *wasn't happy* was an understatement. As she came face-to-face with Kasia, she started to cry as if she'd been holding it back.

Martin stood. To do what, he wasn't sure. There was no place for a strange man in a crying woman's kitchen, of that he was absolutely certain. But the thought hit him hard like a firehose of freezing water. The evening in which Kasia seemed on the brink of giving him everything he wanted and a load of things he hadn't until that very moment realised he did, was officially over.

He didn't need Kasia to come and tell him that. But when she appeared in the doorway, her face a perfect visual representation of a disappointed apology, he knew it was time to go home. *Damn it all.*

She walked to him, her eyes never leaving his, and she lit up a new smile as she got closer. "I don't believe this," she said.

"It looks bad."

"Ah. Not so bad. Her boyfriend has left. He lived here too. Ah, you met him."

"Yeah. I did."

"Yeah. Well, this isn't the first time. It's just something these two do now and then. And this is one of those times. Martin I am so sorry."

*"You're* sorry," he said. He winked.

She shrugged another apology. And then suddenly he was lost. He knew it would be crass to try to grab a feel in the middle of a crisis, but he wasn't certain whether she would call this one. He smiled and shrugged back, buying time as if trying to communicate his next move to her psychically so he could assess whether it was appropriate before he made a fool of himself.

Kasia raised her eyebrows, impatiently, but increasingly amused. He doubted his indecision was as clear as all that ... was it?

And all at once, the voice in his head was his own. Not scolding Sarah's or taunting Rich's, but his own. *"Do whatever the hell you want. Whatever the hell you want."*

He took a step towards her, closing the gap entirely, and he could see her relax though almost imperceptibly as if she'd been watching an opportunity she'd been burning for begin to slip away only to see it re-emerge at the last minute. He leaned in to kiss her and she tilted her head and as his lips touched hers, he felt his pulse begin to surge.

Adrenaline. Her lips were softer even than he had imagined as they brushed his first, her tongue playfully joining in as she opened her mouth just slightly at first and gradually a little more. He slipped his arms around her, pulling her to him as if he could get her any closer, vaguely aware of her breasts pressing against him as their tongues began gently to play with one another.

It was more than a kiss. It was the end of the anticipation that had practically driven him over the edge, but then redoubled with the promise of a second kiss; a feeling his mind could scarcely wrap around; a taste of arousal he knew he'd never be able to describe and a dam-burst of ecstasy that the woman he held in his arms, finally ... *finally* ... was her.

He pulled back slightly to take her in, watching as her eyes slowly open again, this time, for the first time, with all perception of hesitation extinguished.

"Your friend is still crying," he whispered.

She laughed, a whisper laugh just for the two of them. "You need to go."

"I know."

He cupped her face in his hands and touched his lips to hers again as she slowly wrapped her arms around his neck. Even better than the first time, the second kiss was the perfect mix of tenderness and the promise of unbridled, no-holds-barred, manic, unrestrained sex. His excitement became physically apparent and he was torn between hoping she wouldn't notice and hoping she would.

She pulled away this time. "Wow."

"This is hands down my favourite thing to do."

"What?"

"Kiss you."

She laughed, this time more openly.

From the kitchen, the continuing sobs reminded them that there was another matter at hand aside from their demanding lust for one another and Kasia pushed Martin gently away.

"Come. To the door. You need to go," she said.

At the front door, Martin turned before opening. "He'd better not come back to her after this."

"Don't worry. He will. I bet by tomorrow evening."

"Why couldn't he have done it tomorrow evening? Ah man."

She laughed. "You came close tonight. Be thankful. It's easier to get close the second time. You should know this."

"Really?"

"Yes, really." She kissed him quickly on the lips, pulling away before he could take too much from it. "Next time there'll be no crying house mates."

"Tomorrow?"

"Since we have to wait that long it will have to do."

As the door closed, it didn't matter one bit to Martin that he was on the other side of it. He punched the air, triumphant as if he'd just been told he'd won a million pounds. It took him a moment to realise he had to go, but he did so slowly, his lips still tingling from the memory as he stepped through the front gate onto the pavement and wound his way up the road.

He considered knocking on Rupert's door on the way past to tell him his evening ended too soon again, but that this time it was all right. Then he scolded himself. Be cooler than that. It will be so much better if he simply found out from Ania.

He threw himself onto his couch, coat still on, and lay for a moment on his stomach, replaying the kiss. Replaying the moment. And then he began to laugh. He grabbed his MacBook, logged onto iTunes and knew he would have to tell Dave the Legend the next day that if ever proof was needed that love endorsements are more powerful than any other kind, he had it. He did a search on Taylor Swift and downloaded that song.

## Chapter Fifty-One

Dinner the next night was just easy. They were both completely there and both excited and as Martin paid the bill, he suggested they go to his flat for another drink.

"There aren't any crying people at my place. It'll be quiet and we can just relax a little more," he said.

"By which you mean you can take advantage of me, is this right?"

Martin laughed. "Yeah."

She grinned. "Then just say what you mean."

He knew it was childish that he hoped Rupert would appear as he walked her past his door, but he didn't turn up.

What did turn up was an insurmountable joy as he watched Kasia step into his flat and look around. And then he was just consumed, for the first time in longer than he could remember, by a zenlike calm as if having her there was enough to make his world completely flawless.

She turned and smiled. "Nice place."

"Glad you like it."

"It's big."

"Not that big. But it's home."

"Nice home."

"All bought with a lazy way to make a living." He laughed.

She laughed too, one of her silent laughs. "I don't apologise for this. I don't say it's wrong any more though. I know you now, I think."

"And what do you know of me?"

"Well, you don't give up, that's for sure. You should have given up a long time ago."

"Should I have done?"

"No. I'm glad you didn't."

"Honestly Kasia, I don't think I had a choice."

"Why?"

"I'll just scare you if I tell you."

"Tell me."

"I can't."

"You have to, now."

"Well ... does love frighten you?"

"Ah. Maybe you shouldn't tell me after all."

"It does frighten you."

"Are we going to stand and talk or are you going to pour me a drink?"

"It does frighten you, doesn't it?"

"It doesn't frighten me. I just don't think we can think about this."

"Now? Or ever?"

"I don't know. This is a big conversation."

"Yeah. But you need to know this about me. I didn't give up because I didn't have a choice. I couldn't do it."

"You can't love me. You don't know me."

"How well do I have to know you before I can love you? Who makes those rules up?"

She shook her head slowly, but her smile remained.

"Okay, let's call that a big conversation for another time. Let's not kill tonight. But I'm going to suggest that I don't have to know every single thing about you in order to love you. I just don't believe that."

She silent laughed, shrugging as she did so, clearly wanting a change of conversation.

"Sooooo. Wine?" he asked.

"Anything."

He went to the kitchen and she followed him, her eyes landing squarely on the Polish phrasebook he'd picked up casually nearly two months before.

"And this?" she asked.

"I guess that may be some proof of what I just said."

"You bought it when?"

"Around about your fifth day in the office actually."

Her mouth fell open as she took him in. *"Really?"*

"Yeah."

"Ah. Maybe you're telling the truth about this thing then."

"Maybe so. Maybe words don't have two meanings."

She laughed. "You're using my own logic on me."

"Is it working?"

"A man buys a book in my language so he can learn to speak to me, I think that man will get very far with me actually."

He handed her a glass of wine and she took it, placing it immediately down on the counter top as he pulled her towards him.

He didn't lie when he said that kissing her was his favourite thing to do in the world. She gave it all back.

"And again, wow," she said.

"It's you. I can't help myself."

"Say it in Polish."

"Um . . ."

"You must know. Say something in Polish."

"Er. Okay. How about *way yesteshtya pienkni*. Is that right? God, I hope I didn't just insult you."

But he could see from her face he had not. She put her arms around his neck. "You practiced this phrase, yes?"

"Yes."

"And only for me?"

"And only for you, baby."

"Ah. Now I'm baby."

"Is there a better word in Polish?"

"It doesn't matter. This is your word. I like this word. And I like that you think me to be beautiful."

"So I did say what I meant to."

"Yes. Baby. You did."

Martin grinned. Every incredible moment merely laid the foundation for a better one, and it was more than he had hoped for. He breathed her in; her violet scent subtle but more delicious than anything he could think of. Maybe everyone doesn't have a favourite flavor or a favourite smell, but he knew what his was.

"You want to show me around your apartment?"

"Yeah. Grab your wine. There is something I'd like to show you actually."

He took her hand and led her into the living room and around the corner where a darkened room lay beyond an opened door.

"So you've seen the living room and the kitchen. Down the passage there is a bathroom and a bedroom. Nothing special."

He reached in and switched on the light. "This is the main bedroom. This is where I do all my sleeping and dreaming and stuff."

She held her eyes on his as she stepped through the doorway and looked around. Martin thought he might die a happy man right then and there, just having Kasia in his bedroom.

She turned to face him. "What else do you do in here?"

"Oh … you know."

"No. Tell me."

"Actually, not as much as you think. I'm hoping to try some new things in there. Maybe even tonight. With you. Naked.

"It sounds like you're expecting me to have sex you."

"No. Not at all."

"Oh. Okay then, I won't."

"No. I'm expecting you to arch your back and scream and dig your finger nails into my back while I have sex with you."

She stopped, mouth wide open. "Oh. I don't know what to say in response here."

"Actually, that sounds good even to me. I hope I can live up to that."

"It sounds great actually."

"Yeah?"

"How about you stop talking now?"

He pulled her towards him and wrapped his arms tightly around her. "How about I do just that?"

They kissed, deeply, beginning finally to feel each other out as he slowly maneuvered her towards the bed until she willingly dropped back into it.

He lowered himself on top of her, kissing her and drifting his hands slightly, perhaps only setting the stage for foreplay, but delighting at every curve of her body.

Kasia followed his lead, running her hands slowly down his back as if they had a blind man's ability to create pictures just by feeling.

He unzipped her dress and slowly pulled it off her shoulders, to reveal a scarlet bra which he was thrilled to see wasn't a push up, but something to hold her naturally beautiful, firm breasts. He kissed her neck and began to move down her body, kissing her breasts over her bra and moving to her stomach, dragging out every moment as he reveled in her presence.

He could feel her alternately tense and then relax, her body responding to his tongue, her breathing increasing noticeably. As he kissed her stomach and gently caressed her breasts with his hands, he could feel her excitement growing.

His was already out of hand, and he didn't care if she knew it. He gently kissed her neck again, drawing little circles with his tongue, and her breath began to come a little faster and louder.

He moved his mouth back to hers, flashing a grin as she opened her eyes and looked straight into his.

"Martin?" she whispered.

"Mmmm hmmm?"

"You have protection, right?"

"Sorry?"

"We need that if we're going to do this. I'm not on the pill. Please tell me you have some. Please."

## Chapter Fifty Two

As Martin flew out of his front door, his mind was racing. The only place he could think of likely to sell condoms at that time of night was the small shop halfway down Highgate Hill. He'd only been in there once, to buy a lottery ticket in order to test the psychic abilities of a fortune cookie served after dinner at a Chinese restaurant, which simply contained six numbers. He hadn't won of course. The cookie was busking. But he also hadn't noticed when he had been inside, whether the shop sold condoms.

He didn't care if it looked suspicious at that time of night; he ran. He thought back to Kasia's look of impatience as he leapt off the bed and danced around the room, trying to put his shoes on with one hand as he shoved his wallet into his pocket. Until she'd brought it up, the need for protection hadn't crossed his mind, the stupid unprepared bastard. There was no doubt however that he was having sex tonight, and by the most sensational goddess that ever walked the Earth. Him. Martin. And her. Kasia. He stumbled and screamed at himself inside his head, to focus. Over the Archway Bridge, past the school and the Old Crown and down the hill.

He didn't stop running until he got there, but by the time he did, he had to stop and bend over, afraid he would vomit. The last thing Kasia would respond to was that.

His breathing was out of control and his lungs were burning. Gradually, he calmed down, though not nearly as fast as he had been urging himself to do with the thought of Kasia's breasts in her red bra and the supposition she was the sort of girl who had panties to match. That wasn't all that was there. Her lips and her legs and her eyes and her stomach. They were all there, all joined together. It didn't help his breathing.

She hadn't believed him that he'd only had five sexual partners.

"This isn't honest," she'd said.

"Well how many would you expect me to have had?"

"How old are you?"

"What, is there a metric for this stuff?"

"What's a metric?"

"Oh it doesn't matter. I'm twenty eight."

"Twenty eight? And you went to university?"

"Yes. What's your point?"

"What did you do there?"

"Apparently I didn't have as much sex as you want me to have had."

"It's not what I want. I'm just surprised. What did you do? *Study?*"

"How many have you had? Or is that the thing you won't talk about?"

She sat upright, her dress falling all the way off her shoulders. She pulled it up, though it was a pretty pointless gesture considering what they had planned. "It wasn't sex Martin. I didn't fuck for money."

"So what was it then? You don't have to tell me."

"I know I don't have to. Is it a problem for you?"

"No. Not even one tiny little bit."

"We all have a past, you know?"

"Yeah, and you don't think I've nailed enough girls in mine, right?"

"Nailed them?"

"Made love to them."

"No, I'm not saying that. I'm just surprised. This is an honest number, yes?"

"Yes. But let's talk about this later. Right now, you're on my bed, partially undressed and I really need to get to the shop and back."

"Yes you do. Or number six is going to go to sleep."

"And I don't want number six to go to sleep."

"Then go."

After a minute or two that seemed like a decade of non-stop torture, finally he felt able to step through the door of the shop.

A bell tinkled like it was 1950 as he pushed it open, but it wasn't enough to distract the man behind the counter in the hospital lighted interior with its rows of magazines, sweets and cigarettes.

"Hi," Martin said.

"Hi," said the man.

"I need condoms. Urgently. Please tell me you sell them," said Martin, as delighted as he was embarrassed to be able to say all of this.

The man looked at his watch. "It's eleven o'clock."

Martin looked at his own to confirm. "Yeah, and …?"

"Why you need condoms at eleven o'clock?"

"What?"

"Well, the way I look at it, either you've managed to pull a girl at a club or you have a prostitute or else maybe you have the worst preparation in the world."

*"What?"*

"I'm just saying …"

"How about don't say anything. Just tell me where they are."

"You see, because since it is a Wednesday night, it seems unlikely you were clubbing and even more unlikely you've managed to pull for sex because let's face it, we all have to work in the morning, don't we?"

"Mate, are you fucking kidding me?"

"Language, please. And also, it occurs to me that if she was a prostitute she would have her own condoms. I don't know this from experience, but it seems that they are likely to have their own, because they are tools of the trade and they can't do their work safely without them. They're like safety goggles for a welder, you know?"

"I don't believe this."

"So it leads me to believe you just have terrible preparation."

"I just want condoms."

"And I want to sell you some. But it isn't that easy you see."

"Why the fuck not?"

"And again, I must ask you to watch your language, please. The reason why not, is because we don't really know this girl, do we?"

*"We?"*

"The royal we. I mean asking for condoms is a little like asking for something to smoke. Do I sell you a cigar or a box of cigarettes? If it is a cigar, what sort? Most people come in and ask for a packet of Marlboro Gold and even know whether they want tens or twenties. They are specific you see?"

"Mate, I really don't have time for this bollocks. I have a lady waiting. I want plain condoms. Nothing kinky."

"Ah, but what kind of a woman is she?"

*"Condoms. Sell me fucking condoms."*

"Sir, I really must admonish you for this. I mean really, I have asked several times and this is a very respectable shop."

*"Condoms."*

"Fine. I'll sell you some and you can scurry out of here to go and make love to this woman you don't appear to be able to answer any questions about. But I really do demand an apology for the language."

"You demand *what?"*

"There isn't anywhere else to go sir."

Martin considered beating the man to a bloody mass of pulp but realized that he didn't know if he had a bat or something behind the counter. He pictured Kasia, in her red bra, lying on his bed, waiting for him.

"All right. I apologise for the language. I just really, really need condoms."

"And I want to sell them to you as I have said. Now then, I have two brands. I have Durex …"

"Durex. Perfect."

"Durex. Good. Now we are getting somewhere. Now, you say nothing kinky, but do you believe the lady would enjoy something ribbed perhaps?"

"Oh mate, please, just sell me some normal condoms and let me get back to her."

"Okay, so plain ones. But let me ask you, do you think she is likely to engage in oral sex only while you wear a condom or without? I ask because I also have some flavourful ones here. Strawberry, peppermint, I am sure there are others."

"Mate, that's many steps too fucking far, really. I'm starting to get pissed off now."

"All right sir. I understand. You just want plain Durex condoms. Those I have. Now would you like a DVD?"

"A DVD of what?"

The man leaned back to read from behind the corner, entirely seriously. "Sir, I have Nurses Who Dig Cream Six, Soapy Titty Fucks Four and Five and also something called Pussy Bonanza, though I think that one may be low-quality."

"I don't want pornography. Thank you. I just want condoms."

"All right then. Well didn't it take you a long time to get to that?"

Martin tore out of the shop and jogged home, conscious that to over-exert himself might put an end to his whole evening. As he got to the front door of his building, he stopped, wiped his forehead and looked around to ensure he was alone before surreptitiously sniffing each arm pit. Still okay. Nothing she would notice, he was sure.

He let himself in and took the lift to his floor, wandering down the hallway as quietly as he could, this time hoping that Rupert wouldn't notice.

Again, he didn't, and moments later, Martin was safely inside. He closed the door quietly, smiled to himself, and kicked off his shoes in the living room, emptying his pockets onto his couch, but collecting the box of condoms up again.

The bedroom light was still on as he entered the room. The light was on also in the bathroom that ran just off the bedroom.

That was all that was on however. Kasia's stockings certainly weren't, casually hanging over the back of the chair in the corner with lacy elasticised tops that Martin wished he had been able to see around her thighs before he removed them. Her red bra wasn't either. It peeked out from just beneath her dress which had been thrown, apparently carelessly, onto the chair.

He'd have liked the pleasure of removing that too, had he been given the choice, but it wasn't to be. Because Kasia also, was off for the night, out like a light, her chestnut hair up in a makeshift bun, her beautiful face on the pillow, her eyes closed tight and her mouth just slightly open, while her long, willowy body created an almost irresistible line under the blanket.

Resist it, Martin did however. He cursed his luck. He cursed the man in the shop and partly wished he had just gone through with the foreplay even without the promise of sex in the end, just to have been able to play with her. But he quietly undressed, brushed his teeth, put the lights out and resigned himself at least to the enjoyment of sliding into the bed next to her, inhaling the scent of violet and listening to her breathing.

He wasn't sure if he should touch her. Wasn't sure how naked she really was. Wasn't sure if that would matter or not.

Finally, he did nothing. It took an hour, but he eventually fell asleep while Kasia lay with her back to him, not stirring at all.

## Chapter Fifty Three

She kissed his forehead and he stirred from his sleep. She was kneeling on the floor, next to the bed, resting her elbow on the mattress while she cupped her chin in her hand. She was fully dressed.

"Good morning," she smiled.

"Hey."

"When you sleep, you sleep."

"Yeah. Wow. Good morning to you too. Although it could be better."

"How?"

"It could be the morning after."

She grinned. "Well then we still have that to look forward to."

He cracked out a smile and leaned towards her. "Kiss."

She backed her head away and stood up. "No. Because you know why? This isn't a stupid movie and I look like shit because it is first thing in the morning and please don't tell me that I don't when I know that I do. Also, this morning breath thing. It isn't pretty. I don't want you to taste me this way and I really don't want to taste you."

Martin laughed. "We can freshen up. I've got the equipment now."

"Nice conversation for first thing in the morning. Do you wake up thinking about sex?"

"Yes."

She shook her head in mock dismay, but laughed. "Well it's not going to happen this morning. In future you should be better prepared. Right now I have to go home and change so I can go to work. And it's bad enough that everyone will see me on the underground and know I didn't go home last night, but at least it won't be rush hour."

"What time is it?" he looked towards the clock.

It was five am.

"Oh, Jesus."

"It's tough to be a girl. Men don't appreciate what we do."

"It's tougher to be a boy when you're leaving me like this."

"Men are so pathetic."

He sat up. "Which men? You can't mean all of us. Too broad a stereotype."

"Yeah. Pretty much all."

"You know that's something women do, right? This *all men thing* is a feminist statement usually uttered by women who fail to recognise how awesome we are. Men never say they're tired of *all women*. We carefully handpick the ones that piss us off. Madonna is usually on every list. As is Keira Knightley. Other than that though, the lists can be highly individual."

"Whatever. I'll see you at the office?"

Martin nodded and then Kasia leaned in and kissed him anyway. Before he had a chance to react, she was gone. He heard the front door close and fell back on the pillow.

Regardless of the missed opportunity, it was one of the best mornings he had had for longer than he could remember. He wished he'd woken up next to her for real. The scent of violets on the pillow where she had rested her perfect head all night filled his nose and made him smile.

Finally, he jumped out of bed. Since she was going to be at the office, there was nowhere else he wanted to be.

As he arrived, his mood all sunshine, he dropped his bag on his desk and began to head straight down to the first floor for coffee with Kasia.

But the sound from behind him stopped him dead.

It's a simple matter to determine the tone of a reprimand even in a perfect stranger. You have to get to know someone well however to be able to fully appreciate the depth of anger in that tone. All Drake the Robot had said was his name, but it was clear he was at Defcon One.

He turned to face him. Drake the Robot didn't say a word. He simply stepped back into his office, creating an irresistible force as he did so that Martin responded to automatically.

Inside, Drake the Robot remained standing. An even worse portent than the sharpness in his voice. He held up a piece of paper.

"What the hell is this?"

Martin didn't need to look to be able to answer. "It's my column."

"No it isn't Martin. It's shit."

Martin should have known better than to ask, but suddenly he felt like fighting. "What's shit about it? It's a well-written review of a decent book."

"Right. It's a review. Of a book. It is a totally mainstream, pedestrian response to the existence of other people's media. Congratulations Martin, you just killed the goose and made a really shitty omelette with the golden egg."

"I don't feel the shallowness any more Drake."

Drake leaned forward, hissing like an angry swan. "Fuck shallowness Martin. What we have here is a brilliant concept. People don't come up with brilliant concepts. For every Full Metal Jacket there are a dozen Rambos. For every Catcher in the Rye, there are a dozen Mills and Boones. You've just turned a Catcher in the Rye into a Mills and Boone. And frankly mate, there are a thousand sexually-repressed housewives who do that better than you can."

He tore the paper into pieces. "This ... is shit. We're not publishing it. You're going to do it again, properly, the way it works. And if you ever do anything like this to me again, you can forget your column. I'll give it to someone else. I've been warning you."

"Jesus Drake. It's just a change. Maybe it needed one."

Drake the Robot extended his finger, taking on the unambiguous stance of an intractable dictator. "Just get the fuck out of my office."

## Chapter Fifty Four

Martin backed out of the office, stunned as if he'd just witnessed the family spaniel maul a postman. He was used to Drake the Robot pushing to get his way; he hadn't at all anticipated the depth of his interest.

He wandered past his cubicle, his head full of his own social mortality, aware for the first time of where the limits were and how quickly his head could be taken off.

He wound his way down to the first floor where Kasia was whizzing around, collecting the morning's mail. Her eyes were lit up and she smiled to see him. "You're in early," she said.

"Yeah."

He shoved his hands into his pockets.

"What's wrong?" She stopped for a moment, clasping a bunch of envelopes to her chest.

"I just got the verbal kicking of my life."

"The what?"

"I got shouted at."

"Oh. For what?"

"No, but I mean, really, really, yelled at. Like he wanted to kill me."

"Who?"

"Drake the Robot."

"The *Robot*?"

"It's a nickname."

"Is this why he is angry with you?"

"No. He's angry for producing a crappy column."

"More so than normal?" She winked. "Okay, tell me. What did you do? Walk with me, I have to get these upstairs."

She had a pile of packages, and he took them off her, so she grabbed a pile of sorted envelopes instead.

"So I met this writer and I thought she was great and since I never meet the writers, I thought I'd also read her book. Well, sort of read it anyway. She told me what it was about and I flipped through it. So I wrote the review on that. I mean he totally lost it."

"And you thought this was a good idea? Why?"

"I don't know. I thought I'd change it. And you said you thought the Shallow Review of Books is a lazy idea."

"So you listened to what I said about it? What do I know?"

"You said it was a waste of time."

"I did not. I said it was a western idea. But I didn't say it wasn't original. You know what Martin, where I come from all anyone wants to do is stand out from the ... the ... the grey. Do something that can make their name. You've done that here. And you decided to do ... what? Review a love book?"

"Yeah but ..."

"And not even one that you read. Like all other book reviews. It isn't honest this, is it?"

"I don't know. I guess not."

"Look, do yourself a favour, don't mix your life and your art. It is okay to be misunderstood. It is great even to be hated. Or for your work to be anyway. It is better than being ... what word will you use ... normal. No, worse."

"Mediocre?"

"Okay, yes. You understand?"

"So you're saying you think I should keep doing what I do?"

"You said it was successful."

"Yeah ..."

"So what are you doing?"

"Just ... trying to ... oh Jesus, I don't know."

She gave him a quick peck on the cheek. "Yeah you do. Now go do it."

Martin made coffee in the first floor break room and sat down, stirring it slowly. It was a room he had only been in once before he met Kasia. Twice maybe. He didn't feel anything in particular about that one way or another. But the room was symbolic of the rapid changes he had allowed to happen in the intervening eight weeks.

That's all it had been. Eight weeks.

Eight weeks in which he had re-emerged from the shadows he'd been hiding in for more than five years. Eight weeks in which he'd put himself back on the line. Eight weeks in which he'd catapulted himself headlong down a path he couldn't control. In which he'd allowed himself to be pushed, and had done a significant share of the pushing at that.

For her.

Because he didn't have the power to resist it.

He began to laugh. He laughed out loud, and drew an amused stare from a girl who had come in to make herself a cup of tea.

"What's funny?" she asked. She was beautiful. Hair a mixture of blonde and dark with autumn-coloured eyes, gold and green.

He grinned at her. "I think I just realised that *I* am," he said.

She raised her eyebrows, her whole stance good natured. "You know that laughing at your own jokes is the first sign of madness."

"No, I don't think it is, is it? I'm pretty sure that's thinking you have the power to control everything. Laughing at what a dork you are may be the first sign of sanity."

*"Dork?* What kind of a word is *dork?"*

He laughed again. "I don't even know."

She turned around and leaned back against the counter to face him. "You're Martin, aren't you?"

"Yeah, I am."

"I'm Melloney. I'm Terry's PA."

"Terry? You mean upstairs Terry?"

"Yeah. The CEO."

"Oh right. That's where I've seen you."

"You're all the talk up there at the moment, you know?"

"I am? Is it good?"

She shrugged. "Mixed."

"What are they saying?"

"Oh they're pleased enough with the Shallow Review."

*"... of Books,"* he completed her sentence.

"Oh. Particular about that, are we?"

"Sort of."

"All right, fine. Then they're pleased enough with the Shallow Review *of Books*. But you've got them wondering about how to go forward. They think they can take it all the way to a million readers if they can get some more publicity out of it, but that'd need you to be willing to stop being such a hideaway."

"You know a lot."

"I hear everything."

"So what does that mean exactly?"

"You know what you do with this thing of yours Martin? You solve a problem for readers and writers alike. You cut through all the confusion in what must be one of the most obscure areas of modern literature. You make the reviews make sense to the masses. You're like one of those strategists who make sure the Prime Minister enjoys a half pint of ale at a local brewery when he's on the campaign trail so that the cameras can capture the moment and record for posterity that he's an ordinary guy, just like the electorate. What they do is low-information politicking, giving a reference point to the masses who haven't got the interest or even the intellect to make decisions about policy. The end result is that they get their man elected so he can go on and do his job. In your case, the Shallow Review of Books helps writers and publishers shift books to ordinary people. It's the same sort of thing."

He sat back, his mouth agape. "That's interesting."

"Do you want to know what's more interesting? They think you can be bigger than Oprah's book club. You're down-and-dirty Martin, without any of the pretence, if you know what I mean."

*"Really?"*

“Really. But there’s a problem. I bet you can guess what it is.”

“Me?”

“You.”

“You’ll have to be more specific.”

“None of them believe you’ve got it in you. You’re a mole who hides away and never appears. Actually, this business with you and your new girlfriend has them all on tenterhooks like it’s a soap opera. They’ve got Steve Drake reporting on it daily. There’s even a pool running.”

“You’re kidding?”

“You didn’t hear it from me. They say it’s the first evidence you’re actually alive and they think she’s had a good effect on you because of the way the Shallow Review of Books has improved.”

“I don’t know whether to be insulted.”

“Don’t be. Just get over it. It’s better when they’re talking about you.”

“Drake’s such a ... God, he’s such a ...”

“Forget him. You’re the talent, he’s just the agent. His job is to make sure you deliver or it’s his balls on the line. He’s a good guy. He’s a big defender of yours upstairs you know?”

“He is?”

“You’re not laughing anymore. You should be. You’re the man of the moment.” She looked at her watch. “Got to go. If it means anything to you, the girls all prefer this version of you too. You seem like you’re more, somehow.”

She winked and was gone.

Martin took a sip of his coffee and recoiled slightly. It was cold. It was disgusting. And anyway, he didn’t have the time for it.

## Chapter Fifty Five

He got to his feet and, taking the stairs the entire way, found himself outside Drake the Robot's office.

Drake the Robot had seen him coming all the way across the floor and appeared to have calmed down, Martin was relieved to see. He knocked, but it was a mere courtesy. He already had Drake the Robot's attention.

"Hi," he said.

Drake Robot nodded in acknowledgement.

Martin took a deep breath and then just let it all out. "You know, even if I'd had the chance, I probably wouldn't have read the Angela Knight book."

Drake the Robot sat back, but didn't say anything.

"I think there's something happening to me Drake. I mean, the fact that we're even having this conversation. It's interesting that even Kasia hates this week's column."

"She's read it?" Drake the Robot looked solidly affronted.

"No. She just hates the idea."

"I see. Go on. Don't let me interrupt."

"Look, I think I've been getting stuff all mixed up is all. Anyway, I'll do this week's column again. You're absolutely right about it. But I just ... I'm making a lot of changes at the moment as you well know, and those are going to come over in the Shallow Review of Books. The sneering has to go because I just don't feel it anymore."

Drake leaned forward, one eyebrow raised. "Martin, until recently, you've been scurrying around the world and putting together a solid review every week and we've all been very happy with the work. It's been growing and it's been consistent and I don't think I've ever missed an opportunity to tell you when you're getting it right."

"No, you haven't."

"But along the way I've been wondering when you're going to flame out. Nobody can hold onto that sort of isolation forever without going mad. However, I've never stopped worrying that when you finally do so, you'll simply go bat-shit crazy and balls everything up. Yesterday, apparently, you did so. And I don't know what to do next. I'm adding to my worries now that apparently you'll take advice from Kasia as opposed to me and that concerns me greatly."

"How can it be otherwise? I'm sitting here in front of you because I care about what you think and I want you to know that I'm over my brief deviation. But don't expect me not to care about what she thinks because that's ridiculous. The good news is she's on the same wavelength as you and that seems to put me solidly in the minority in the category of people who know best how not to make a total fuck up of my career."

Drake the Robot exhaled noisily. "So what are your next steps?"

"Right now, re-write the column, then when the day is over, take Kasia out for a few drinks. Maybe something to eat. Tomorrow? Go see the Peepers and see what goods they've got. Business as usual. Non-business stuff, not as usual at all."

Drake the Robot nodded. "All right. I'm looking forward to the new column."

"Good," said Martin.

"Good," said Drake the Robot.

"Things are going well with her you know. We're really starting to click."

"Ah."

"I thought you'd be interested to know that."

"All right. Good for you."

"You know. Because of the pool upstairs."

The shock on Drake the Robot's face was as amusing as it was unusual. "How do you know about that?"

"Let's just say I don't have my head down any more."

Drake the Robot slowly sank back into his chair. "Noted."

"Can I ask you a question?"

"No."

"Why don't you ever go home?"

"I do."

"No. No you don't. Or if you do, it's to shower and shave and come back."

"Maybe babysitting you is a full time job."

"And maybe it isn't. Come on."

"I spend time at work because unlike you, Martin, I'd rather not handle baggage of any description."

"Oh."

"Things are as they are. I'm working them out."

"Sorry Drake."

"Just make this good, will you?"

## Chapter Fifty Six

Martin unlocked his front door and rolled his eyes when he realised the lights were already on. *Oh God.*

Isabel was lying on the couch, staring at the ceiling.

"Hello Martin," she said.

"Isabel. What are you doing here?"

"Oh dear. Another frosty greeting. And just last week you were buying me flowers."

"Don't you think it would be a good idea to call to say you're coming once in a while?"

She sat up and even managed to look hurt, though Martin could see all the way through it. "Would you like me to go?"

"No. Of course not. I couldn't ask you to put up with the wretchedness of the Connaught."

"Quite right too."

"I have plans though Isabel. I can't entertain you tonight."

"I see. And what makes you think I was looking to be entertained?"

"You have something to do?"

She stood up and extended her arms. "At least give your mother a hug, will you?"

He sighed, but hugged her anyway, giving her a little squeeze as he did so.

"So," she said, pulling away, "What plans do you have?"

"Plans."

"You never have plans."

"I do lately."

"Oh, I see. Is this with the Russian girl?"

"Polish. And yes, it is."

"I see. Am I to expect a future of Polish grandchildren with unpronounceable names?"

"I don't think that's likely, to be honest Isabel, no."

"Well don't keep her hidden. Bring her along to dinner."

"I'm already taking her to dinner and you're not invited."

Again, the look of mock hurt. Maybe it was real. Martin wasn't certain this time.

"Look, you can't just turn up in my flat unannounced all the time and expect me to drop everything. If I'd known you were coming, I could have made plans to spend the evening with you, but as it stands now, I can't."

"Oh don't be absurd Martin. What kind of a restaurant can't find one extra chair?"

"That's not the point. It's a date."

"Oh I see. I'm sorry, I misunderstood. This is your weekly date night."

"We don't have a weekly ..." Martin stopped himself, recognising the trap.

Isabel folded her arms and blazed him with a trademark tried-and-perfected non-verbal scolding that had rattled many a witness in court.

"It's just that we never get time together," he said, annoying himself with his own whining.

"It's fine. I understand. I'll order some take away or something. You must have a pizza menu around here, haven't you?"

The buzzer rang just as he was about to fold.

"Hold on," he said.

It was Kasia. *Shit.* He buzzed her in.

"Is that her?"

"Just be polite, will you?"

"Why wouldn't I be polite?"

"Can't imagine," said Martin as he opened the door. A moment later, she popped out of the lift and grinned to see him waiting.

"Hey," she said as she came towards him.

"Hey yourself. Everything okay?"

She kissed him. "Mmm hmm. Well no, actually. There's too much drama at home. Tom's back so they're getting very emotional and I needed to get out. It's okay?"

"Of course it's okay. Your timing is interesting, anyway. My mother's here."

Kasia peered into the flat and Martin could feel her tense up. He followed her gaze to a still challenging Isabel and he threw her a look of most urgent plea.

To his relief, Isabel relaxed, but he was irritated immediately at her second act which was way overboard.

She smiled warmly. Too warmly. As warm as ground zero after an atomic blast in fact.

"I believe you're the lovely creature that has stolen my Martin's heart," she said, extending a hand.

Martin could feel Kasia tense up further. He guessed she could see right through the act too, which was unsurprising.

She offered Isabel her hand anyway. "Kasia. So nice to meet you."

"My, what a lovely name. That's a new one for me. Russian is it?"

"Mother," said Martin.

"It's Polish," said Kasia.

"Oh Polish. Lovely," said Isabel.

"And I hear you live in Paris and work there as a lawyer?"

Isabel was taken aback. "Well yes I do. My son speaks about me then?"

"Yes," said Kasia.

"And it's all good Isabel," said Martin.

"Oh I have no doubt," said Isabel with a wink that chilled Martin to the bone.

"Will you be joining us for dinner?" said Kasia.

*Noooooooo!* Martin groaned silently as he watched any chance of a simple evening and absolutely any chance of sex afterwards, fly out the window.

"Well if Martin doesn't mind," said Isabel.

They both turned to him.

On the spot, he could do nothing but nod.

## Chapter Fifty Seven

Dinner was awkward.

It was Scott's again, the same as it always was. Despite her pretence, Isabel had already made a reservation and made a show of organising an extra chair for Kasia.

Martin could see that Kasia was embarrassed by the prices and Isabel didn't help.

"Just have anything you want, my darling," she said.

Kasia nodded.

"And don't worry about the numbers. Just think of them as a rating for how delicious the dish is that you'll be ordering."

*"Isabel,"* Martin warned.

"What dear?"

"Do you like lobster Kasia? It's great here. I'm going to have that.

You should try it," he said.

Kasia smiled. "Okay. Sounds good."

Isabel smiled saccharine sweetly. "Oh dear. Is my son teaching you to speak English darling? Because you're uttering such incomplete sentences, I have to imagine it comes from him."

Martin watched Kasia's face fall and suddenly he was genuinely angry.

*"Isabel."*

Isabel feigned surprise at his tone but gave the conversation another quick spray with verbal itching powder. "I don't see anything wrong with attempting to help her. You don't mind, do you Kasia?"

Kasia was like a trapped owl. "Maybe we all calm down, yeah?"

"You missed the word *could* dear," said Isabel.

"She missed the word *should*, Isabel. And it doesn't matter, because as a word, it is way overrated."

"Do you two fight like this all the time?" said Kasia.

Martin smiled sarcastically, another one for his Dave the Legend evidence list. He put his hand gently on Kasia's to take the sting out. "Only when we're together."

"He's always on edge around me darling. Apparently I have that effect on everyone who is trying to keep information from me. It's very useful in my line of work."

"What am I keeping from you?" said Martin.

"Well for instance, you're in a romantic relationship with this lovely, lovely girl and this is the first I'm hearing about it. I have to assume you've been hiding it from me. Forgive me if I'm a little hurt."

"Oh stop the act. You're never hurt. You're devious. I told you about Kasia months ago. You didn't want to know. I didn't think it was worth filling you in on the rest."

"You didn't think she was worth mentioning?" said Isabel.

"You mentioned me *months* ago? *Really?"* said Kasia.

"Don't twist my words Isabel."

Kasia grabbed his hand and gave it a squeeze. He smiled back, weakly.

Isabel did a mock bow with her head. "All right then. Allow me to apologise. I didn't mean to offend anyone and I see we're all over the place now. Why don't we just go back to the beginning? Would that be all right with you?"

Martin sat back, Kasia still ignoring Isabel and giving him her full attention. For her sake, Martin let it go with a shrug.

"Fine," he said.

"Fine? I mean it's not a warm response, but it'll do," said Isabel.

"Isabel, *Jesus*," said Martin.

She turned her attention to Kasia and forced another smile. "So Kasia, what brings you to the United Kingdom?"

"She's trying to better herself mother and that is to be commended. I think more English people should take that attitude. We can all learn a lesson from her."

Kasia pulled her hand away.

"What do you mean *better myself?*" she asked, her tone of voice suddenly appropriate for the table.

Martin didn't grasp it. "You know. Getting out of Poland, working in England and getting ahead?" he said.

"I have a first class degree in Art History and Russian Literature from the Nicolaus Copernicus University. I speak three languages, Martin."

"Oh really? I mean, I didn't know that. Why are you doing what you do then?"

"Why do I do ... whoooow! You look down on my job? I didn't know this."

"No, I don't. I don't look down on it. I just ... I don't know, you said you needed the job. I didn't like to ask."

"Ah!" She laughed. He'd heard this one before. It wasn't her rich swirl of warmth and chocolate. *"You didn't like to ask?"*

"I mean I don't mean to pry."

"What's *pry?"*

"I think he means he's not ready to share yet dear," said Isabel. Martin swung on her, but her face said it all. She wasn't stoking the flames. She was annoyed. With him.

Kasia pushed her chair back and folded her arms. She was ice cold.

She turned her attention to Isabel. "So here's what I'm doing in the UK. I'm here to learn English. I guess you don't think it's good, my English, but it's better than it was six months ago because six months ago, I didn't know anything. Not one word. So laugh if you want when I forget words, but I tell you this, I am learning it fast and already I know enough so I can tell you both to fuck off if I want to. Well, maybe I should."

She swung on Martin.

"This is my third job since I got here. First, I was a cleaner. How do you like that? It hardly paid at all but it's okay because you don't need to be able to speak much in this job. I did a course with some headphones and I learned enough English so then I could work in a shop. Worse money actually, but all day I can speak English and practice what I know. Then, finally I get to this job that you think is no good. But you know, with this economy, this is the kind of work there is. I don't mind. I take it. It is like I am paid to learn English and with that I can use my degree to make something big of my career. Yes, I like to *better myself* as you say, but I'm not some poor Polish girl who doesn't have nothing and has to try to do anything to survive. Six months of English and I can say this to you. Not bad, eh? What have *you* learned in these last six months?"

Martin felt the heat of embarrassment in his cheeks. This was unexpected. "I don't know. I've learned stuff. I've learned to fall in love again, so that's something."

"Oh for Christ's sake Martin," said Isabel.

Kasia's look of derision was absolute. "What bullshit, Martin. Here we are again. I ask you to tell me something and the answer I get is ... what? Something you tell to someone so they will stop asking questions. Nothing. You see? Still nothing."

"What's this chorus of criticism. Are you two quite done?" said Martin.

"No. Not done," said Kasia. "Tell me why we're doing this."

"Doing what Kasia?"

"You and me. Why? Why bother?"

"No. No, no, no. We're not continuing with this. We're done with this," said Martin.

Kasia pulled the napkin from her lap and threw it onto the table. "Yeah. We're done," she said.

She stood up and did what Martin felt sure was what writers mean when they say she stormed out. There was nothing hurt about her demeanour. She was spitting-fire angry.

Martin swung back to Isabel with horror. She met his gaze with open delight.

"I meant we're done with the *conversation.*"

"Well what do you know? Perhaps she isn't just a pretty face after all," she said.

"I told you that."

"Martin, may I ask one thing of you?"

"What Isabel?"

"For the love of God, will you please go and fucking get her."

## Chapter Fifty Eight

He shot to his feet and tore out onto the street, aware as he did so that the tables around theirs had been unwillingly dragged into the entire spectacle. *Whatever*, Isabel would easily handle that.

Kasia was halfway down Mount street, outside Christian Louboutin and moving fast towards Berkeley Square. He broke into a run to cut her off, calling for her to stop.

"Kasia. I'm sorry. I'm so sorry. My mother ... I told you she's a nightmare."

He cracked a smile, reflexively, but when she lifted her face, his heart leapt to see she was crying.

Her anger hadn't subsided one little bit.

"What do you mean your *mother*? You think I'm upset with her? I mean I must say, she could have been nicer, but at least she didn't assume I'm so stupid that I do this nothing job because I can't do anything else."

"I don't think you're stupid. How can you say that?"

"Ah. You're just talk Martin. Still, even now. Even after I am now throwing myself towards you. Still only talk."

"What are you talking about?"

"Tell me about my life. Tell me about *your* life. Tell me *anything*. You're just standing by the side of the swimming pool when I am already swimming. I don't care that you like me or that you think I'm beautiful or that you can tell some good jokes. I believe you when you say these things, but this isn't anything. I told you I didn't want this, but you made me do it. And I don't care that you didn't know that I have a degree. Well, you never asked, but I don't care about that. What I care about is that you don't think I am clever enough to have one. And that kills me."

"Kasia, for God's sake, you're going way overboard here. You're making a big deal out of nothing. That was a totally ridiculous situation and I don't think you're too stupid to have a degree. I could have asked, you're right. But you also could have told me if you thought it was so important."

*"If I thought it was so important?"*

"No, don't do that. Don't do that whole words don't have two meanings thing. Just try to understand what I'm saying, will you? Once again we're standing here at the end of a burnt out evening and I really don't get why."

"That's true."

"What's true?"

"You don't get why. Typical man. Typical fucking self-interested idiot. This is what I didn't want."

She pushed past him and raced off again, the same demeanour she'd had leaving the restaurant. Panic grabbed Martin by the throat and began to punch him in the stomach. Hard.

He went after her and stepped in front of her. She tried to push past, but he blocked her path and she lifted her face to him once again, this time with what looked close to blind fury.

"Get out of my way," she said.

"Kasia stop. Listen to me. Don't tell me I haven't given anything. I've dumped an entire life that I built deliberately and studiously, for you. I did it willingly because I think you're someone I really want in my life, but I've done it and it's been traumatic. Don't go around telling me I don't care or I'm not making an effort ..."

"Well it isn't good enough," she interrupted.

"Then what would be?"

"Nothing. From you, probably nothing."

Martin took a step back. He could see her body gently heaving not with the exertion of the physical activity, but with the sheer flood of adrenaline coursing through her.

"Well, that's what we have then my love because honestly, maybe I've just been wrong about all of this," he said.

"Maybe," she said.

He swallowed hard to keep from throwing up. Then he turned and walked away, back towards the restaurant, hoping that she'd stop him, that she'd put her hand on his shoulder or shout "wait" or ... anything. But at the restaurant entrance, before he stepped through the door, he looked back down the street. She was gone, and the bottom dropped out of his world.

## Chapter Fifty Nine

*"Well?"*

Isabel had been waiting impatiently and had ordered a large scotch on ice, Martin assumed because she didn't want to drink champagne alone.

He was aware of the eyes on him as he walked through the restaurant as if he had a neon loser sign bolted firmly to his head. He dragged himself back to the chair opposite Isabel and collapsed into it.

"We broke up."

"Why?"

"What do you mean why? Did you just miss all that?"

"No, I didn't. I saw a girl who is gaga over you put up a fight apparently in defence of your rather breathtaking lack of sensitivity."

"Oh bollocks Isabel. Like you know anything about anything."

He snapped his fingers for one of the black waistcoated waiters, and demanded the same as she was having.

"I know *you* son."

"Do you?" His sarcasm was so thick you could have plucked it out of the air and rolled it into little balls. "You think so?"

"Martin, has your world collapsed this evening?"

"It feels a little like it, yes."

He looked around with frustration for his drink.

"So who broke up with whom?"

"I did."

"*You* did? Well, well, maybe I *don't* know you."

"Told you."

"Why?"

He sucked in air, audibly as he threw his hands into the air, only narrowly avoiding knocking the tray bearing his drink. The waiter skilfully pulled it aside without spilling a drop.

Martin took a long sip of his scotch and then put the glass down with a thud.

"Because I can't take the complications."

"So you're running away? Actually, I take it back. I do know you."

"No you don't, Isabel. You don't know anything about me. You see what you want to see. I'm not running away from anything. I just don't want this particular relationship any more. I'm done with the constant fighting."

Isabel leaned forward, her stare menacing.

"Rubbish," she said. "You're giddy when you're around her. I've made some suggestions about her generally Martin, but you don't know your own mind if you allow that to influence you. Frankly, the only thing worse than that, that I can think of, is that my son is a martyr who'll let a girl like Kasia walk out of his life."

"I thought you didn't like her."

"This isn't the Shallow Review of Women, Martin. What the hell difference does it make to you whether I like her or not? Since when is that a criterion? Are you in love with her?"

"*Do* you like her?"

"Are you in love with her?"

"Do you *like* her?"

"Martin, my mind on this matter is irrelevant. I'll answer that question another time. Your mind is what matters here. You're a man and I'm fairly sure you have one. But from what I can tell about what just happened, your mind isn't in this at all."

"How can you say that?"

"Are you in love with her?"

"I don't know. Maybe."

"Oh, well then, if you're going to insist on being dishonest about these things, that's your problem. But you're not going to be happy until you can start to make the commitment."

"It's been a couple of dates, Isabel. It isn't marriage territory. I'm not planning on settling down with her."

"I see. So you only give one hundred percent for the end run then?"

"What the hell are you talking about?"

"I mean she's not Charlotte, Martin. I mean love the girl like there is no tomorrow. Just do it. Just take the risk. If you break up, what of it? But at least you'll grow from it."

"Where the hell do you get off giving me love advice?"

"You're asking me that? You're the one with the ridiculous nickname."

"No, just answer the question. Just once in your life, answer a fucking question."

Their waiter appeared and cleared his throat.

Martin looked up at him. "Just the bill. This evening hasn't gone as it should have done."

"Oh no you don't. We're eating. If we leave now you'll just be mopey and I can't stand that." Isabel waved the waiter away impatiently. "Just bring us bisque. Both of us. We'll get to the rest in a moment."

The waiter ignored the slight, smiled and thanked them. Martin thought it was a wonder they allowed them to keep coming back.

He sat back, arms folded and waited for her to speak.

"You like bisque, don't you?"

"I'm no longer hungry."

"You will be when you smell it."

"Answer the question."

"Martin, I don't know what you would like to hear. I really don't. I'm your mother and if I give you a hard time it is only because a part of you is a half-hearted, non-starting, vacillating disaster and I know you're better than that. I don't worry about your intelligence and I don't worry about your ability to build a career and make a living even though you know I think this Shallow Review nonsense is beneath you. But I do in fact worry about the fact that you don't have a single clue how to make a lasting human connection. Apparently you think you've made one with this girl, and you have to ask yourself why you've gone to the trouble since you're flinching at the first threat of hard work."

The soup arrived. Martin regarded it with distaste while Isabel tucked straight in.

## Chapter Sixty

Martin didn't sleep that night. Neither did Rupert, though his plan had been for an early one. Isabel went to bed as soon as she got back, unwilling to spend another minute in the company of a man, even her son, who apparently had descended into a puddle of inky blackness.

Rupert was almost atop his beanbags, a newly acquired bootleg copy of an as-yet-unreleased DVD of cheetah attacks primed and ready for viewing, when Martin knocked at the door.

"Oh fuck, not again," he said as the cloying odour of Martin's failure wafted off him the moment he opened the door.

"I don't know what to do anymore."

"I take it you had a bad dinner again?"

"Must you be so smug?"

"I'm not smug. I'm absolutely astounded however. What's the matter with the pair of you?"

Martin's ears pricked at the words. It hadn't fully occurred to him that she might bear some of the responsibility for their repetitive non-starts.

"Rupert, can I come in?"

Rupert seemed surprised to discover that they were still in the doorway and stepped aside, though Martin could see it was a reluctant gesture. He couldn't help but notice that Rupert was carrying a little weight around his face and the makings of what was beginning to look suspiciously like a stomach. Snickers bars no doubt, the fucker.

"You got time for this?" Martin asked.

"Time to listen to more tales of disaster? I was going to get into bed actually and watch a DVD."

"Well I won't stay then. I just need your advice."

"No you don't. You need to think your own shit through. Really you do."

"Every time I try that, it goes tits up, Rupert."

"Then maybe she isn't the right girl, Martin."

Rupert's reaction told Martin he hadn't hidden his shock well at all.

"She *has* to be."

"Why does she *have* to be?"

"Because I can't stand the thought of being without her. She *has* to be."

"No she doesn't. You're just getting yourself in an emotional tangle because she's here and she's fantastic and you don't want to think of being without her. But in six months time, you won't even remember her name, trust me."

"You're wrong."

"No I'm not."

"Yes. You are."

"Why?"

"Because ... Christ, I just can't stand the thought of being without her. I can't."

"You're without her now."

"We'll sort it out in the morning."

"Then why are you here?"

"Because what if we don't?"

"What do you want me to do Martin?"

"Tell me what to do . . ."

"No."

"What do you mean no?"

"You don't hear that word much, do you?"

"Are you joking? It's all I ever hear."

"So you know what it means then. But let me elaborate if you're determined to play stupid. It means that I will not help you with this. You're a man. That's what she wants you to be. Act like one."

"What the hell does that mean?"

"Martin, listen carefully because this is the last time I'm going to try to help. Because you're not really committed to winning Kasia, so there isn't much point in any of this. But since you're here, I'll take one last stab at it. No matter what you think women want, they really want nothing more than for you to be a man. Not a guy Martin, a man. You're a good enough guy. You watch sports and drink beer and if I can give you credit for doing anything right over the course of these past few months it's that you've begun to embrace your guyness if that's even a word. You're doing the wildest, whackiest, craziest shit and it's almost worth writing some of it down. The flowers and the chase and all of that. It's real stupid guy stuff, and girls like that. She responded to it and frankly, I think you may have picked the toughest nut of all of them. I wouldn't have got within spitting distance of Kasia. She's loved the chase and she's loved the way you've stepped way out of your zone in going after her. You can rest assured of that. She's so into you she keeps giving you extra chances. But you're going to have to actually get involved at some point if you want her to stick around.

And if *I* can see that mate, multiply it by a million for her."

"What are you talking about?"

"I'm talking about being a man and taking some control. Not a thug who bosses her around, but a man who doesn't constantly hide in the shadows in the hope that she'll make all the effort. She's not just going to go with the flow mate. She's Polish. They grow up tough. You can't rip those barriers down because they're very fucking gifted at building new ones. You have to massage them down. Do you want to know the most macho thing a guy can do? Love. Trust. Totally. Completely. Unconditionally if you're able. It's a brave thing and it isn't for everyone. But doing that, even knowing that you run the risk of having the living crap kicked out of you emotionally is the mark of a man. There is nothing braver that a man can do. That's what someone like Kasia needs. And I haven't seen any of that if I'm totally honest."

"I do that."

Rupert laughed and it wasn't kind. It was laced with such contempt that Martin recoiled with heated anger. It didn't bother Rupert in the slightest.

"You're not in it at all mate. You're not. You handle her like she's a fucking Faberge Egg. She needs you to stand up *to* her as much as you stand up *for* her. It's a mark of respect Martin. It's a way of saying that you're confident enough that you're not expecting this to end any time soon. That you can risk the confrontation because you're not pissing yourself with fear that it'll all be over if you do. It doesn't take long for any woman to go from loving that you respect them that much to wondering if you have any self-respect of your own. They don't like that. At all."

"Yeah but I'm not interested in being confrontational. That's not the sort of relationship I want."

"Then Kasia's not your girl."

"This is bullshit. This is shit advice. You're saying fight with her or don't have a relationship with her?"

"It's not shit advice and if you don't want it mate, I was on my way to bed anyway."

"I'm not that confrontational Rupert."

"Then Kasia's not your girl, Martin."

"There has to be more to it than that."

"I'm not saying fight with her. Who the hell wants a relationship like that? I'm saying stand up *to* her as much as you're willing to stand up *for* her. Be in the relationship completely. Commit to the damn thing if it's worth a single fucking thing to you. She wants you to have a pair of balls Martin. Sweetness and kindness and funniness is all well and good, but she can get that from any number of friends. You've yet to put your stamp on this at all."

"I sent flowers for a month."

"Yesterday's news mate. If you were eighteen you could snuggle in the back seat of your car for weeks on that. In a real adult relationship, that's just the ticket to the show."

"So you're saying Kasia isn't the girl for me then?"

"Yes. About four times now."

"Well fuck that."

*"Fuck that?"*

"Yes."

"Well what are you going to do about it?"

"I don't know."

"Are you going to stand there and tell me you've never thought about it? That you haven't thought about it tonight even?"

"I don't know. All right, listen, you're on your way to bed so I ought to leave you to it."

*"You're the one that came here Martin.* I don't know what you expected. Did you want me to wave a magic wand and make you all better and make her come back and right all the wrongs in your little universe? Because I can't, and I wouldn't even if I could because it will not help you."

"So what would you do?"

"In your position right now, I'd avoid her like the plague and hope she goes away. You sure as hell can't face her tomorrow with the attitude you brought in here tonight."

Back in his flat, Martin grabbed a beer, cracked the top and gulped it, enjoying the coldness of the liquid despite his mood and letting out a long belch when the bubbles began to pop their contents all at once.

He closed his eyes and bent forward to rest his head on the kitchen counter top.

And then it hit him all at once.

“All right then,” had been his sole response to Charlotte. No play to keep her. And he had never spoken to her again.

No fire.

No assertion.

No anger.

No challenge to her notion that she was better off with someone else.

It might have shocked her if he had made one. It might have delighted her. It might have put her in the dilemma of having to choose instead of him carrying all the fallout.

Rich went to Japan for the faintest chance of love. Martin had simply walked away without a word.

He glanced to his left. His iPod sat on the countertop, the white earplug cable having got itself hopelessly knotted in his pocket the way only iPod earphones can.

And another thought hit him as his eyes traced the cable, trying to mentally untie it. He grabbed his keys and raced out of his flat.

## Chapter Sixty-One

The buzzers for the flat numbers were confusing. He just picked one of the four second floor ones, glancing at his watch as he did so and noting with a pang of guilt that it was after midnight.

A man’s voice answered.

“Hello?”

Martin tried to find his most painfully embarrassed voice.

“Hi, sorry to bother you at this hour. Is this the right number for the flat facing the road, to the left?"

"Is it what?"

"I'm looking for the occupant of the flat facing the road, to the left."

"What do you mean?"

"Sorry, I know it's really late, but I just need to speak to the occupant of that flat. Blonde girl? Very pretty?"

"Are you drunk?"

"It's not strange or anything. I just need to speak to her."

"Wrong flat mate."

"Oh right. Sorry about that then."

"Brilliant."

The intercom went dead.

Martin looked around the pavement. He couldn't find what he was looking for, so he ran his fingers around his pockets, knowing before he did that they were empty. *Bollocks*. He ran back across the road, up the stairs to his flat and grabbed the pile of change he'd emptied from his pocket onto the coffee table when he had got home.

Back downstairs and across the road, he hurled a fistful of coins at the windows above, caring little for what the coins actually were.

There was no response, so he scouted around the pavement for all the coins he could find, and threw them again, cupping his hands to his mouth and shouting her imaginary name, as loud as he could.

He didn't even notice the silver and orange Vauxhall Astra as it drifted slowly to a halt on the road behind him.

Martin stared up at the windows and shouted once again, falling to his hands and knees on the pavement immediately afterwards to collect his rapidly diminishing collection of coins.

He got a real fright when he turned and saw three pairs of legs.

"Everything all right?" said the first man. He was dressed in the navy and white of the Metropolitan Police but his face and his stance said he could just as easily have been bodyguard to a mob boss.

Martin got to his knees and looked up at the policemen.

"Yeah," he said.

"Is that your flat, sir?"

"No. It isn't. It belongs to a friend."

"What's the friend's name, sir?"

"Um. I don't know."

"You don't know? Is it male or female, sir?"

"Female. But it isn't what it looks like."

"What's your name, sir?"

"Martin. White."

"And where do you live?"

Martin pointed to his flat.

"There. The one with the light on."

The officer looked to where Martin was pointing.

"What's the address?"

Martin gave it to him and faced a barrage of other questions, all leading up to the main one which was: what the hell was he doing throwing coins at the window of a girl he doesn't know, at nearly one o'clock in the morning.

It was only the sound of a window opening above them that saved him from certain overnight detainment. As they all looked up, Martin was more relieved than he had ever felt to see Polly's face peering down at him.

Not that she made it easy on him. By the time he gained admission to her flat, he'd had to explain in front of the police officers and for all the neighbours who'd been dragged from their beds by the noise, that he wasn't as big a dickhead as he appeared.

Polly's face as she stepped aside to let him in, said she still wasn't convinced.

He looked briefly around the flat. It was vaguely interesting to see it from a different angle, but he was much more interested in her.

She was in her pyjamas; little shorts and a little top. Martin wondered if she ever wore anything else in summer. She stood with her arms folded, not saying a word.

"Polly, I need to explain myself to you because I know how badly I've let you down."

Her face said she didn't care, but she also didn't interrupt him.

"When you came over that night, I really needed you. I know it's selfish, but I did. And what we did ... what *I* did ... it doesn't mean anything. Oh Jesus, what am I trying to say here? I mean that I think you're a really amazing friend from across the road and I've never had one of those before and I love having you to wave to and to say good night to and to laugh at. Or with. Both. Whatever. But we've lost that because I was a total prick and I want to say that I'm sorry."

Again, no reaction.

"See, what I mean is that, okay, so until recently, I didn't want anyone to be anything but arms' length away. You, across the road, were the perfect sort of friend. I wasn't ready to take anything seriously or treat anything with the respect it deserved and I just basically fucked up everything I touched. Including you. I'm really sorry and I'm sad that you're no longer at the window, and we're no longer across the road friends because I think you're amazing and I absolutely hate that I hurt you."

She nodded, but he could see she wasn't going to offer up anything more than that.

"Okay. Anyway. And if it makes any difference, I think you're incredibly brave for doing what you did. I'm only learning now how to be that open and that honest. I wish things could have been different."

He went to the door and pulled it open.

"Polly?" she said. "Is that the name you've given me?"

He turned to her. "Yeah. I hope you like it."

"It's my real name."

"It is?"

"You didn't know that?"

"No."

"That's odd, isn't it?"

"It is an amazing coincidence."

"I call you Woody. You know, from Toy Story."

He couldn't help himself from laughing out loud. "Woody? Really? Why? He's a plastic cowboy."

She laughed too. "He's tall and he's skinny and he's got a sweet face. Mostly though, you dance like him. There's no chance that's your name then?"

"No." He extended his hand, laughing harder now. "Martin."

She shook it. *"Martin?* I suppose that could work."

"So anyway Polly, I don't know if we can go back to how we were or even if we can maybe be actual friends, but I cannot let another night go by with someone as nice as you thinking I'm a wanker."

She smiled. "Thank you. I still do. But you're a slightly nicer wanker now."

He winked. "All right. I'll take what I can get."

When he got back to his flat, he went straight to the window. Her flat was dark, but as he looked, he could just about make out her silhouette looking back at him, perhaps just checking to see if he would check.

That was the trial run. He knew he could do this. Now there were more important things to do.

## Chapter Sixty Two

He dialled her number. It went to voice mail. He didn't leave a message. He tried again. It was the same. Finally, he began to type a text. *I'm guessing you'll read this because I don't think this is anything like over. I'll have to tell you my newly-adopted theory of Love in Hollywood Time one day but as crazy as it may seem and because it might be over and because I don't want to miss the chance to say this: I'm in love with you.*

Martin didn't get to bed until three and was up at six, anxious to be in the office before she was. When she arrived, she looked like she hadn't slept either. She gave him a smile, but there wasn't much feeling in it.

"Good morning," he said.

"Morning," she said.

"Did you get my message?"

She shrugged.

"Okay. Here's what I need from you. I need until Sunday. I need today and I need the weekend and I need you to meet me on Sunday. In the mean time, don't go anywhere, don't leave town, don't get married, don't join the foreign legion. There's something I need to do, that I should have done for you right at the start and all I want is a chance to try this again, the way I mean it. Can you do that?"

"Martin, whatever, you know?"

"I'm taking that as yes. 48 hours. Give me that commitment."

"How's it going to be different in 48 hours?"

"Just give me the commitment."

A frustrated flick of the hands. "Fine."

Isabel picked up on the second ring. "You were out early this morning."

"I'm no longer flinching at the threat of hard work."

"Oh. Well done."

"And I need a favour. I need a gallery and I don't have time to search myself. Do you know anyone?"

"Tell me what you need."

Drake the Robot wasn't in his office. Martin dialled his mobile. He too, picked up on the second ring.

"Hello Martin," he said. "You all right?"

He sounded downright chipper.

"I am. Are you? Where are you?"

"Taking the day off," said Drake the Robot. "I think it's about time."

"Wow. Well done. What's brought this on?"

"You have actually, mate. You got me thinking yesterday. If your head's up your ass, mine is even further. I'm taking the day off and spending it with my wife."

"I'm ... I'm blown away."

"Thank you. Now what do you want?"

"The day off. I've got things I need to do."

"Do I want to know what they are?"

"No."

"Fine. See you when I see you."

## Chapter Sixty Three

It was a busy two days. He didn't sleep much. It was way harder to get together even than he thought it would be and several times he wondered if he should have requested a day more.

When Sunday morning dawned and he knew he was going to be ready for her, he called.

"It's early," she said.

"This won't wait. I've been busy. I have something for you. I want to give it to you today."

"What do you mean? What do you have?"

"Just do me a favour and trust me on this. Meet me on Wardour Street this afternoon, say around three. I'll be here. You're looking for a sign saying Gallery Martin."

"Martin what is this? What are you doing?"

"I'm doing what I should have done right from the start. I'm diving headlong into the pool and I'm swimming."

She came around the corner a little before three. He saw her the moment she appeared and she caught him too. She put her head down a little as she approached, but she moved quickly towards him. When she arrived, her eyes said she was intrigued.

"Welcome to Gallery Martin," he said.

She looked up at the sign above. It was hand-painted and even he had to admit it was a crappy sign with the red paint running into the green and making a sort of sludgy colour in the middle. She looked at the windows, covered with black material and entirely hiding the interior.

"What is this place?" she asked.

"It's my gallery."

"You have a gallery?"

"Only for the evening. They want it back tomorrow. I think they're letting it to a fruit and veg seller."

That made her laugh. "So it's a top class place then?"

"Well I wouldn't want you to think I'm a show off."

"Okay."

He grabbed her hand and led her to the door. "Come on. I want to show you. This may take some time."

It was dark inside. The sheets covered up almost every glimmer of daylight save for the corners where he hadn't attached them properly. As he closed the door behind him, it was almost pitch black.

He squeezed her hand and reached for the light switch. "You ready?"

"I hate the dark."

"Then let there be light."

Twelve miniature spotlights came on, eleven of them each shining directly onto a painted canvas on easels spread throughout the small interior of the makeshift gallery, the twelfth onto an icy bucket with a bottle of chardonnay and two glasses next to a tray of clumsily-made snacks.

Her mouth fell open as she looked around. The setting was impressive, even if the art wasn't.

"It's amazing," she said.

"Thank you. I'm thinking about sending the collection to New York when we're done here this afternoon. It's a pity for them to only have one showing."

"Did these come from small children? What am I looking at here?"

*"Small children?* No. They didn't."

She turned to him. Her hands said *so tell me.*

"This is what I've been doing for the past day and a half. I'm hurt you don't appreciate my art."

Her mouth fell open again. She looked around. She was confused.

"Baby, each of these is a story about my life. Something that's about more than shoplifting bars of chocolate. These are things I want you to know about me. For starters, anyway. There's always more. Now, it's obvious that I can't paint to save my life, but if you can see the story of a small girl in a canvas covered in nothing but red paint, you can certainly see a story of a small boy falling out of a tree house in a really badly painted picture of a small boy falling out of a tree house. That was the first time I realised my mother's work was more important to her than I was because she didn't come to the hospital for a day-and-a-half. We'll get to that though. There's lots to talk about this afternoon if you'll listen. First I have wine. You want?"

She was trying not to cry. "How do you do this? How do you go from being the biggest asshole on the planet to ... to all of this?"

He shrugged. "I'm just a guy. This is what we're like. We don't show it because we've got ourselves all fucked up in this world. I get it wrong a lot. But don't doubt that despite all that I'm absolutely determined that you know that I love you. I want you to be my girl. What do you say?"

***

# THE NINTH

*Nathan White knows he is going to die on the ninth. He just doesn't know the day, the month or the year. It's hard enough to deal with as it is, but then he realises that it may not be a date. It could be the ninth of ... well, anything. The ninth bus of the day. The ninth meal from a restaurant kitchen. The ninth angry football fan to pass him on a random street. His life is about counting and the expectation of a terrifying death and he lives in a constant state of panic.*

*Then he meets Victoria.*

*Victoria knows she's going to die on the 27th. She just doesn't know the day, the month or the year. Or even if it's a date at all. She faces the constant threat of death with defiance, choosing to face down the 27th every chance she gets, as a challenge to a twisted universe.*

*Then she meets Nathan.*

*Joining forces to deal with a fate that neither of them can stand to face alone any longer, they begin to upset the balance of the force that has singled them out for punishment.*

*But are some people actually just cursed?*

*The Ninth is the second book by Colin Browne and will be available mid- 2012.*

www.ingramcontent.com/pod-product-compliance
Ingram Content Group UK Ltd.
Pitfield, Milton Keynes, MK11 3LW, UK
UKHW041431210726
13854UKWH00010B/1855

9 780957 203907